All the Wild Obsidian stories in one place

Wild Obsidian: Complete Collection

Vic Raven

Publisher: Vic Raven Author LLC

Cover Design: Vic Raven

ISBN paperback: 979-8-9934170-4-2

IBSN eBook: 979-8-9934170-5-9

First Edition

www.vicravenauthor.com

Also by

The Scars We Carry series

The Final Letter

Only If I Stay

Even If We Shatter (June 2026)

Wild Obsidian Series

Wild Obsidian: Complete Collection

Temptation

Menage

Overload

Ritual

Run

Recover

Knife

Bruise

Taken

Contents

Author's Note

Welcome to the tantalizing world of Wild Obsidian.

In this book, you will find nine stories about nine different couples (one menage) that all have some sort of trauma they are working through.

But the most important thing I can tell you is that these stories are FICTION! Yes, in the kink community negotiation and consent are key. BUT I need you to remember these stories are fiction and reading them does not give you the education required to do these scenes. Hurting yourself or your partner (without consent) will lead to a charge. So let's not do that.

And please remember that a lack of knowledge immediately revokes consent. If you don't know what you are getting into, you cannot give consent.

These stories are just the...tip, if you will. There is so much more to the community, so many more dynamics and play types. If you are interested in the kink or BDSM community, reach out. I can hopefully point you in the right direction. If you are like me (extremely introverted) a quick Google search can get you started in finding a community.

These stories are in order from least to most kinky. Yes, there is a CNC story. If that isn't for you, please don't read it. It's not for everyone and that's okay.

As always, remember, your safety is number one and enthusiastic consent is mandatory.

Love you to the moon and back

—Vic Raven

Trigger Warnings

LISTEN, WE ALL KNOW that we are bad bitches who love to read about the darker side of romance. But mental health is important, especially in a book with heavy emotional themes.

If I missed one, PLEASE email me at vicravenauthor@gmail.com so I can add it to this list.

Take care of your brain, it's the only one you get, and fixing it is expensive.

Full List of Trigger Warnings for *Wild Obsidian: Complete Collection*

Each book will have it's own TW prior to each book. Feel free to skip a story if doesn't fit.

Food shame (not by MMC)

Body dysmorphia

Religious trauma

Repression

Mention of past sexual trauma

Childhood trauma

Narcissism

Off page abuse (not by MC's)

SVU detective

PTSD/ Anxiety

Off page mention of rape

Chase/ Primal

Fire play

Impact play

Sacrifice play scene

Master/Slave relationship

ON PAGE Consent non consent (CNC)

Dedication

This is for all my millennials who thought sex was supposed to be boring.

Welcome to paradise.

Will she give into temptation?

Wild Obsidian: Temptation

Vic Raven

Trigger Warnings

Temptation

Food shame (not by MMC)

Body dysmorphia

Religious trauma

Repression

Temptation Chapter 1

Elise

I hadn't planned on helping Claire cover this event tonight, but saying no to five hundred dollars isn't something I can afford to do. My business does well, but having the extra cash in the slow season is critical.

So instead of being laid up in bed, reading one of my smutty romance books, I'm in a black dress with long sleeves and a high neck and heels. I'm having to remind myself that helping Claire manage this event is good for both of us. But I'm struggling to maintain my composure.

The art on sale tonight is beautiful and erotic. People of all shapes, sizes, cultures, and genders have gathered to celebrate that art. No one is judging anyone else. Everyone is comfortable in their skin. And I'm standing here against the wall, feeling like a twenty-six year old virgin at their first formal dance.

But my job tonight is management; making sure that the servers clear tables, the bar stays stocked, and the food is replenished before it has a chance to run out. I've run these events with Claire so many times, I could do this half asleep.

But there will be no sleeping tonight. My brain is breaking that there are people in this world, hell in my local community, that feel free enough to express themselves and their sexuality.

I love that for them, the freedom. But I couldn't imagine feeling free enough to not only embrace my sexuality but also my wants and needs as a human being.

I just came back into the ballroom to make sure that the staff had enough help clearing dishes, but what has left me speechless are the burlesque dancers on the stage.

They are all shapes and sizes, and in various stages of undress. Everyone is clapping and shouting, and I am struggling with what I am seeing.

"Art is the purest form of self expression," a man says as he steps up behind me.

I turn around to ask him if he needs anything but stop dead in my tracks, my voice dying in my throat. The man standing before me is stunning.

He's tall, dwarfing my five foot eight frame, and thickly muscled. He's not wearing a shirt, instead a leather harness crosses over his chest, highlighting the geometric tattoos all over his torso and arms.

His blonde hair is long and thick, braided back from his face. But the sides are shaved to the skin, and tattoos cover the sides of his head. His eyes are a startling shade of green, almost like sea foam but with little red flecks in them.

I clear my throat. “Can I help you with something?” I try not to stare, but it’s hard when those eyes feel like they are peering into my soul. I step to the side, putting him in front of me.

“Just making conversation.” His eyes track my movement and a grin slides across his face. “Do I make you nervous?”

“No, I just wanted to be out of the way if someone needed to pass.” I press my back against the wall behind me.

“Would being in the way be such a bad thing?” He steps in closer to me, his scent filling my nose with something citrusy, along with a hint of musk.

“It is if I’m in the way.” My throat is suddenly thick with tension. I try to shrug it off and act like him being so close doesn’t bother me. But it does. “I need to get back to work.”

I take a step to the side and he lets me. He takes a step back, noticing my discomfort. “I’m sorry, it was not my intention to make you uncomfortable. I saw you staring at the dancers and thought that maybe it was in awe.”

He stands next to me, mirroring my image; hands clasped in front of my waist, shoulders back, head high.

“You didn’t make me uncomfortable, I just need to work.” I take a deep breath and let it out slowly. I let my eyes move over the crowd, checking on the staff.

“Do you always lie to yourself to make others more comfortable about their bad behavior?” He says it causally while watching the dancers. “Because I *did* make you uncomfortable, and I will gladly accept and apologize for that.”

“I’m not lying to myself. It’s just not a big deal.” I keep scanning the crowd, making sure that everything is still running smoothly, also secretly hoping that I can escape.

This man is right. He is making me uncomfortable, but not because he’s being creepy. I'm uncomfortable because he is attempting to look past the carefully built facade that I have been wearing for years.

"How long have you been in the catering business?" he asks as he leans against the wall behind us.

“I’m not in the catering business. I’m just helping out a friend tonight.” I see a server struggling with a pile of plates. “Excuse me, I need to get back to work.”

As I walk away, I can feel his gaze burning a hole in my back. But I keep my back straight and ignore it. I’m used to being stared at—it’s the curse of a redhead.

When I get to the server that is struggling, I take a couple of plates from her and gather up the rest that were left on the table. We make our way to the kitchens down the hall, dodging guests and exhibits as we go.

We deposit the plates and she murmurs a quick *thank you* before heading back out to gather more plates. I stand in the kitchen, helping the dish washer scrape plates and get them loaded in the dishwasher.

“I’m not paying you to help the dish washer scrape plates, ya know?” Claire is standing in the doorway holding a plate loaded with food.

“I know, but he looked like he needed a hand.” The dish washer gives me a side eye, clearly not understanding that I needed a minute to gather myself. I put my hands up in surrender and walk towards Claire, wiping my hands on a towel before tossing it in the linen bag.

"I'll bet he did. Here," she says as she hands me a plate of food. "Don't even bother with the excuses, I know you haven't eaten yet."

This is why I love Claire. She knows that I don't eat until I'm about to drop. "Thank you," I mumble as I start forking food into my mouth.

We met in a creative writing class in college. She was taking the class as an elective, and I was trying to feed my soul. My parents hated that I was taking the class because it didn't fit their plan for me, but I told them it was an elective. They didn't know that I needed to let off some steam before I exploded.

"Who was the guy you were talking to? He's fucking hot." She pulls me out of the wash area and into the hallway.

"I don't know, just someone who decided to strike up a conversation, I guess." I don't taste the food as I eat, just trying to get calories in. I'll have to work out harder tomorrow to make up for the extra meal.

"What do you mean you don't know? You didn't get his name? His number?"

"Claire, you know me better than that. My parents would revolt if I brought a guy with tattoos to meet them." My parents are extremely conservative, super religious people. They believe that women should be at home raising their children, not running their own businesses. The fact that I am twenty-six and still not married and having babies is abhorrent to them.

"When are you going to learn to live for yourself and not your parents?" She lets out an exasperated sigh. We've had this conversation many times over the years and it always ends the same—her shaking her head.

"I *am* living for myself. I'm here, aren't I?" I let out my own sigh and take the plate into the washroom before coming back to the hallway. "I'm not interested in a hookup, though."

"Getting his name and number doesn't mean you have to hook up with him. It just opens the door for a date. You know, the thing you haven't been on in years after Shane walked out on you for being too *boring*."

I can't cover my wince. Shane and I had been together for over a year and I thought we were headed for engagement. But one day, out of the blue, he told me that he had hoped that I would be more adventurous, more sexual, more everything.

"Elise, you are a beautiful, strong, sexy woman. If I had a dick, I'd be gunning for you. But I don't. Instead, I watch you hide yourself from others. I watch as all the things you were taught as a kid and teenager hold you back from being who you truly want to be."

I lean back against the wall, tipping my head back to look at the plain beige ceiling tiles. For a minute, I sit with what she said, and has been saying for the last couple of years. And finally, it dawns on me, *I'm a ceiling tile*.

Sturdy, utilitarian, following the ridge pattern set up for me my entire life. I *am* boring.

I used to love bright colors, literature, music. I volunteered at the animal shelter and women's shelter. I used to write poetry, music, and stories. Five years ago, I would have loved an event like this, one that supported literally everything I cared about.

Now, I hide in my apartment. I wake up at six am to work out, not because I want to, but because I have to stay in shape to land a husband. I work on my clients' books until my eyes cross. Then, and only then, do I allow myself a small window to read or write. But only for a short time—I have to go to bed early so I can wake up and do it all again.

I am one hundred percent positive that those people in there, the ones that are actually enjoying themselves, have day jobs. Some are probably doctors, lawyers, teachers, and any manner of *normal*. But they are here, having fun, and being themselves. And no one is judging them.

"You're right," I tell her as I continue to stare at the ceiling tiles. "I am boring."

"You're not boring, Elise. You just fell into a routine that doesn't suit you."

"I'm going to see if I can find that guy, maybe get his number." I start walking down the hall towards the ballroom.

Claire lets out a quiet 'thank fuck' before heading back to the kitchens to make sure that the desserts are ready to roll out.

I walk back in and scan the crowd. Everyone is still entranced by the dancers, and the servers have cleared all the dinner plates. The bartenders nod at me, indicating that they are good.

I continue to scan, looking for the man with the long blond hair, when my eyes land on a large photo on the exhibition side of the ballroom. I hadn't seen it earlier as I was moving through the room.

I am drawn to the photo, stepping around guests and staff. It's the most beautiful photo I've ever seen. When I come to stand in front of it, I can't help but stare. My eyes move over every inch of the photo.

It's a black-and-white photo of a woman laying on her back, her hands covering her breasts and her leg pulled up just enough to cover the most intimate part of her. Her head is tilted back, eyes closed, and her mouth is barely parted. It looks like she is on the edge of an orgasm.

My eyes rest on the small white card attached to the bottom.

L. Hart - Temptation

Below the photo is a clipboard with names and amounts listed out. The last bid was for four thousand dollars. I tried to hide my surprise, but I'm pretty sure the sound of my jaw hitting the floor was heard throughout the ballroom.

I'm still staring at the photo when the scent of citrus and musk surrounds me.

"This is one of my favorite photos." The man from earlier is back. This time, though, he isn't standing as close.

"It's beautiful," I tell him, peeking over my shoulder to look at him. He's not looking at the photo, but at me.

"Thank you," he says with a nod.

"This is your work?" I ask, surprised. At his nod, I pull my eyes away from him and back to the photo. "You're a photographer?"

"I am," he says, his tone cautious. "Does that surprise you?"

I think about that for a second. "Not really. I don't know many photographers, so I don't really know what one would look or act like."

"That's fair. Yes, I'm a photographer. I work with all types of people for a variety of different portraits. Can I show you?" He holds out his arm, offering to show me the other photographs in the exhibit.

Despite what I told Claire, I'm hesitant. He's not even wearing a shirt, for heaven's sake. But I don't want to be a ceiling tile anymore, so I take his arm. He leads me around the exhibit, not only to his photos but to the other art that is up for auction.

He tells me about each artist: the silversmith, the glassblower, the ropemaker, the painters. He tells me their stories and how they got started. But the thing that hits me the hardest is his photos.

Each one is different, and they're not all sensual. One is of a prosthetic leg and a woman's boot. Another is a wide, thick collar on a man's throat that has *Darling* stamped on the front and a woman's painted nail tilting up the man's chin.

I'm staring at that photo, trying to figure out what it means, when he points out another one. This one is also black and white. It's of a woman's back with something melted on her back, a tattoo that says *His Angel* inked into her skin.

Her hair is up in a messy bun, and she is naked. Her hands are tied to a hook above her head, and there is a man's hand caressing her jaw.

"This is one of my favorites. The woman struggles with sensations and being touched. But when it's her partner touching her, she melts." He stares at the photo for another minute before turning to me.

"My name is Elise," I blurt out before I lose my courage.

I watch as a smile takes over his face. "I'm Lucian."

"Do you want to get coffee?" I ask him, my face flaming.

"You beat me to it. Yes, I would love to get coffee."

Temptation Chapter 2

Elise

Last night was wild. Not only was the event a new type of experience for me. I asked out a man. My parents would be livid if they knew.

But because I was working the event and Lucian was a vendor, coffee would have to wait until today. We would both be too busy finishing the event and then tearing down. We decided to meet at a coffee shop in downtown Franklin.

Turns out we are both locals. He lives in an apartment above his studio, and I'm in the apartments on the main street through the art district, less than a quarter mile between our homes. But I had never seen him in the five years I had been in my apartment.

I leave my apartment early, hoping to get to the coffee shop before he gets there. They have the best muffins, and I want one desperately.

I have just placed my order and sit down to eat my muffin when I hear him place his order at the register. I look down at my muffin longingly. He comes over with his own muffin and sits down in front of me.

Today, he's dressed in jeans, a band shirt, and a flannel. His hair is pulled up and back in a topknot that puts my own messy bun to shame. When we discussed going for coffee, I had assumed it would be casual, but I still feel over dressed, sitting across from him in slacks and a button down.

"Hey, pretty lady." He notices my muffin. "Oh, did you get the blueberry or the banana?"

"Banana," I say quietly. I push my plate towards the center of the table.

"Do you not want it?" He looks at me with sadness in his eyes.

I look at him and try really hard not to pout. I really wanted that muffin, but my struggles with my weight over the years have caused me to be very careful about what I eat. The fact that my parents and past boyfriends have made comments about my weight make me uncomfortable eating in front of people.

In short, I am now in a situation where either I tell him the truth about why I can't eat the muffin, or I eat the muffin and deal with the shame and guilt.

"Mmmm...I think I know the problem." He pushes his muffin to the middle of the table next to mine. My gaze drops to the two muffins. "If I had to guess, based on last night and what I've seen in the last five minutes, I'm going to say there is a lot of shame around food."

I raise my gaze to meet his, and I can feel my eyes fill with tears. He reaches over and takes my hand. My pulse jumps at the easy contact.

"You don't have to eat the muffin in front of me if it is going to cause you distress. However, I need you to understand that I think you are beautiful no matter if you eat the muffin or not. Your value is not measured by your weight or what you look like."

"I wish it was that simple," I murmur.

"Do you want to talk about it?" he asks calmly, but I see his hand clenched around his mug of coffee.

"Not really," I answer honestly.

"Then we won't talk about it, at least not yet." He takes a sip of his coffee. "What do you do for work?"

I let out a small sigh of relief that the topic of food is over. "I run my own bookkeeping business."

"Are you accepting new clients?" he asks with so much hope in his voice that a small laugh escapes me. I expect some sort of criticism or condescending comment, but I'm pleasantly surprised.

"I might be willing to take a look at your books... are you sure you can afford me?" I take a sip of my tea, barely hiding my grimace at the bitter taste.

"Probably not, but if you can straighten out my books, I will figure out a way." He stares at me for a moment. "What do you do for fun?"

"I hate to disappoint, but I'm pretty boring. I wake up, work out, work on my clients' books, and go to bed." I keep smacking myself in the face with my own ceiling tile reference.

"Do you read? Watch TV?"

I can feel my face start to heat up. Another curse of being a redhead.

"You read, don't you?" He lets out a small laugh. "Let me see if I can guess your favorite author."

He leans back in his chair, grinning like a maniac. "Part of me thinks you read the old-school bodice rippers from Rosemary Rogers. But the other part of me thinks that you are reading something darker and deeper, like J.T. Geissinger. Am I close?"

I know that my face is the color of a tomato. But while Lucian is grinning like a maniac, I don't feel like he's making fun of me. I clear my throat delicately. "J.T. is my favorite author of all time."

Lucian barks out a laugh. "I knew it. Was I at least close on Rogers?"

I let out a small laugh. "Yes. I started my romance journey with Nora Roberts but quickly moved to the darker, smuttier stuff. But I had to hide my books at school and friends' houses. If my parents ever find out what I read, I would be in so much trouble."

“Why would you be in trouble with your parents? You’re an adult.” His face falls so quickly, I’m surprised he didn’t pull a muscle.

“It’s not appropriate,” I say automatically. Sometimes I forget that other people grew up outside of the ultra-conservative and religious groups. "I was a rabid reader as a kid, and I still am. But I had blown through all the books that were deemed "appropriate" by our church by the time I was ten. I started reading fantasy when I got to middle school and started asking questions. Needless to say, that didn't go over well, and my books were confiscated. I wasn't allowed to read at home anymore unless it was the bible."

"How did romance get involved?" He's still clutching his coffee like he's trying to strangle it.

"I was at the thrift store with a friend and the classic romance novel cover. You know the ones, the man is ripped with his shirt open and the woman is clutching him like he's her savior. Anyways, I was curious and picked it up. That was the day my love affair with romance started."

"Did your parents ever find out?" He places his coffee mug in the center of the table.

"Never." I finish off the rest of my tea and place my mug next to his.

"What are you doing for the rest of the day?" he asks.

"I was going to finish up my client's books and then hit the gym again." I stand up and gather my purse and jacket.

"Do you want to hang out with me today? I've got a couple of errands to run before I have a meeting tonight and I'd like to hang out with you more." He looks so earnest, his smile genuine.

I stare at him in disbelief. I've really enjoyed myself and talking to him, but I've never slacked off or played hokey. I've never done the fun thing. Hell, I waited until I was twenty-one before I had my first drink.

"Yeah, I'd like that. But I need to run home to change. I'm not running around with you in heels." I watch as he snags two to-go containers from the napkin station. "Do you want to meet me back here?"

"Probably a good idea. Do you want to meet at my studio? It's only another block down, just past the tattoo studio." He hands me a to-go container before putting his muffin in his. "By the way, did you have a meeting before we met for coffee?"

"No," I say slowly. I'm speechless for a second. He listened and took action instead of making me feel bad about my food issues. "I just wanted to dress nice."

Lucian cocks his head to the side. "And you're comfortable dressed in slacks and a blouse?" He seems genuinely confused. He looks down at himself.

I laugh. "No, which is why I'm going to change when I get to my apartment." He holds the door for me as we walk out.

"Then why would you wear it?" The confusion has morphed into understanding. "Elise, this is a date, and yes, I want to get to know you. But in my world, casual is jeans and a t-shirt. Hell, getting dressed up is jeans and a button-down if I can find one."

"In my world, jeans are worn by slobs and degenerates. T-shirts should only be worn by men under their dress shirts." I take a deep breath and continue. "But I hate slacks, blouses and heels. I much prefer leggings and a baggy t-shirt."

"Then meet me at my studio in whatever you are most comfortable in." He looks down at the container my muffin is in. "I'll be honest, Gorgeous, I don't like the world you come from. But I do look forward to corrupting it."

He winks at me before backing away. "Go get changed."

I can't stop the grin that takes over my face, and I start the short walk to my apartment, keeping a death grip on my muffin.

The trip to my apartment to get changed doesn't take long. I get changed into jeans, a t-shirt, and a hoodie as I wait for my muffin to warm up. I'm not ready to run around outside the house in leggings just yet.

I inhale my muffin over the kitchen sink as I think about everything that happened at the coffee shop. Lucian is different from every guy I've ever dated, at least so far. He actually paid attention to me, not the phone that I could hear vibrating in his pocket. He noticed my discomfort in eating in front of him and didn't make a big deal out of it. His level of casual is going to take some getting used to, but I like it.

I'm enjoying the crisp weather on my walk to his shop when a door opens and he steps out onto the sidewalk. I'm momentarily stunned. "This is *your* shop?" I know my jaw is on the ground, but I can't help it.

Lucian grins at me. "It is. Would you like to see it from the inside?"

I nod, still dumbfounded. He pulls me inside and shows me around. The studio is set up like a house. Living room, kitchen, bedrooms—everything is set up as if you could actually live in the studio. But there is extra lighting and props against walls and shoved into random spots.

"I've always wondered what it looked like in here. I've seen the pictures hung in the window and always thought it was beautiful."

"It's my second home, and for a time, my first." He steps into the kitchen and I follow him, still struggling to take everything in. Every room is warm and full of texture; leather couches, exposed brick, plants tucked into mismatched pots.

It smells exactly like him, citrusy with a hint of musk but there's coffee, vanilla, and cedar too. Touches of a home that can't be sold in a bottle.

But it's the bedroom that stops me in my tracks. He comes to stand next to me as I take in the space. The bed is unmade, and the sheets rumpled. There are several lights positioned to act like windows and add extra lighting.

“It feels... real,” I murmur.

“That's the point.” His voice is closer now. “People relax when a place feels real. They stop performing and show me who they are.”

I glance at a camera perched on a tripod in front of a chair. There are ropes on the armrest and legs, a crop resting across the seat. Next to it, a folded blanket and a half-empty mug.

My pulse trips. “You photograph all this?”

“Not all.” He gives me a knowing smile. “Just what’s honest.”

He moves past me and adjusts a light near the faux window. “You can touch anything you want. This isn’t a museum.”

I reach out, fingers brushing a length of rope. It’s smoother than I expected.

Lucian’s voice breaks the silence again, softer this time. “You okay, Gorgeous?”

I swallow, not sure what to say. “It’s just... intimate.”

He nods. “That's the point of art, isn't it?”

"What don't you photograph?" I ask as I continue around the room.

"I'll photograph just about anything that interests me." He leans against the bed frame as he watches me move around the room. "But I cut my teeth on family portraits."

"You don't strike me as the type for family portraits." I come to stand in front of him. I'm not a short woman, but when he straightens to his full height, I feel tiny.

"I stopped doing family portraits after three years of dealing with shitty parents." My confusion must show on my face because he continues. "I can't tell you how many times I had to listen to the dad bitch about having to get dressed up. Or how many times the mom would end up in tears and heartbroken before I even got the first picture."

"You probably would have loved my family then. We were all in matching sweaters. No one complaining, just ready to take orders." I meant it as a joke, but the look that crosses his face is full of sadness.

"Honestly, I don't know what was worse. The dad complaining, the mom showing off her kids like prized cattle, or the kids whose eyes were empty."

"Yeah, I can understand why you wouldn't want to do portraits after that."

"I still do portraits," he corrects. "I just do them how I want to do them."

"What do you mean?"

"You said you would run errands with me, right?" The sadness is gone, and his mischievous grin is back.

"Yeah," I draw out slowly.

"Good. Then you'll see what kind of portraits I do." He leads me out of the shop and locks up.

"Why do I have a feeling I'm going to regret this?"

He doesn't answer, just grabs my hand, and we start down the street.

Don't be a ceiling tile, I remind myself. *Just don't be a ceiling tile.*

Temptation Chapter 3

Elise

I should have asked more questions when I agreed to run errands with Lucian. He said that he had a shoot first thing in the morning and needed to get props. As we walk to the first stop, he asks me how he would go about having me start working on his books.

He says that he has an accountant, but they are always getting onto him because he just hands them a stack of receipts. They recommended a bookkeeper to keep his expenses on track.

We talk about my coming over later in the week to go over his system to see what needs to be tweaked. He says to prepare for a disaster, and now I'm concerned.

When we get to the first shop, I'm surprised that it's a bookshop. He asks me what is the darkest romance that I had read to date. I show him a couple, and he buys them without even asking twice. Then he asks which are on my list that I haven't gotten around to buying yet.

He buys those too.

But it is the second store that has my heart racing and my face the color of a stoplight. We are at a small adult store at the end of the art district that specializes in handcrafted items.

Lucian doesn't even think twice before going in and dragging me along with him. I don't even know what to look at; the glass dildo, the vibrating cock rings, the bullwhip. It is a little much for me, but Lucian acts like it was totally normal to be picking out toys.

And maybe it is. Maybe I am too sheltered, too much of a prude. A ceiling tile.

But I decide to go out on a limb and embrace the freedom that I am feeling. I buy a vibrator, and Lucian looks so damn proud. Sure, I am still embarrassed, but I don't want to be sheltered or a prude or ultra-modest anymore.

Lucian and I walk out of the store, arm in arm, and start heading back to his studio. We are laughing and joking about my first vibrator when I hear my name called.

"Elise Marie Anderson!"

I freeze, my shoulders bunching up to my ears. Lucian looks down at me in surprise. *Marie*? he mouths at me with a grin. But the grin quickly disappears when he sees the look of absolute terror on my face.

I turn around to see my mother striding towards me with a purpose, a look of horror on her face. She goes to grab my arm, and Lucian steps in front of me, blocking her.

"Can I help you?" he asks, his voice deep and menacing. He uses his arm to keep me tucked behind him.

"Get your hands off my daughter." She lunges at me again, but I shrink further behind Lucian's broad back.

"Ma'am, you need to stop grabbing at her." He says it calmly, but I can feel the anger vibrating through his back.

"That's my daughter, and I will do to her whatever I need to protect her from the likes of you," she screeches.

My fear of being caught coming out of an adult store with a man clearly not good enough for my mother evaporates.

"Don't you dare insult him," I say as I step out from around Lucian. "He hasn't done anything wrong."

"How dare you talk to me like that. This heathen has corrupted you! You need to come with me right now, Elise Marie."

I grab Lucian's hand and pull myself up to my full height. "No. I'm tired of being told what to do. I'm twenty-six years old and I don't need my mother treating me like a child. If I want to hang out with Lucian, I'm going to."

I look up at Lucian and see that he's glaring daggers at my mother. "Come on, Doll. Let's go."

I take his arm and steer him around my mother, who is gaping at me like I've grown a second head. "Wait until your father hears about this."

"Be sure to tell him that I said hello." I wave over my shoulder and keep walking. Lucian places his arm around my shoulder and pulls me into his side. He rubs my shoulder until we have gotten far enough away from my mother for us to stop.

He turns me until my face is buried in his chest. He wraps his arms around me, and I can feel him bury his face in my hair. I start shaking like a leaf in a storm. I keep the tears back, but only just barely.

It takes a while, but once the shakes finally dissipate, I pull back. Lucian looks down at me with a grin. "Doll, huh?"

"I'm so sorry," I mumble, and my head drops back down.

"Hey." He lifts my chin with his finger and presses a kiss to my forehead. "Don't do that. You aren't responsible for her and her words."

"But I hid behind you like a coward." I feel the tears prick at my eyes.

"No, you didn't. You were shocked and terrified. But you stood up to who I assume is your biggest bully. That takes a lot of strength." He presses another kiss to my forehead. "I'm really proud of you."

I just nod because it *did* feel really good to stand up to my mother. I also know how much trouble I've just landed myself in. But there is freedom in standing up to my mother that I never expected to feel.

"Now, do you want to continue letting me corrupt you, or do you want to go home?"

I am thankful that he is allowing me to make this decision. He's not taking the choice away from me. "Well, I'm already in deep shit, might as well finish off the rest of the day."

"Good choice," he says. He threads my arm back through his and we continue back to his studio.

When we get to the shop, he tells me about his shoot tomorrow. It's of a woman who left her abusive ex and is now with another man who absolutely adores her. She wanted to do the shoot to close one chapter and start another. Apparently, she's a freelance romance editor, so the bookstore stop made more sense.

I spend the next couple of hours helping him set up his studio for the shoot, and it's coming up on dinner time.

"I'm getting pretty hungry," Lucian says as we sit on the couch in his office that doubles as another shooting space. "I understand how you feel about eating in front of people, but I would love to take you out. There's a group of us that goes to this really great noodle place down at the end of the art district."

I'm silent for a minute as he watches me. "In it for a penny, in for a pound, right?"

I should not love the feeling of butterflies that takes over my stomach. But the grin that takes Lucian's face is equal parts devious and pride.

"Hell, yeah!" he crows. I can't help my answering smile. "I've got a jacket you can borrow. We usually eat on the patio, and it's supposed to get pretty cool tonight."

He jumps off the couch and grabs his jacket. He helps me into it, and it smells like him. All I want to do is bury my face in it. He grabs a thicker hoodie and pulls it on. He adjusts his topknot and we are out the door again.

He threads my arm back through his as we walk to the noodle place. I've seen it in passing a couple of times but couldn't bring myself to go. We round the corner to the patio, and there are about twenty or so people hanging out. When they see Lucian, they start calling out his name, and he greets everyone.

He introduces me to his friends, and it's not long before we are all talking over each other. I expected to feel overwhelmed, but everyone is welcoming.

When the waiter starts taking orders, I'm at a loss. I have no idea what any of the things on the menu are. Lucian orders me a glass of wine and a simple ramen bowl. I give him a grateful smile.

But the real test comes when it's time to eat. Bowl after bowl of ramen hits the table, not to mention the sushi, and the appetizers. Old habits are hard to break, even when you make the decision to not be a ceiling tile.

I look over at another woman who is struggling with her own bowl. I can't remember her name, but she looks really familiar. I think she might live—or used to live—in my building.

I watch as her boyfriend switches out his jammy eggs for hers, finds the fermented garlic shoots and puts them into his bowl. He works on her bowl until she smiles at him like he hung the moon.

Lucian leans over and whispers in my ear. "That's Maggie and Vex. She has some pretty big food aversions. Vex is a human garbage disposal. So he will eat whatever she doesn't or can't."

I watch as Vex places a quick kiss on her lips and she digs into her noodles. It's not long after that she is dancing in her seat and he's grinning at her.

I pick up my chopsticks and look around the table. No one is paying me any attention, too busy eating their own food and talking to their neighbors. I carefully grab some noodles and place them in my mouth. Flavor explodes across my tongue, and I can't help the moan that escapes me.

"Good girl, Gorgeous," Lucian whispers in my ear. I almost melt into my seat. He goes back to eating like he didn't just rock my entire world with that praise. He nods at my bowl, silently telling me to eat as much as I want. I dig in.

The rest of dinner is amazing, and I clear my bowl. I've ordered a second glass of wine and I'm leaning against Lucian. Maggie, Becca, and I are all talking about books we've read and what they are working on.

I'm pleasantly buzzed from the wine when I let slip that I've been writing stories my entire life. Lucian jerks in surprise and looks down at me. I smile up at him sheepishly, suddenly embarrassed to admit it.

Becca and Maggie start gushing about wanting to read them, but I tell them it's just a hobby. They must sense my discomfort because they tell me that they would love to read my stories whenever I am ready to share.

One by one, couples pay their checks and head out. When Maggie stands up, I can't help but stiffen when I see the tattoo on her back, *His Angel*. I look over at Lucian, and he gives me a small smile.

Lucian pays our check and stands up. He helps me to stand, and we start walking back towards my apartment.

"Your friends are pretty amazing," I tell him. I've got three potential new clients and a couple potential friends.

"They are pretty amazing," he says as he opens the exterior door to my building. "We've all been friends for years. Some I knew before the club, and some I met at the club, but they are the best group of people to have in your corner."

"What club?" I ask as I start up the steps to my floor. My head is slightly fuzzy from the wine, and I'm holding onto the banister for dear life.

He pauses before answering. "Obsidian."

I stop on the stairs and look over my shoulder. Lucian is a step below me and looks me in the eye. "The sex club?"

He raises his eyebrow at me. I wince when I realize that sounded really judgmental. "I'm sorry, that came out way worse than I intended. I just don't know what else to call it."

His posture relaxes, and he gently urges me to continue up the stairs. "It's a private dungeon, but I understand why people call it a sex club, especially if they aren't in the lifestyle."

"I really am sorry, Lucian. I didn't mean to offend you." I'm mentally kicking myself for ruining an entire day.

"It's okay, Gorgeous." Lucian sighs. "It is hard to figure out what to call it if you're not in the lifestyle. But I would caution you to just call it a club or dungeon from now on. Especially if we continue to see each other."

Relief floods me, and we finish the climb to my apartment.

"Are you in the lifestyle?" I ask, suddenly terrified of his answer. But also intrigued.

"I am," he says, his voice low.

I reach into my purse and grab my keys. I unlock the door and turn back to look at Lucian. He stands tall, his shoulders back and chin high. There's a gleam in his eye that wasn't there before. Like he wants to let me in on a secret, but can't just yet.

"I'd really like to see you again."

"Then that's what we'll do." He gently pushes me inside my apartment. "Lock the door, Gorgeous. I'll see you tomorrow."

I step into my apartment and lock the door. I look through the peephole and watch him. He's staring at the ground, deep in thought. He stands there for a minute before he looks up at the peephole, a smirk on his face. That gleam in his eye turns predatory.

"I'm going to corrupt you, Gorgeous. I hope you're ready."

Temptation Chapter 4

Elise

Tonight, I'm getting ready for another date with Lucian, and I'm finishing up my makeup when my phone chirps.

Be there in five

I can't help the grin that takes over my face.

The last several weeks have been the weirdest but most gratifying of my entire life. I called Claire after my date with Lucian. If the squealing on the other line was any indicator, she was one hundred percent on board with me seeing him.

I've been ignoring the phone calls from my parents for the last couple of weeks. I just didn't want to deal with them and their opinions on how I chose to live my life. They even called Claire when they couldn't get in touch with me, and she went off on them.

Lucian and I have seen each other every day. We usually meet for coffee in the morning after my workout and then have dinner together every night. My food shame issues are almost completely gone, and I've been trying every new restaurant that Lucian takes me to.

We've also started discussing the elephant in the room when it comes to Obsidian and his kinky side. I've been up late every night doing research and figuring out what I want, if anything, from the kink community.

A week after we started seeing each other, I started going over his books, and he wasn't lying when he said that it was a disaster. But that's okay. I got him straightened out and on a new system that works for both of us.

The best part of the last four weeks have been the changes within myself. I've hung up the blouses and slacks, and honestly donated over half of them. I live in my jeans or leggings and t-shirts and hoodies. I've even started wearing leggings out in public. I've never felt more comfortable in my life.

There's a knock on my front door, and I smile. The changes that have taken place over the last four weeks have truly been amazing. And it's all thanks to the man at my door.

I check the peephole and see Lucian standing with his hands in the pockets of his leather jacket. He's staring at the ground like he always does. I flip the lock, and I watch as his eyes lift, like he knows I'm watching him. My panties melt when I see those light green eyes hit mine through the peephole.

His hair is braided back from his face instead of in his usual topknot, and his face and the sides of his head are cleanly shaven. When he smirks, I see those dimples that I love so much appear.

I open the door, and he moves into me, picking me up and pressing a hot kiss to my mouth. My core clenches, and I gasp into his mouth. He's been teasing me with touches, kisses, and looks for the last couple of weeks.

He pulls away, gently placing a kiss on my forehead. "Hey, Gorgeous," he says with a grin. I learned early and quickly not to bother with lipstick, it only ends up ruined within a few minutes with Lucian.

"Hey, Doll," I answer back.

"You ready?" he asks as he sets me back on my feet.

"Whenever you are." I grab my purse and leather jacket. "Where are we going for dinner?"

He takes my keys from me and ushers me out the door. He locks the door, and we start down the stairs. "Well, you've got two choices. Option one—I take you to the new Thai place. Option two—is a complete surprise."

This is one of the things that I love the most about Lucian. He gives me options. He pushes when he feels he needs to, but ultimately, it's up to me if I'm willing to do or try something.

"Can I have a hint for option two?" Lucian stops on the steps and turns to look back up at me.

"That would take the surprise out of it." He presses another kiss to my lips and starts walking down the stairs again.

"Will I like option two?"

"Have you ever not liked option two?" he asks with a laugh. We reach the bottom of the stairs and exit the exterior door.

"Good point." I still get nervous with surprises, but Lucian hasn't let me down yet. "Option two."

"Good choice." He takes my hand and we head towards the art district and not the restaurants.

We continue walking through the art district, and I'm getting more confused as to what the surprise is as we go. He stops in front of his studio and unlocks the door. He leads me through the studio. There's thumping bass playing over the speakers, and I can see the glow of the candles in the back of the studio.

"What's this?" I ask when we step into the bedroom. But I already know the answer. The bed is covered in black silk sheets, candles of all different sizes are lit all over the room.

"I want your picture, Gorgeous." He stands behind me and wraps his arm around my waist. He tugs me back against him. His breath is warm against my neck as he says, "I want to watch as you come apart for me."

"Okay," I say on a breath. He presses a kiss to my neck and releases me.

"I've got an outfit for you in the changing room. Go put it on while I finish setting up."

I nod and start walking to the changing room but pause when I watch him strip out of his leather jacket and throw it on the bed. He starts setting up his camera and tripod. He looks up and sees me watching him.

"Go, Gorgeous." He goes back to his camera, like he knows I'll do what he says.

When I get to the changing room, I see the black silk and lace teddy on the hanger by the door. There's a box under the teddy as well. For a moment, I'm the old Elise. *I can't wear that. I'm too fat.*

But then I shake myself. I can wear it or I can wear nothing. Either way, Lucian will love it, and I will learn to love myself.

I struggle to get the teddy on without ripping anything. I open the box and inside are a pair of patent leather high heels, a set of leather cuffs, and a tube of my favorite lipstick.

I pull my hair out of the messy bun and shake my hair out. I put on the shoes and cuffs. I walk over to the counter, careful not to look at my body in the mirror, and paint my lips. I step back and look at myself in the full-length mirror.

I'm stunned at the vixen staring back at me in the mirror. I can't believe that this is me. I'm fucking stunning. Suddenly, I'm not nervous about being in front of the camera. I'm not worried about the thickness of my waist. I don't care that my breasts and hips are too large.

I look like a bombshell.

I open the door and strut out into the bedroom space, walking straight to Lucian. His eyes widen slightly before his pupils dilate, and he gives me his signature grin.

"Oh, Gorgeous, I think I've finally corrupted you." He adjusts himself and motions for me to move towards the bed. "I'm going to run you through a series of poses. Relax into them. I'll adjust you as needed, but I want you to be as natural as you can be. It's just you and me here."

At first, I'm stiff in the positions and poses he puts me in, the click of the camera making me nervous. But it's not long before I'm relaxed and turned on. He pulls off his shirt and tosses it on the bed next to his jacket, and suddenly, I get an idea.

I crawl to his jacket and slip it on. It smells like him; citrus and musk, and I breathe in his scent from the collar. I raise my eyes to him at the growl he lets out. I let one of the shoulders drop off mine and lean back against the headboard, my legs spread wide.

"My turn," is all the warning I get before he jumps on the bed, crawling over me. I hear the click of the camera and look up at him. "It's set on a timer. I want pictures of us, too."

He kisses down my jaw, careful of my lipstick, before moving down my neck and over my chest. The teddy is no match for him, and he rips the silk like it's made of paper. I gasp when his mouth closes over my nipple and he sucks.

"So responsive," he murmurs before he moves to the other, using his fingers to pinch my nipple.

He moves his hands over my curves; grabbing and kneading before his hand reaches my core. "Is this pussy drenched for me?"

He slips his fingers through my wetness, and I'm arching off the bed. He plunges two fingers into me, thrusting deeply. His thumb presses on my clit, and I go off like a rocket. Stars explode behind my eyes.

I whimper as I watch him pull his fingers out from between my legs.

"So noisy." He brings his fingers up to his mouth and licks me off them. "You taste so good, Gorgeous."

He gets off the bed and unbuckles his belt and kicks off his boots. His tattooed fingers unbutton his jeans, and they hit the floor with a thud. I watch as he strokes his dick, and I'm concerned that he isn't going to fit.

"It'll fit, Gorgeous," he says with a chuckle. He climbs back up on the bed and rubs his hot head through my wetness. He notches himself at my core and slowly starts to push in. My back bows off the mattress, and I can't stop the moan that escapes me.

"You're doing so well, Gorgeous." He pushes in more before sliding back out. "Relax for me."

He presses a kiss to my lips, his tongue stroking mine. I relax into the kiss, and he slides the rest of the way in. I've never felt so full. He pulls away and starts to pound into me. He's hitting every spot in me just right, and soon I can feel myself building towards another orgasm.

Suddenly, he rolls and brings me on top. He lands a slap on my ass, and I can't help the moan that escapes. "Ride me," is all he says before he starts moving my hips. It doesn't take long for me to pick up a rhythm that has both of us on the edge.

"Come for me," he says as he pulls me down and pushes himself deep inside me. I come with a scream, and he is right behind me, coming with a roar.

I slump down on him, trying to catch my breath. I look down at him, and I can't stop the giggle that escapes me.

"Scarlet is your color, Doll," I tell him. He grins up at me and reaches for his t-shirt. I really need to get some smudge-proof lipstick because I really like wearing lipstick, but not on him. He hands me the t-shirt, and I gently wipe the lipstick off his face before taking care of my own.

Once that's done, I snuggle back into his chest, and he wraps his arms around me. I don't know how long we stay like that, but I must have dozed off because I startle at the sound of beeping from the camera.

"The battery is dying," he murmurs into my hair. He gently pushes the hair off my face and presses a kiss to my forehead. "Let me get it shut off."

I watch as he climbs off the bed and turns off the camera. He's the gorgeous one—the tattoos, the muscles, the long blonde hair. But it's also the kindness, the unrepentant self-love, and passion for people to actually see themselves.

"When can I see the photos?" I ask quietly. He looks up at me and grins. He walks out of the bedroom and into his office. He comes back with his laptop, plugs in the card, and pulls up the photos.

"Let me get our food, and I'll be right back." He hands me the laptop and leaves the room. He comes back in with a bag of takeout from the Thai place, passes out our food, and starts a slide show of the photos.

I watch as picture after picture of myself slides across the screen. Despite the fact that I've seen Lucian's work and I know how good he is, I didn't think my pictures would look like his other pictures.

But I do, they do.

I look over at Lucian, and he wipes a tear off my face. "That is how the world sees you, Gorgeous. You are the most beautiful woman I've ever seen, and I'm so sorry that the people that were supposed to build you up made you feel less than."

I watch as the photos transition from me to us. The look of ecstasy on my face is earth-shattering. The look of awe on his face as he watches me come undone rocks me to my core.

"I'm not sorry," I whisper. I look at him. For the first time feeling like I am good enough. "Because I have that now."

Temptation Bonus Chapter

Elise

I am stressed to the max. It's the holidays, and I have been trying to get all of my clients' end-of-year documents together. That's not a big deal. I do that every year.

But this year, I am juggling that, a newly published book, moving in with Lucian, and now going to my parents for Christmas. Initially, I didn't want to go, but Lucian said that we could try and see if they would be civil. If they can't, then he won't try to make me deal with them.

I highly doubt that they are going to be civil, but family is important to Lucian since his entire family disowned him when he decided to pursue photography as a career. He made his own family with the club, but still.

So I'm getting ready for a nightmare lunch with my family.

"You ready, Gorgeous?" Lucian calls for me. He walks into the bedroom, and I giggle when I see him. My family is going to throw a fit when we show up.

"What?" He spins in a slow circle, and I have to admit, he looks damn good. He's in a new pair of dark-wash jeans, his boots are clean, and he even managed to dig up a button down. But jeans are a *no no* in my family, especially at holiday functions. Not to mention his long hair is pulled back in a topknot and his new tattoo is peaking over the collar of his leather jacket.

"Nothing, Doll. You look great." I had planned on wearing a dress for this shit show, but now I've decided I would go in jeans, my knee-high leather boots, and a t-shirt. I get dressed and shrug into my leather jacket. "In for a penny?"

"In for a pound," he says back with a grin. He grabs my hand, and I grab the two bottles of wine. "Do you remember the signal?"

"Yes, green is *fine*. Yellow is *get me out of this*. Red is *get me out of here*. Black is *call the club, we're burying a body*."

We go down the stairs at the back of his studio and exit onto the street. He locks the door and then leads me to his blacked out sixty-nine Dodge Charger. He holds the door and helps me inside before rounding the hood and starting it up.

The loud *whomp*, *whomp* of the cams rattles the car. I grin at the noise and vibrations. This is going to either be a lot of fun or a total nightmare. Once the car is warmed up, he pulls out of his parking spot and we start the drive down to Crescent. We talk about upcoming projects, how my book is doing, and the exhibit he has in February.

The drive passes in a blur, and before I know it, we are pulling into my parents' driveway. I see my father pull back the curtain and shake his head, letting the curtain fall back into place. Lucian gets out and helps me out of the car. He presses a light kiss to my lips, and I'm instantly settled.

If this goes sideways, then my life won't be any different than it has been over the last six months. If it goes better, then maybe my parents will love me despite the fact that I refuse to toe the line they have laid out for me.

I walk up to the front door and turn the knob. It's unlocked. I turn to Lucian with my eyebrow raised. He gives me a thumbs up, and we walk inside. "Hey, Mom. Dad."

My mother comes out of the kitchen, dressed like a good suburban southern woman, complete with pearls and a cream cardigan under her apron. She stops in the hallway that leads to the kitchen and stares at me.

"What are you wearing, Elise?" she asks like I'm naked.

"Clothes," I say simply. "I can leave if it bothers you and not come back."

I threw down the gauntlet. It's up to her if she picks it up.

"Who is this?" she asks, and I tense.

"This is my fiancé, Lucian." I lift my chin and dare her to say anything. "Again, if you don't like it, we can leave and not come back."

"Frank, Elise is here with her... fiancé," she calls into the living room. "Elise, you can take off your jacket and come help me in the kitchen. Lucian, you can watch the game with Frank and Connor in the living room while we wait for lunch to finish."

I look up at Lucian. *Color*, he mouths at me. "Green?"

His grin is slow. "Try again," he whispers.

"Green... for now. Let me introduce you to my dad and brother and then ask me again." I place my coat on the coat rack, and Lucian follows suit. I take his hand and we head into the living room.

We make it into the living room, and I see my dad sitting in his recliner and my brother sitting on the couch. Their eyes are glued to the game, and I have to wait for a commercial before getting their attention, or they will riot.

"Dad, this is Lucian, my fiancé. Lucian, my dad, Frank." I look at my brother, who is sizing Lucian up for a body bag. "Connor, this is Lucian. He will kick your ass, knock it off."

"Elise Marie! Watch your mouth!" my father barks at me.

"Don't talk to her like that," Lucian says in a low voice.

"She's my daughter—"

"Then treat her like it," Lucian says firmly.

"Frank, leave it alone." My mother is standing in the doorway. "She's made her choice, and she's an adult. Lucian, have a seat. Elise, come on and help me."

Lucian sits down next to Connor. *Color*, I mouth at him with a grin. He gives me a thumbs up and turns his attention to the TV. He hates football, and I'm pretty sure I'm going to get a text here in a few minutes telling me to save him.

"Are you happy?" my mother asks me when I walk into the kitchen. For the first time in my entire life, I feel like she's actually looking at me.

"Unbelievably happy."

My mother stares at me for another minute before she nods. "Set the table. The ham is almost done."

When two becomes three.

Wild Obsidian: Menage

Vic Raven

Trigger Warnings

Menage

Light MM

Anal penetration

Menage Chapter 1

Maris

Tonight is demo night, and we have been preparing this demo since last year's event. The demos tonight are a little bit of everything; with breath play, Shibari, primal, and impact play being the most popular.

I am rushing to get ready but Rhett isn't home yet. And I am still working to get my bags packed. I have gotten all three boys settled and in bed while the sitter cleans up dinner and gets laundry started for me.

Rhett said that he would be home after dinner, but we are already an hour past that. I am struggling not to get nervous, and I really need him home soon.

It doesn't matter how long I've been a kinky sex educator. It doesn't matter how many times I've spoken publicly or given demos or panels. I am always a wreck until I lay eyes on Rhett and he tells me it will all be okay.

Tonight, I am hosting a talk on primal play and I need to have all of my stuff together. Primal play isn't necessarily a toy heavy kink, not like impact play or Shibari. But there is the after party, and that needs bags.

I hear Rhett's truck pull up and start getting the rest of our bags together. The boys are already in bed, and the sitter is settled in for the night. All we have to do is get Rhett showered, dressed, and us out the door.

"Maris?" Rhett calls for me.

"In the bedroom," I call back. I hear his heavy boots clunking down the hallway. He laughs at something the sitter says and continues towards our room.

"Sorry, I'm late getting home. We had an engine that took forever to get torn out." He leans down to give me a quick kiss. He goes to grab me, but I scurry out of his reach. He's grubby and grimy, and I do not have time to change my outfit.

Thankfully, our sitter is well-versed in corsetry and helped me get into my corset dress. It is my favorite dress because I had altered it for pockets, but getting out of this one and into a new one would have taken time we didn't have.

"Absolutely not. You need to get your ass in the shower first," I tell him. He grumbles but backs away. "Did you get the engine fixed, or just needed to get it out tonight?"

He takes off his baseball cap and runs his fingers through his black hair. He needs a haircut, but I'm loving this look on him. The top is long and just barely brushes his jaw, but the sides are short with a fade. Seeing all that inky black hair flop down into his face only brings out his startling blue eyes.

"Just out tonight. The new kid is struggling with the mechanics of mechanic-ing but he's getting it. Are you ready for tonight?" he asks, scratching his chin with his thumbnail while looking at the disaster our bed has become.

He recently shaved his beard, and I have to admit, I love being able to see the face that I fell in love with, not to mention the dimples that show up when he really smiles. But the black five o'clock shadow that is gracing his jaw is panty-melting.

I turn around before I jump his bones. "Just about. I've got your rope and rigging for you to do your demo in your leather duffle bag. I've got my iPad to keep track of my notes for my primal panel in my satchel. Oh, and I got all our bags for the after party later tonight in the rolling suitcase."

I hear the clunking of his boots as he heads into our bathroom before I hear the shower turn on.

"Gorgeous, you didn't have to pack all of that. I could have helped."

"We would have been two hours late for the demo if I hadn't packed. Plus, you always forget something. Usually, your rope, which is weird," I laugh. I get the rest of our stuff into the bags and then stack them by the bedroom door and go into the closet to start getting his clothes out.

Our club, Obsidian, has only a few ironclad rules: one, enthusiastic consent, always. And it can be revoked at any time for any reason. Two, vanilla to the door, which has saved many of us from indecent exposure charges.

Even in the middle of summer, jackets and other coverings are a must. We have changing rooms, but most of the time, it's easier to get dressed at home and cover up until we are inside the club.

We are lucky that we were able to purchase the warehouse that we use as our dungeon. Our club is run by a committee, and we have a steep membership fee. But it has allowed us to remain a private event space.

Obsidian is on the outskirts of Franklin, a small mountain town in North Carolina. Because we are privately owned and operated, we don't have to worry as much about laws and local ordinances, but we still need to be very careful.

We were also able to purchase the land and cabins next to our property to open up a primal play park. Obsidian Wilds, or The Wilds for short, was previously a resort that was getting ready to go into foreclosure.

Rhett and I knew the previous owners, and they offered for us to buy the property for cheap. They didn't want some developer to come in and put in subdivisions, and neither did we.

We went to our members to see if they were interested in having a resort so that we could not only have a safe place for our primal community but also host educational retreats and other conferences. It was by far our most lucrative investment as a club.

Our primal community loved having the ability to run around a safe property and not worry about being caught by the police. We are also happy to have the extra income.

The Wilds has six cabins and twelve miles of hiking trails throughout. Plus, there are twelve foot tall fences that surround the entire property along with fast-growing conifers to keep sight lines to a minimum.

Not that it was necessary, especially with over thirty of those fifty acres being heavily wooded. But the extra peace of mind was worth it.

Between the two locations, we have a fair amount of money to invest into programs and charities to help the kinky and queer community.

I hear the shower turn off as I put out Rhett's outfit for tonight. He doesn't love getting all dressed up for any kind of event. So a nice pair of blue jeans, his favorite cowboy boots, and his corset vest are all he needs or wants.

He comes out of the shower fresh and clean, his black hair still dripping. His towel is wrapped around his hips and water beading down his chest before trailing down his six-pack. He had trimmed the stubble on his face into a more groomed beard, and I am instantly wet just looking at him.

It doesn't matter that we have been together for over ten years. It doesn't matter that we have seen each other at our worst. He is still the hottest man I have ever seen.

He has fulfilled every fantasy I'd ever had. Except one.

A few years ago, after the club bought The Wilds, I told him I wanted him and another man to chase me down. To be hunted, caught, and taken under his control. I wanted his rope on me while someone else's hands left their mark.

Rhett only shook his head. That wasn't something he wanted, and that was the end of it. A hard limit. And I respect that, respect him. I'm not willing to risk what we have for a fleeting fantasy and an hour of play.

I watch as he gets ready. First, dropping the towel. His cock is on full display, thick and long. He pulls his jeans on without underwear, then he sits on the bed to put on his socks before his boots. When he stands up, he picks up his corset vest.

This is my favorite part of watching him get ready for club night.

I watch as he puts his arms through the armholes and latches the front of the corset closed. I am damn near drooling as I wait for the next part. He doesn't let me help him tie into his corset. Not because I can't, but because he knows I like having a front-row seat to the next part.

Rhett reaches behind him and grabs the ties at his lower back. He takes a deep breath, rolls his shoulders back, and lifts his chin before he pulls the ties tight.

I watch as his already trim waist becomes trimmer. I watched as his already broad chest widened. His arms seemed even larger, the tattoos on his arms and neck more pronounced.

He shifts his shoulders to get the corset to sit right before he turns away from me. As he ties off the excess string in the back, he gives me the perfect view of his back and ass.

The steampunk style mechanical spine shows through the space between the panels on his back. The tattoo continues up over his neck, and when he has a fresh haircut, you can see it disappear into the base of his skull.

He glances over his shoulder at me and chuckles.

"You have a little bit of drool, Gorgeous," he says. He walks up to me and runs his thumb over my bottom lip. His cologne envelopes me with the scent of leather, cedar, and a touch of motor oil that always clings to him.

"Stop it," I say breathlessly. "We don't have time for any shenanigans. We are already running late."

He runs his hand down my jaw and grips the front of my neck, pulling me closer and lifting my face to his. My breathing picks up as he lowers his head down to me. His lips are a breath away from mine when he releases me and starts toward the bedroom door.

"You coming?" he asks as he grabs his leather jacket and shrugs it on. He grabs his cowboy hat off the hook by the door and looks back at me. He rakes his hair back from his face and puts his hat on.

"Yeah," I croak.

He laughs and picks up our bags. I quickly grab my own leather jacket and put it on, following him out into the living room.

Layla, our sitter, is reading her book with the TV playing softly in the background. She never even looks up as she says, "Don't start. You're already running late and I've been watching those boys since they came out of your vagina. Go."

We laugh and say our goodbyes and 'be safe' to each other.

Rhett throws our bags into the back of my Suburban before helping me into the passenger seat. I've been wearing corsets since I was nineteen, and it never ceases to amaze me how difficult it is to climb into tall vehicles.

Of course, Rhett never acts like it bothers him at all. He says that it's like wearing a tight t-shirt. I don't think we tie our corsets the same though.

Rhett starts up the Suburban, and the gentle rumble is soothing. He pulls down the rutted road that leads us down the mountain, one hand maneuvering the huge rig like it's second nature while the other is on my thigh.

"Are you ready for tonight?" I ask him. Rhett has been working with rope damn near his entire life. First, as a kid helping his dad with his tree company. Then taking Shibari lessons in Asheville when he moved there after his dad died.

When we moved to Franklin after getting married, he had just started teaching classes when the instructor couldn't make it. Now, he is the premier Shibari instructor in the southeast. He makes his own rope, and we sell it to the community.

"Yeah. I've got a new set of rope made for you after the demos are done for tonight." He glances over as we hit the main highway leading to Franklin. "Did you match your corset to the rope?"

"No, I haven't seen the new rope yet. I just got my favorite corset because it's got pockets and you know how I get when I'm nervous." I watch his profile as he continues the forty-five minute drive from our house to Obsidian.

"Good, that's your first surprise of the night then."

"There's more than one?" I ask.

"Oh, yeah. And you'll love both." He continues watching the road, the hand on my thigh rubbing soothing circles. "Are you ready for tonight?"

"I'm as ready as I'll ever be." I have always had an issue with public speaking, and not just to big groups.

If there are more than one or two people around me, I clam up and stop talking. It's one of the reasons I continue to push myself and speak at panels and events.

"I won't start my demo until you give me the signal that you're okay."

"I know. I don't know why I still get like this. I've been doing this for the last twelve years and I still can't shake being afraid to talk to people."

"Gorgeous, you've made a ton of progress in the last twelve years. You used to not be able to talk to anyone. Now you can talk to huge groups of people. You just need support, and that's okay."

Rhett is right. I have made huge progress. When I first met Rhett, I had to have a friend help me negotiate with him about a rope scene. I had so much trauma around men and sex that I couldn't talk to anyone without someone there to help me.

My past is the entire reason I am a sex and kink educator now. I am passionate about having a voice and helping others find their voice too.

We spend the rest of the drive to Obsidian in silence. Just the murmur of the radio and the hum of the tires keeping us company.

When we pull up to the club, we are the last of the educators to arrive, which means we will have to hurry to get our stuff set up. Since my demo is mostly discussion, I'll help Rhett set up his demo before we move to my area.

Rhett helps me out of the rig and gets our bags out of the back. He leads us to the side entrance where a member of security checks our badges and then lets us inside.

Then we walk into the chaos of demo night.

Menage Chapter 2

Maris

Obsidian hasn't always been a dungeon. The warehouse used to be part of Franklin's old textile industry, back when the town's lifeblood was cotton and denim. For decades, machines clattered across the floor, turning raw fiber into fabric.

When the mill closed in the early 2000s, the building sat empty, collecting dust and graffiti. A group of us were tired of driving to Asheville all the time and decided it was time to open our own place. We bought it cheap, scrubbed it down, and rebuilt it into something new.

The best part about the kinky community, beyond safety and inclusivity, is that just about everyone has a day job. Rhett is a mechanic and I am an educator. Cam is a general contractor and Ashley, his late partner, was an event planner.

Our members all bring something to the table, and it really helps to make Obsidian shine. Not just the club, but the community. We have lawyers and doctors who keep us safe medically and legally. We have techies to help run everything from club night setup to educational seminars.

When it came time to build Obsidian, our community came together and made it an amazing and safe place for our members. Obsidian has kept the old beams, creaky wood floors, and exposed brick. But instead of a place where workers toil for minimum wage, now we freely dole out pleasure and pain in equal measure.

The club crew has already gotten the floor plan laid out for the demos tonight. The various active demos like Shibari, the three impact sets, the fire demo, and others are all partially walled off so that people can talk to the educator and participant without interrupting, or being interrupted by, other demos.

But the discussion-based demos, like mine, are being held in the back classrooms. No one needs to hear a bullwhip being cracked and then try to learn about the intricacies of primal play and consent-non-consent.

Rhett and I walk over to where his demo is taking place. He is stationed next to Cam, who is setting up his Saint Andrew's cross and has already unpacked his toy bag. His is one of the impact demos that is happening tonight. His partner for the night is helping him set up.

Rhett and Cam have been best friends their entire lives, and when Cam lost Ashley, we were there to help him and his boys get through it. He hasn't taken another submissive in the three years since Ashley died, and no one blames him.

Well, he's taken partners over the years occasionally, usually keeping everything at the club. He said it is hard to find someone who is willing to be a submissive, step mom, and all the other things he needs.

Rhett gives Cam the manly handshake and hug combo, and I wave at him before I start pulling out the rope and rigging Rhett needs for his demo. I can barely hear them over the music that had started up since we walked in, but I take a moment to take them both in.

They are imposing men, both standing at six two and packed with muscle. They are both covered in tattoos, but that's where the similarities end.

Where Rhett is fair-skinned, with black hair and blue eyes, Cam is tanned from years of being outside working construction. He has dark green eyes and long blond hair that he ties back in a bun. It is like looking at night and day.

They finish talking, and Rhett comes over to me. He takes his cowboy hat off and places it on the table. His hair falls into his eyes, and he moves into me, causing me to back up into the table. He brings his finger to my chin and forces me to crane my head back to look at him.

"Tonight, you have two surprises. You will get both as long as you are a bad girl," he says with a knowing grin as he looks down at me. "You can have one drink at the bar, no more. I need you sober for what I have planned."

"Okay," I murmur. While I am Rhett's Submissive, I am not a submissive. Throughout our relationship, and the various things we have tried together, one thing is perfectly clear: I will follow if he leads. Neither one of us is interested in a Dom/Sub relationship. He leads, I follow. That's it.

He turns back to the table and continues to lay out his rope the way he wants it, dark to light colors from left to right. Long to short lengths from top to bottom. One of the club crew pulls over a ladder and helps him hang the pulleys and hooks on the exposed metal beams.

I watch it all with a smile on my face as I remember back to when I had finally gotten the courage, and a friend to help me, to talk to him about tying me up. I thought Shibari was beautiful, but the thought of being restrained after the trauma I had been through made it incredibly difficult to actually go through with it.

Samantha had finally convinced me to talk to him after the third rope class we attended. I had talked to her about how much I wanted to be tied up, but all of my issues and trauma made it damn near impossible.

Not to mention the whole talking to people thing.

I had given Samantha the go ahead to tell Rhett about some of my issues and hoped that he would be willing to negotiate with me, even though I had to have Samantha help me.

Samantha had gotten Rhett's attention after class and told him that I wanted him to tie me up. At first, he was hesitant, and I couldn't blame him. If I needed help with negotiating a scene, then would I be willing to safe word if I needed to? He didn't want to traumatize me more than I already was.

Instead, he asked me out for coffee, no rope. He just wanted to get to know me and where my head was, why my trauma made it so I couldn't talk to people. We went for coffee, and after the second cup, we were chatting like old friends. I gave the signal that Samantha could leave, and we stayed and talked for hours.

The second negotiation was at a steakhouse and we closed out the restaurant. I told him what I was looking for in regard to being put in rope, and he explained what he could do for me.

By the end of that night we had agreed to a semi-public rope scene the following Friday night at the club in Asheville. We negotiated the scene down to the most microscopic detail; I wanted to be fully restrained but my hands had to remain free. I wanted to fly, but only if he kept a hand on me. I wouldn't be completely naked and would stay in my bra and panties. On and on the details were set until both of us were comfortable.

When that Friday came, I was a wreck, but in the best way. We had requested one of the rigging stations in the back of the club where most people didn't wander, but would be open enough for people to see us and us to see them. Plus, Samantha would be there to keep an eye on things.

When I showed up to the club, I was a jumble of nerves, both fear and excitement. I walked to his station and saw that he had the most beautiful jade-colored rope laid out. He had the rigging hooks pulled low enough for him to grab them, and he had a couple of wooden boxes stacked so that he didn't have to break his back trying to tie up my short ass.

He looked up as I walked to him, and the lust in his eyes gave me pause. Not because I was scared, but because no one looked at me with that kind of lust. I was too short, too curvy, too awkward, too shy. But the lust in his eyes made me feel like a goddess.

The music in the club was heavy drumbeats that throbbed through me. I stopped in front of him, waiting for him to make the first move, letting him take the lead. He took my hand in his much larger one and led me to the wooden boxes that he had stacked up.

He asked permission before he unzipped my dress. At my nod, his big hands deftly lowered the zipper. I shivered as he lowered the straps from my shoulders and then helped me step out of it.

He asked if I wanted my boots removed, and at my nod, he lowered himself down and untied my combat boots. He gently pulled them off my feet, followed by my socks. He placed everything under the table where he had his rope laid out.

As I stood there in just my underwear and bra, he looked up at me. At first, I thought it was so that he could figure out how he wanted to tie me up. But as the seconds ticked by, I was left wondering if my curves were too much, if I wasn't good enough.

But he laid that to rest with one gruff word, "Gorgeous."

He helped me up onto the stacked boxes, where I stood looking out over the rest of the club. I could see Samantha at one of the tables watching us. But no one else was paying attention.

I watched as he grabbed the first section of rope and started at my feet. He tied one leg, then the other, before moving up to my hips. I felt his fingers brush my skin as he tied knots or laid down more rope.

I closed my eyes and listened to the drumbeats, a primal urge rising up inside me.

On and on he worked, moving up from feet to shoulders, making sure to leave my hands free. He checked in with me constantly, making sure that I was comfortable, that the rope wasn't too tight, that I was mentally okay.

I gave him greens until he got to my arms. That's when I stiffened and had to breathe through the panic. When he hooked my arms to the harness he had created on my chest, I called yellow.

Rhett stopped instantly and moved in front of me. Even with me standing on two boxes, I could barely look him in the eye. He placed his hand on my chin and raised my face to his. He placed his forehead on mine and took a deep breath. I leaned into him and did the same.

I don't remember how long we stood like that. Breathing together. But after a while, I gave him a green, and he finished securing my arms to the harness. I closed my eyes and let the drumbeats take me away.

The weight of the rope on my skin was tight but not painful. The restriction of movement in a way that was finally safe. I felt myself let go.

I hadn't even noticed that I was flying until I felt Rhett's hand on my thigh. He was gently pushing me into a swing that made me feel like I could touch the stars.

I couldn't tell you how long he pushed me or how long I remained restrained. But I can tell you that after that night, I finally felt a sense of peace that I had been searching for since I ran away from home at sixteen.

I come back to myself as Rhett is finishing up. It's almost time to start my demo.

"I'm going to go to the bar. Do you two want anything?" I ask Rhett and Cam. They both nod and follow me over. I place my order for a cranberry vodka and two beers. I feel them approach from behind as they come to stand on either side of me.

When the bartender hands us our drinks, I turn and lean back against Rhett. He wraps one arm around my shoulder and chest and rests his chin on my head. I look at Cam as I take a sip of my drink.

Sometimes there is no urge or desire when I'm around Cam. Other times, I can't help but be attracted to him. Tonight is one of those nights where I am attracted to him. It's hard not to be when he's got the 20s *Gatsby* vibe going on.

His black slacks are hugging his muscled thighs. The emerald shirt matches his eyes. His sleeves are rolled up his forearms, showcasing his tattoos that seem to move when he flexes. He's got leather cuffs on his wrists and a thick silver chain with a dual raven pendant that rests at the hollow of his throat.

His leather vest hugs his narrow waist and emphasizes his broad shoulders. He's got a long chain that runs from his wallet to his belt loop. His shirt is unbuttoned at the top, showing part of the wolf howling at the moon tattooed on his throat.

Cam leans down to whisper in my ear and I'm instantly wrapped up in his cologne. The scent of leather, pine, bergamot, and sawdust envelops me. "You're drooling, Little Moth."

I stiffen and pull back from him, taking shelter in Rhett's arms.

Rhett has never made me feel bad about being attracted to other men. But this felt like crossing a line. Especially after he denied bringing a third into our bedroom.

"Breathe, Gorgeous. I've got you," Rhett grumbles in my ear.

I do as he says, taking a deep breath and trying not to look at Cam.

"You can look, Little Moth. Sometimes getting close to a flame isn't so bad," Cam says. He's gotten closer. I can feel his body heat on my back as I cling to Rhett.

"And sometimes, a Little Moth will burn," I mumble back.

"Let's get you set up for your presentation, Gorgeous," Rhett says as he wraps his arm around my shoulder.

I just nod as we walk over to his table and I grab my satchel.

"Gorgeous, you don't have to be embarrassed for being attracted to him."

"I'm not. I just felt like I was crossing a line and I don't want to disrespect you like that."

"You're not disrespecting me by being human, Gorgeous. I know that you are mine and that's not going to change because of him."

I just nod and allow him to lead me back to the classroom where my demo is being held. I stand at the doorway for a second as I watch the room slowly fill up and as people take their seats. My nerves are starting to creep in, but instead of allowing them, I hand my iPad to one of the tech guys and we set it up.

He hands me my microphone and I walk to the front of the classroom with my drink.

As I take my place, the projector pops on, and it's go time.

Menage Chapter 3

Rhett

I watch from the back of the room as Maris gets into the swing of her demo and wait for the signal that she is okay. If she sticks to her routine, the signal will come in about five minutes. If not, then my demo will be pushed back or canceled.

Either way, she is my priority, and Obsidian knows that. Which is why the few times that I've had to cancel a demo, and new members get upset, the other members step in. Maris is well loved in our community and no one is allowed to fuck with her.

As I lean back against the wall, I hear the distant crack of the bullwhip. Cam has gotten started on his demo. His partner tonight, Henley, is a true masochist.

She loves being restrained and whipped. They have a regular scene twice a month where he whips the shit out of her and she comes on his cross. But there is nothing between them beyond the pleasure and pain. They tried briefly, but it just didn't work out.

I think back to the conversation that Cam and I had about six months ago. He had come over for the weekend with his boys while Maris was at the Wilds for an authors' retreat.

We let all five of the boys run around the shop while we worked. I had just gotten a new shipment of rope in, and I was working on getting it boiled and ready to dye. Cam was working on a custom bullwhip for one of the members.

Both of us were keeping one eye on the boys and one eye on our works in progress. It was chaos. But here in about twenty minutes they would start crashing out in front of the TV one by one. It happened every time.

As we were working, I thought about asking him if he would be interested in helping me surprise Maris. She loved when I chased her in the woods. She loved when I turned her into a Shibari work of art.

But she also loved being spanked, and the few times she had been caught and punished with a flogger, she had come so hard I had to carry her back to the house. I knew she was happy with what we were doing, but I never wanted her to shrink herself for me. If she needed more, I wanted to give it to her.

When we first started dating, we made a deal that if we had a fantasy, we would try to make it happen. It didn't matter what the fantasy was—we created an open space for each other to try it.

After she opened up to me about some of her fantasies, I told her that sometimes I wanted to be chased. Sometimes, I wanted to be on the other end of the rope. In the time that we had been together, we had explored all manner of kinks together.

But when she opened up to me about being chased through the woods by me and another man, I shut down. It wasn't my finest moment, and I apologized profusely when I realized how much it had hurt her.

It was something that I had sat with to try to figure out. Did I not want someone touching her because she is mine? Was I insecure? What was the reason that I had immediately shut it down?

Over the last couple of years, she has really grown more comfortable in her body, skills, and wants. It has been amazing to see, and I want to give her every last fantasy that she has.

"Maris and my anniversary is coming up," I say out loud. "I need your help with a surprise."

Cam looks up from his whip. His dark green eyes are direct but open. "Okay...."

"Maris wants to be chased by me and another man. She told me about it years ago, but I was an asshole and shut her down without even thinking about it. She was good about it, and accepted my apology, but it didn't sit right with me."

"Are you asking me to be the other man that chases her?" Cam asks in his normal, direct way. "Because that is a big ask. You know how I get on a hunt and how hard it is for me to pull off."

"I know, that's why I wanted to bring up a two-fold surprise. First, I want to bring you in after demo night. I want to Top both of you. Give myself a chance to be okay with it. Give her the chance to be okay with it."

"Go on." Cam is skeptical. He's a Dom through and through. I don't think he's ever been told what to do.

"Then, if it goes well and I can handle it, I want to reserve the Wild's for the weekend. We could do it here, but that would mean sending the boys away for the night, and I don't want to upset the boys' routines. Plus, Layla loves your boys."

"But that still doesn't answer my biggest issue. What are you going to do when I go full primal with her? Because the only thing that will be able to pull me off is her safe wording."

"I've been sitting with this for years, Cam. Why did I say no? Was it knee-jerk? Was I being an alpha-hole? What I realized is that I don't trust anyone with her. Too many people have hurt her that should have protected her. You won't hurt her, not in a way that she doesn't want."

"And if she doesn't want this?"

"Do you want this, Cam? Are you even willing to do this?" I answer him. Because if he isn't, I don't know that there is another man that I would trust enough.

"At the risk of sounding like an asshole, Maris is smart, sexy, and drop-dead gorgeous. I would have to be dead to not notice and want her. But she's yours, she's off-limits."

"But would you do this for us, with us?"

"Let me think about it. I'm not saying no. I'm only saying that while you are my best friend, she is also my friend. This crosses lines that can't be uncrossed no matter how relaxed people are about sex. Hell, it took Henley and me months to get back to just being friends after the disaster of dating."

I realize that I have been leaning against the wall for longer than I intended. I catch Maris' attention and she nods that she's good.

I leave the classroom and walk over to my demo. My student is already there in a bodysuit, like we'd discussed. I have one rule when tying up other people—keep yourself covered. I am a happily married man and don't want breasts or penises in my face as I work.

My station already has a group formed around it and one of the members looks pissed to have been kept waiting.

"Nice of you to show up, man," the asshole says. He's shorter than me by a lot, damn near Maris' height, and he's got that mean guy energy. I'm not in the mood for it.

"That's strike one on a two-strike club. I haven't seen you around here before, but let me educate you on how shit works here. When someone is nice enough to put on a demo to educate you, they are taking time out of their lives to do so. It's called patience. Learn some, or you won't stay here long."

"Whatever, man. Let's get this going." He puffs up like he's trying to impress someone.

"And that's strike two. Get the fuck out." I nod to the bouncer set up next to our station. "Get him the fuck out of here. He's officially banned."

"You can't ban me, I'm a member!" he roars at me.

"And I'm one of the founders of this club. Last chance before you are thrown out on your ass. Get the fuck out of my club."

He goes pale, like he realized that he fucked up. The bouncer leads him out and radios to the head of security for the night that this member was officially banned by me.

"Are we ready to get started?" I ask everyone else. They all nod, and my student gets up on the wooden boxes I have laid out. "Then let's do this."

I get to work, starting at her ankles and working my way up. She has no limitations when it comes to Shibari, so I get her contorted into a harness that bends her backwards and essentially hogties her. I make sure that my work is set and she's comfortable before I pull down the rigging.

I hook her up and slowly let her fly. The new members and other onlookers ask questions as they watch in awe as she slips into that meditative state that allows her to let go of every thought and she settles into her body.

I answer questions as I keep an eye on her. I watch her breathing patterns and measure her body's fatigue and stress. I spin her around and push her so that she swings out into the crowd a bit more.

I glance over at Cam and he's snuggled up with Henley on the small couch next to his cross. Aftercare is Cam's favorite part of any play scene. He needs it just as much as his partner does.

He's brushing her hair from her face and drying her tears. He's already applied ointment to her welts and snuggled her in a blanket. Knowing Cam, he's probably already got snacks and water off to the side for her.

Henley's girlfriend, Beth, is next to them, rubbing her leg and murmuring in her other ear.

I turn my attention back to my student and slowly start lowering her from the rigging and hooks. Her boyfriend steps forward and helps me release her from the restraints.

This is the second rule of working with me—you provide your own aftercare. I will make sure that you are physically okay, but anything beyond that is on you to provide. The only one I'll provide aftercare to is Maris.

I've worked with my student several times, and her boyfriend is really good at making sure she is okay after any rope play we do.

I pack up my bag, making sure that I have the rope that I dyed for Maris on the top. I grab my hat and push my hair out of my face before putting it on. I finish cleaning up my station and throwing away trash left behind.

I walk over to Cam's station to see if he's ready. The club is starting close down for the educational portion of the night and the after party is getting ready to kick off. Everyone is helping clear stations and partitions. Some of the stations will stay open and people will play, but for the most part, it's a party now.

Cam bundles Henley off to her girlfriend and starts cleaning up his space. He cleans all of his equipment and stows it into his toy bag. Next, he wipes down the cross and makes sure that the area around his station doesn't have leftover drink cups or trash.

"I'm going to go get Maris," I tell him.

"I'm coming with you. I need a minute of normalcy after that scene."

"Is everything okay?" I ask him. He is a true sadist, but sometimes, he has Dom drop from inflicting pain and needs a second or two to get his bearings.

"Yeah, aftercare helps a lot, but sometimes the endorphins are a bit much." Cam gathers up the rest of his stuff. "Henley has been going through some shit with her therapist and she needed more of a release than normal. It took almost twice as long to get her to drop than I was prepared for."

"We can do this another time, Cam." I give him the out. I'm suddenly nervous about what is coming next. We approach the back classrooms and see that Maris' class is still going on. The door is open and I can see that she is wrapping up.

"Nice try. I've been dying to get my hands on her since we agreed to this. Plus, I think being Topped would be good for me tonight. Who knows, I might be your next Sub," he jokes.

"I couldn't handle you as my sub, you don't listen for shit." I laugh, but the image of Cam tied up in my rope, on a bondage bench, flashes through my mind. His ass cheeks spread wide as I slammed into him. Maris on her hands and knees in front of him as he takes her.

I clear my throat and watch as Maris' class releases and people start filing out. I discretely adjust myself, the image weaving a new fantasy for me.

Cam looks over at me with his eyebrow raised, but says nothing. Instead, he turns back to take in Maris.

Maris grabs her drink and iPad, putting the latter in her satchel. She lifts her head and sees Cam and me standing just outside the door. Her eyes darken as she takes us both in.

I'm not an egotistical man, but I know what I look like. I take care of my body and appearance. Cam is the same way.

But I take a second to take her in. She is a petite woman, standing at only five-two, but she is a bombshell. Her corset dress pushes her big tits up and emphasizes her tiny waist and big ass.

She has her long, curly red hair pulled back into a high ponytail. Her makeup is soft, but her light green eyes are lined in thick black liner.

Maris slings her satchel over her shoulder and starts walking towards us. Her combat boots are loose and clunk on the ground as she walks. This woman has held my heart since that night almost thirteen years ago when I tied her up in my rope the first time.

She stops in front of me, her body so close that I can smell her arousal over her perfume. I take the satchel from her and hand it to Cam. She lifts her eyebrow at the handoff but doesn't say anything.

Maris loves educating. She loves teaching about primal play, being prey, and non-con. But one of the things that sets Maris apart is that she really gets into her classes. She gets turned on, and it makes our time at the after party a lot of fun.

"My gorgeous girl, I'm going to give you a choice. We can go out and mingle, dance, and party. Or we can start our night in the private room."

Maris looks from me to Cam and back.

"Yes, Gorgeous, all of us."

A blush heats her cheeks and she nods.

Menage Chapter 4

Cam

As we walk upstairs to the private rooms, I stay in front of Rhett and Maris. I know that Rhett is grounding Maris, keeping her from getting too much in her head. To be honest, I wish I had someone grounding me.

Maris isn't just a piece of ass and a good time. Yes, she is absolutely stunning. Yes, she is wicked smart. Yes, her kink lines right up with mine. But there is so much more to her than that. Maris truly cares about people. She's a fantastic mother. And after everything she went through as a kid, she has every right to be bitter and cold.

But she is patient and kind. She loves with her entire heart, and if you are lucky enough to be in her circle, she will do anything for you. I am lucky enough to be in her inner circle. But I am terrified that tonight will change everything.

I unlock the door to my private room, hoping like hell I'm not making a massive mistake.

I open the door and step inside. One of the perks of being a founding member of Obsidian is having a private, studio style apartment. Any member can rent the smaller rooms for the evening, but they are pretty basic. Just a big open room with a bed, half bath, and a bondage bench or cross.

The founder's suites each have a bedroom, an en-suite bathroom, and a small kitchenette. Nothing flashy, just a small refrigerator, microwave, and breakfast nook. The goal is that if we want to play all night long, we don't have to leave our rooms. Or if we are too deep in a drop, we don't have to go far to come back up.

When Rhett and I were discussing our plans for tonight, we decided that we would have our play scene in my rooms. If this didn't work out, or if it was too much for Maris, we didn't want their rooms tainted for her.

While Rhett and Maris were setting up their demos, one of the club crew took all our bags to my room. Rhett and I didn't want Maris to have to worry about a thing tonight. This is about her pleasure, nothing else.

I place my keys on the small table next to the door, and Rhett does the same for their room next door. Everything tonight is planned down to the most minute detail. Contingency plans are in place. But everything stops if Maris says the word.

Rhett leads Maris to the center of the room. He takes a step back, and I watch as this goddess of a woman stands there with her head held high, but picks at her fingernails. She is a study in contradictions.

I take a second to look at her in my space. My rooms are plain but masculine; minimal furniture and dark colors.

The bed is pulled away from the walls and has no head or footboard to allow for easy access. The St. Andrew's cross in the corner next to the bondage bench. And finally, my pride and joy, a wall of my favorite toys. Everything from floggers and whips, to ball gags and cuffs.

I bring my gaze back to Maris. I won't lie and say that I haven't fantasized about this. About the three of us together. I just never actually thought it would happen. But here I am, watching this woman fidget in front of me.

Rhett comes over to stand beside me and crosses his arms over his chest, mirroring my stance. Tonight will be the first night in damn near twenty years that I will Bottom. I'll be letting Rhett call the shots. And I am surprisingly okay with it. Mostly because I get to have my Little Moth, if only for the night.

At Rhett's nod, I take a step towards Maris. Her gaze snaps to mine, and I hold it as I take another slow, measured step. I watch as her pupils dilate, swallowing up the beautiful jade green of her eyes. Her hands stop picking at her nails and drop to her sides. I take another step towards her, hunting her.

She lifts her chin even higher, indicating that she needs me to earn her submission. I grin as I take the final step into her. Her head is craned back and I'm staring into the eyes of the most beautiful prey I have ever seen.

I grab her by the throat and start moving her backwards towards the bed. She tries to spin and break my grip, but I pull her to me and pick her up. She weighs next to nothing but fights like a hellion. Pushing at my shoulders and wiggling to break free.

This is her favorite part. I've seen her go toe to toe with Rhett and lose every time. She ends up restrained in his ropes and coming until her legs give out.

But that's not how I like to play. I won't restrain her with rope or cuffs. I want her to fight me. I want her to beg and plead. And only after she has worn herself out will I take her again and again.

I throw her on the bed and watch as those glorious tits bounce. Maris lands and scrambles up. I dive on top of her, pinning her arms over her head. I leave her legs free on purpose, hoping that she will continue to fight.

I pin her hips with mine and watch as her eyes widen, and I know she can feel my cock rubbing against her cunt. She lets out a low moan and starts grinding against me, but after a second or two, she catches herself and stops. She bucks her hips and tries to roll me off her, but I've got about a hundred pounds on her. She's not going anywhere.

I hear Rhett's boots on the hardwood floors as he comes closer. He steps up to the bed and I release her just enough so that he can slide her to the edge of the bed. He positions her so that her head is hanging over the side.

She continues to try and buck me off, thrashing her head, trying to get away. But Rhett grabs her by the throat and forces her head still. I start unhooking the swing hooks on the front of her corset, watching with awe as inch by inch her skin is exposed. Her heavy breasts are bared to me, and her nipples tighten into little pebbles.

I continue to hold one arm down while Rhett controls the other. I use my other hand to part the corset the rest of the way and cup her breast, bringing the nipple to my mouth. Rhett unbuckles his belt while keeping a firm hand on her throat. He releases himself from his jeans and strokes himself before shifting so that he can shove his cock down her throat.

I watch as he face fucks her, and when he moves his hand from her throat to grip her ponytail, I see the outline of his cock sliding in and out of her throat. Maris stops struggling against us and starts swallowing. Her throat convulses and Rhett's head falls back on his shoulders.

I take the opportunity to remove the corset the rest of the way and look at my prize. Maris is a gorgeous creature, all curves and soft skin. I trail my mouth between her breasts, licking and kissing my way down to her sweet cunt.

I pull out my knife and drag the edge of the blade around her nipples. She moans and Rhett shudders. Maris has grabbed onto Rhett's thighs and he continues to pound into her throat, only giving her a second to breathe before he's right back in there.

I trail my knife down her belly and watch as it quivers. Making quick work of her thong with my knife, I trace my finger along her outer lips before dragging my knife along the same path. Maris whimpers and I can feel my cock starting to drip with precum.

With a signal from Rhett, I dive face first into her soaking cunt and eat like a starving man. I lick and nip at her outer lips, bite at her clit, and within minutes Maris is arching off the bed, her screams of pleasure muffled by Rhett's cock.

Rhett pulls out of her mouth and I climb off her and go to stand next to him. She looks at us with dazed eyes. I turn towards Rhett and start working the swing hooks from his corset, revealing his massive, tattooed chest. I hear Maris' moan over my shoulder. I slip off Rhett's corset and let it drop to the floor.

I trail my hand over his pecs and tweak his nipples. Rhett lets out a groan and steps closer into me. He starts to work the snaps of my leather vest, pushing it off my shoulders and dropping it to the floor. He starts to unbutton my shirt, and it follows my vest.

His calloused hands are rough against my chest as he runs his hands down my chest, making a beeline for my pants. He makes quick work of the button and zipper, and before I know it, I am standing naked in front of him.

He takes my cock in his rough hand and strokes it, and I let out a low moan. Behind me, I hear Maris whimper. I take that as my green light that we can continue. Rhett lets me go and walks over to the bed. Maris gets up on her knees and reaches for Rhett, but he shakes his head.

He unbuttons his jeans and pushes them down his legs. After he steps out of them, he lays down on the bed and pulls Maris to him. She climbs on top and starts grinding herself against him. He grabs her hips to still her and I climb up on the bed. I reach into the small shelf built into the bed and grab the bottle of lube.

Rhett draws Maris' mouth to his, which gives me a perfect view of her tight asshole. Thankfully, Rhett has already done the prep work with Maris over the years, and this won't be uncomfortable for her. But I am a bit wider than Rhett, and need to make sure she is ready.

I drip some lube onto her asshole and start to massage it in. Maris lets out a low moan and starts grinding against Rhett again. I slip my finger into her ass and I feel her clamp down on me. I keep working my finger, and within minutes, she's coming again.

Slowly, I add a second finger, and I feel her relax. Rhett does too, because he lifts her hips just enough to enter her. Maris lets out a loud groan of pleasure and I am damn near ready to explode.

I place my hand between her shoulder blades, forcing her to lie flat on top of Rhett so that I can enter her. Rhett is murmuring sweet nothings in her ear, and she is nodding along. Rhett pulls her ass cheeks apart and gives me another nod.

After rolling on a condom, I lube up my cock and notch it at her asshole. I slowly start to push in, feeling resistance. "Relax, Little Moth." At my words, she melts into Rhett and I'm able to push the rest of the way in.

She feels incredible, and I can feel Rhett through the thin tissue of her anus. First, Rhett starts to move, and I hold still. It doesn't take long for Maris to push back against me, giving me a signal that she is good.

When Rhett pulls back, I push in. We keep that rhythm, and I reach up and grab Maris by the throat and squeeze gently. Rhett palms her breast, and with a tweak of her nipples, Maris comes again with a scream.

I can't hold back any longer, and when I look at Rhett, he nods like he is right there with me. I continue to stroke my cock in and out of her, both of us drawing out her orgasm.

Finally, I erupt, filling the condom with rope after rope of come. I feel Rhett push into her one last time and he comes with a shout.

Maris collapses on top of him and, after taking a second to catch my breath, I gently pull out of her. I tie off the condom and take it to the bathroom. I grab a washcloth from the stack and wet it with warm water, then I walk to the fridge and grab a couple bottles of water.

I come back to the bed to find Maris snuggled into Rhett's side. I take the time to clean her up, making sure that I didn't hurt her. When I am satisfied, I throw the washcloth into the bathroom and snuggle up on her other side.

I throw my leg over hers and run my hand up and down her arm.

"Are you okay, Little Moth?" I ask. I'm not going to lie to myself, I want to do this again. I want to hunt her, to tie her up, to flog her. And if I am being really honest with myself, I want Rhett as well. I want the whole thing.

But Maris doesn't answer me—she just nods.

"I need the words, Little Moth."

"Gr...gr...green," she stutters out.

Rhett and I chuckle. I'll take it as a good sign that we fucked the stutter right back into her.

"Good Little Moth."

Maris snuggles back into me, allowing me to wrap my arm around her. And Rhett runs his hand up and down my side.

"How are you, Cam?" Rhett asks me. There is hesitation on both of our parts about us touching each other. Every one in this bed has experimented with all kinds of kink and people, but crossing the line of friendship could destroy it.

"I'm surprisingly good. You?"

"Never better."

He shows her she's normal just the way she is

Wild Obsidian: Overload

Vic Raven

Trigger Warnings

Childhood trauma

Neurodivergence (AuDHD, ODD, etc)

Overload Chapter 1

Maggie

Since I was a kid, I knew I was different. I didn't like to be touched. I didn't like certain fabrics, foods, or noise. I was labeled a picky eater, a slob, and anti-social. I didn't realize that all the quirks that I had dealt with, and been made fun of for, for my entire life were actually signs of autism.

I don't like small talk, and often my directness makes people uncomfortable. I don't like to wear pants, and even in the coldest of weather, I wear dresses. And, at best, I am reluctant to try new things.

A couple of years ago, I found myself at a crossroads of sorts. I had just read an article on BDSM and trauma awareness. It felt like my brain was starting to link up everything I knew about myself and my sexuality and the traits that most of the kinky community have.

The negotiations, direct communication, and consent were all things that I felt like I was missing in my normal life and relationships. So I attended a couple of munches at Obsidian and got to know the people. And I realized I wasn't alone.

The people I met made me feel welcome and accepted. For the first time in my life, I wasn't a weirdo. I was among friends.

I applied for membership and after attending the classes and finding a mentor, I became a full member of Obsidian. I continued to explore and learn, not just about the community, but about myself.

The one thing that I continue to struggle with, though, is overstimulation. But I want to change that.

It's club night at Obsidian and I'm tucked back on one of the couches watching everyone play and mingle. The music is quieter back here and there aren't as many people. I requested that security let Vex know that I am looking for him when he comes in. I take a quick sip of my drink as I continue to people watch.

I see Vex look around before spotting me. And I watch as Vex approaches the couch I'm curled up on. He's a total stunner. Inky black hair that hangs in his eyes but is skin-short on the sides. Ice-blue eyes that are so light they are almost white. Snake bite piercings on his lip.

He must have just come from work because there are white and pink ink stains on his forearms and a black smudge on his jaw. He's an award-winning tattoo artist that owns a shop down the street from my office.

I continue to check him out as he stands in front of me, towering over me. He's got tattoos that run from his jaw to his hands. He's tall, probably just over six foot, and stacked with muscle, but he's lean.

"You done eye-fucking me, Magpie?" he asks, his voice low.

"Not yet." I laugh as he sits down next to me.

"I heard you wanted to talk to me." He stretches his long legs out in front of him. "What can I do for you?"

This is the hard part. The part where I clam up because I don't like talking about how different I am from normal people.

"I want to play with you," I start, but then stall out. I fucking hate talking about this stuff. I had a whole conversation planned in my head, but now as I stare at him, I just can't do it. I start picking at my cuticles, pulling the skin until it breaks.

Vex reaches over and places his hand on mine. I look at him and I see the understanding on his face. "Did you know that my sister is autistic?"

I shake my head, unable to speak.

"She struggled for years before she was officially diagnosed. It was like being hit with a ton of bricks. All the things we missed: her meltdowns over clothes, food, or noise. The sensory aversions to food, needing constant comfort but hating touch. But when she was diagnosed, everything made sense."

"What did she do to get over it?" I ask quietly. Because that's what I want. I want to get over being different.

"What do you mean, *get over it*?" He looks confused.

"How did she learn to accept touch, wear normal clothes, and just be... normal?" I ask, my voice small.

Vex cocks his head and looks at me. I start to fidget under his stare, feeling like a bug under a microscope. His hand is a steady presence on mine. "Magpie, you are normal."

"I'm really not, Vex." I move to stand up, but he puts a bit of pressure on my hands, silently telling me to stay put. "My entire life, I have dealt with people telling me that my symptoms were just quirks, that I was weird. I just want to be normal."

"Just because your normal looks different from other people's doesn't mean that you aren't normal. It just means that you don't like certain things. And that is normal."

"Vex, it isn't normal to feel like your skin is crawling when people touch you." I pointedly look down at our hands.

"Does it feel like your skin is crawling right now?" he asks, his tone gentle.

I think about what he asked. "No, but I'm not overstimulated yet." He pulls his hand away, and I immediately feel the loss.

"So you know your triggers, that all touch isn't bad, just when you've had too much sensory input."

I think about that for a second. "No. If I knew my triggers, I would be able to control it and not be a fucking spaz when I get overstimulated."

"Alright. Let's back up. What can I do to help you?" His voice is commanding but not harsh.

"I want to have a scene where you overwhelm me with sensations. My goal is to treat it like immersion therapy, like they do with OCD patients? I want to do that."

He stares at me for a minute, and I start to fidget again.

"So that you can be 'normal'?" He makes finger quotation marks in the air when he says normal.

"Let me think about it," he says softly. "I want to play with you, and I've been watching you as you learn your way through the club. But there are a couple of issues at play here that I want to make sure we both understand."

"Issues?" I ask. I didn't think there would be any issues with the type of play I am asking for.

"Sensation play is all about feeling your body, grounding in the sensations, and giving yourself over to them, not trying to control them. It's about intent. Why do you want to be overwhelmed with sensations? Is it because you like it or because you are working through something?"

He pauses and leans into me, never touching, just in my space. I feel his body heat on my arm and goosebumps form all over my body.

“But you aren’t asking for sensations to be erotic, you are trying to overcome your brain. That’s a totally different type of play. And I need to make sure that I am capable of doing that for you. The last thing we want is for you to regress in your triggers.”

He stands up and looks down at me. “You aren’t broken, Magpie. You’re different, and that’s okay. You just have to be okay with your differences. Maris has my number. Your first task, if you want to play with me, is to text me tomorrow.”

Vex walks away, disappearing into the crowd.

This is not at all how I imagined tonight would go. Hell, any time I had negotiated with other Tops or Doms, we played that night. But this is different. Maybe because I am asking him to help fix me.

I look around for Maris to get his number before I go. It’s getting late and I have to get up early for a meeting with a new author. I find her in the corner watching Rhett tie up one of his students. She is snuggled into Cam as he rubs her very pregnant belly.

I walk over to where they are sitting and Maris looks up at me. "Hey, Magpie. What's up?"

"I am planning a session with Vex, and he told me to get his number for you." Cam pulls his phone out of his pocket and within a couple of seconds I feel my phone vibrate.

"Enjoy playing with him. He's a sadist when it comes to sensation. You're going to love it," he tells me before cuddling Maris.

"Thank you." I turn and start to walk out of the club, suddenly very concerned about what I have gotten myself into.

This morning has gone to hell in a handbasket. I met with a potential new client, an indie dark romance author, and it went great. She was excited to purchase a package from me that included rebranding her entire catalog. The commission on this was going to be huge for me.

But throughout the whole thing, my dress wouldn't sit right and my hair was in my face. I managed to keep my cool long enough that I didn't have a complete meltdown, but it was close.

When I got home, I cried on the couch until my basset hound, Harley, came up and cuddled with me, licking my face and burying her face in my chest. I desperately wanted to be normal.

I want to wear cute jeans and not feel like my skin is being rubbed raw. I want to eat the foods that look so damn good, but I can't stand the texture. But that's not the life I was dealt.

After forty-five minutes, I am finally calm enough to text Vex. This is getting out of hand.

I would have texted sooner, but I had a meeting this morning.

I put my phone down and head to my office. I live in an apartment on the third floor in the artistic district in downtown Franklin. I got a great deal on the apartment and it feeds my soul to be around all the artists in the city. Even if I can’t stand to be around too many people for too long.

But if I look out the window in my office, I can see Vex's tattoo shop. The lights just turned on and I can see him moving around, getting the shop ready for opening.

I kind of feel like a stalker as I watch him move through the shop, but I have caught him watching me right back. I'm getting ready to start working when I hear my phone ring in the living room. I race into the living room, hoping that it's not the author calling to cancel before I even get a chance to send out the contracts.

It's Vex.

"Hey, Vex," I answer, a bit breathlessly. I make my way back to my office. "I was expecting a text back, not a call."

"Well, I saw you staring at me from your window and figured you weren't very busy if you could stare at me while I open the shop."

"I was just thinking about what kind of covers I am going to create for the new client I just landed."

"Hell yeah, Magpie. That's fucking awesome." I hear him moving around the shop and say hello to the other artists that are trickling in. "I don't have an appointment for a couple hours. Want to celebrate with lunch? My treat."

"Uh, I don't think that's a good idea." I look down at myself. My dress is still driving me crazy and I'm not in a good headspace for more socialization.

"Are you already in your muumuu?" I watch as he steps outside and leans against the wall of his shop. He lights up a cigarette as looks up at my office window.

"Not yet, your phone call interrupted that," I would love to be embarrassed by him noticing the boxy, super unflattering house dresses that I wear around the house, but I just can't drum it up today.

"Mmmm," he says into the phone. "I have an idea. You get in that sexy muumuu and I'll be right back."

He hangs up and disappears into the shop. I don't know what's going on, but this dress is driving me crazy and my muumuu sounds like a great idea.

It's not long after I'm changed and sitting in my office that I hear a knock on my door. Harley starts going nuts, barking and howling, generally acting like she's a guard dog and not going to roll over for belly rubs as soon as I open the door.

I check the peephole and see Vex standing there with a bag of takeout in his hand. I manage to get Harley pushed back enough that I can open the door.

"What are you doing here?" I ask. But he's not answering me, he's too busy staring. "Vex, are you okay?"

He nods as he takes me in. His eyes run from my bare feet up my legs. I see his nostrils flare as he takes in my muumuu. When his gaze reaches my face, I take a step back at the intensity that I see there.

"Oh, Magpie, you have no idea how perfect you are, do you?"

Overload Chapter 2

Vex

I watch as Magpie starts to fidget with her muumuu, twisting the cotton around her fingers. I wasn't lying when I said that she is perfect. The boxy dress covers most of her curves, but I know they're there. I've been watching this woman come and go from this apartment for the last four years, since she moved in.

Her long blond hair is pulled up in a messy bun with a headband, probably to keep flyaway hairs out of her face. Her dark chocolate eyes are rimmed red, like she's been crying. My heart clenches.

Magpie's basset hound takes that moment to bark, and it snaps me out of my stupor and I notice that her dog is jumping on me, trying to get my attention. "Hey, pretty girl. Let me put this down and I'll give you some love."

Magpie steps back from the door and lets me inside. I see her trying to check out the logo on the takeout bag and I know what she's thinking. That there won't be anything in here that she can eat.

But I was being honest when I told her about my sister. While I don't understand the intricacies of autism, since I'm not autistic, I do have a frame of reference. My sister loves noodles, and I took a chance that Magpie would too.

I see her couch in the living room and head towards it.

"Kitchen table, please," she says softly. I stop and turn towards her. She is picking at her cuticles again.

"Okay," I say as I switch directions to the table off the kitchen. Thankfully, her apartment is more of a loft with everything being open, so I didn't have to ask for directions.

"Vex, I don't want to offend you, but there's probably nothing in there that I can eat." She's got her head down. She's starting to twist the cotton of her dress in her fingers again.

"Magpie, I know that. Did you forget what I told you last night? My sister has a lot of texture issues, but she loves noodles. Do you like noodles?"

She nods but doesn't come into the kitchen.

"Okay, then come in here and see what I brought." I hold out my hand for her and she slowly makes her way to me. "I got a basic ramen noodle and three different kinds of broth. I had them keep everything in separate containers so that nothing touched. There's jammy eggs, four different kinds of meat, and various toppings and addons. I also got fried dumplings if you prefer those."

I start to unload the takeout bag and then think better of it. Alex, my sister, would panic if there were too many choices and end up eating nothing. Instead, I pull out the noodles and broth and place them on the table.

Magpie is just standing there, dumbfounded. I don't want to pressure her, but I also want to push her boundaries just a touch. If she is serious about playing with me, and her intentions are pure, I need to know how far I can push her. I hold my hand out for her again.

She takes my hand and I pull her the rest of the way to the table. She sits down in her chair, and I place the noodles in front of her.

"Pork, soy, or miso broth?" I ask her.

"Miso," she says softly.

"In the noodles or on the side?"

"In the noodles, please."

"Beef, pork, chicken or shrimp?" I ask. I watch as her nose curls up at the chicken and shrimp.

She takes a minute to think before saying, "Beef."

"You are doing perfect," I tell her. I'm mentally logging her answers for next time. "Do you want to keep going or are you happy with this?"

She relaxes back in her seat. "Are the jammy eggs really soft or more firm?"

I open the container with the eggs and look at them. "Which would you prefer?"

"The really soft ones," she replies. Her voice is still soft, but she's not as guarded. Instead, her voice soft as she gently rocks in her seat.

"Okay," I pick out the softest of the eggs and put them in her ramen bowl. "Anything else?"

"Corn and the bamboo shoots?" She asks like I would forget those toppings.

I pull both out and put them in the bowl. "Is that enough, or do you want more?"

She looks in her bowl and asks for a bit more. When she's satisfied with her bowl, I pull out the chopsticks and hand them to her. She snaps them apart and starts rubbing them together as I make my ramen bowl. I put everything that she didn't want into my bowl and sit down.

"Do you want the fried dumplings?" I ask her. Alex loves fried dumplings, but the texture can be odd if you aren't expecting it.

"I've never had them." She digs into her ramen and moans.

That moan goes straight to my cock and I adjust in my seat to make room for it in my jeans.

"Do you want to try them?" I ask. She nods, and I put one on a lid and slide it to her. She stares at it for a second before returning back to her ramen. She starts wiggling in her seat and I grin.

"Is it good?" The grin she sends me is fucking adorable. Her cheeks are full, and she looks like a chipmunk. I lean forward and press my lips against hers.

She freezes.

"You are so damn cute, Magpie." I tuck into my ramen and let that kiss just linger in the air between us.

I watch from the corner of my eye as she swallows the food in her mouth. But I don't say anything about the kiss. I don't want her putting more thought into it than necessary.

Not yet, at least.

We continue to eat, and I clear my bowl and start on the dumplings. She still hasn't touched hers and is staring at it with longing.

"Would it help if it were a smaller bite?" I ask. She raises her eyes to mine, and the look of defeat is written all over her face. "Magpie, it's okay if you don't or can't try it."

"But it looks so good." She pouts. She *actually* pouts, and it's fucking adorable.

"And it will be good the next time you have ramen. And if you can't try it then, it's still okay."

"Can you make it smaller?" she asks, her voice back to being small, like she's afraid to use it.

"Yes." I take a fork and cut the dumpling into bite-size pieces. "The dipping sauce is a mix of soy sauce, mirin, and sugar. It's sweet but has the tang of soy sauce.

The dumpling casing is firm from being fried, but the inside is hard to describe. It's soft, but when combined with the casing, you don't notice it. There isn't really a taste to what is inside the dumpling. Most of the flavor comes from the dipping sauce."

She pauses, her chopsticks hovering over the smallest piece. "What if I don't like it?"

I look at this woman, who is trusting me to explain the textures of food. Who trusts me enough to make her food for her. Her cheeks are stained pink, and her eyes are glistening with tears. I take her hand and put down the chopsticks.

"Magpie, you are perfect just the way you are. Your ability to try new foods is not tied to your value. If you want to try the dumpling, then try it. If you don't like it, spit it out. You expanding your palate is great. But there isn't some award for putting yourself through hell just to please someone else."

I watch as her shoulders slump, like the weight of maintaining other people's expectations is sliding right off.

"Did you think that trying the dumpling would impress me?" I ask, my voice gruff. She shakes her head, her head hanging down.

"No, it really does look good. But I'm worried that the inside will be too soft and the casing too hard, and the sauce too tangy." She sniffles and looks up at me. "I hate this about myself."

"That's understandable, Magpie, but you don't have to pretend with me. You trying new food doesn't matter to me. As long as you are healthy and happy, I don't give two flying fucks about you eating a dumpling. But if you want to try the dumpling, or anything else, I will be happy to be there with you."

I watch with awe as she picks up her chopsticks and picks up the dumpling. She dips it into the sauce and freezes before she brings it to her mouth. I stay silent, waiting to see what she will do.

She puts the dumpling in her mouth, and her face immediately twists in panic. I grab a napkin and hold it in front of her mouth just in time. She spits it out and immediately starts apologizing.

I toss the napkin into the takeout bag with the rest of the trash and grab her hands. I tug until she gets up and stands in front of me. I pull her into my lap and hold her as she trembles. I gently rock us until her trembling stops and she takes a deep breath.

"I'm so proud of you, Magpie," I tell her softly as I rock her. I brush the hair back from her face, my thumbs brushing the tears that have fallen. "You did so well trying something new."

"But I spit it out," she mumbles.

"So? You didn't like it."

"But spitting it out is rude and gross. I should have just swallowed it."

I grin at her, hoping that she catches her own innuendo. I'm glad to see her roll her eyes and swat my chest. The tension eases from her just a touch.

"No, Magpie, it's not rude or gross." I laugh at the look on her face. "You think it's okay to just gut it out and force yourself to do things that you don't like? Sure, sometimes it's necessary. But a dumpling? You don't have to eat a dumpling."

She snuggles into my chest, and for the first time in years, I feel complete. Like I've actually helped someone.

"Why do you want to play with me?" I ask her quietly. Her body stiffens, but I continue to rock us.

"My entire life I was told that I was too much or not enough. I was too sensitive, too picky. Or I was weird for not talking as much as the other girls," she mumbles into my shirt. "There was always something wrong with me. I was recently diagnosed with AuDHD and it felt like everything clicked into place."

She pulls back from me and goes to stand up. Reluctantly, I let her go, knowing that what she is about to tell me will probably have me ready to lose my shit.

"I started therapy to try and figure out how to fix me, but she would only offer coping strategies. But I don't want that. I want to be normal."

"Magpie, you are normal. Just because your normal doesn't match someone else's doesn't mean you aren't normal." I can see she is getting agitated with the conversation, so I switch the topic. "I want to play with you, and I think I can help you with your sensory aversions. But you aren't going to like my methods. I enjoy taking Bottoms to the very edge of their limits."

I watch in fascination as her pupils dilate. "But I will not abide by you calling yourself abnormal. We will push your boundaries. We will learn to work with and around your triggers. But you will be punished when you degrade yourself."

I stand up and walk over to her. She has to tilt her head back to look at me as I walk into her space.

"Only I'm allowed to do that," I whisper in her ear. I bend down and pet Harley. "I have to get back, my client is waiting for me at the shop. But we are going to continue talking about what I expect from you and what you want from me."

I grab the takeout bag of trash and walk out the door. I turn to look at her over my shoulder as I open the door. She has stopped fidgeting and is standing tall. Her nipples are straining through the thin cotton of her muumuu. I grin. My job here is done.

I shut the door behind me and make my way back to my shop, tossing the takeout bag into the trash on my way. My brain is going a million miles an hour with everything that I have learned about Magpie.

I think back to when Alex was younger. No one could understand why she would cry when my mom would put her in certain clothes. Or why she would only calm if I held her pinkie, but she would push away hugs.

As she got older, my parents realized that something was different about her. Her meltdowns over the smallest things didn't make sense to us. She wasn't eating appropriately, and the doctors were worried because she didn't talk much.

My parents had Alex tested when she went into middle school, and they, and the doctor, realized it wasn't a phase. When she was diagnosed, everything clicked, and we were able to help her.

Alex and I are incredibly lucky. Our parents would move heaven and earth for us. Even now, as a thirty-two-year-old man, I can call either of my parents and ask for help.

But I don't think Magpie is that lucky. Not with all of her talk of wanting to be normal. I meant what I said when I told her that she will not be allowed to degrade herself. I won't stand for her talking badly about herself.

A plan starts to take shape in my mind: the tools that I'll use on her, how I will overload her senses. But most importantly, how I will ground her during the process.

When I get back to my shop, I set up for my client. It's not long after my client sits down that I am lost in my own world. The buzz of the tattoo machine is soothing, and watching my creations come to life on skin is a high that can't be replaced.

As a Sensation Sadist, I get pleasure in creating sensations in my play partners. It's just one of the many reasons I love being a tattoo artist. But with Magpie, it will be more important to teach her how to ground during that overload.

I finish up the tattoo I'm working on and go over aftercare instructions with him. I get my station cleaned up and pull out my sketchpad as I wait for my next client. It's not long before her gorgeous face takes shape on my pad.

"Oh, this is going to be fun, Magpie."

Overload Chapter 3

Maggie

It's been a whole day since Vex came over for ramen, and I'm not sure how I feel about what happened. I'm not as concerned about him knowing which apartment is mine. I'm more freaked out that he took everything that happened in stride.

I have never felt more seen or cared for in my life, which is sad if I'm being honest. But when I look back at everything that happened, he never made me feel less than or too much. He just handled it.

He texted me yesterday when he was closing up shop and asked if I preferred texts to phone calls. When I explained that I had a hard time on the phone, he just said *okay*. No explanations, no harsh words, just acceptance.

My therapist used to call it "safe exposure." Letting people get close in small doses. But nothing about Vex feels small.

I'm not used to people respecting my boundaries. Hell, my mom still calls me every week to make sure I'm alive, despite me begging her to text me. My dad? He hates talking on the phone too, so he just shoots me a text asking how everything is going.

Today, though, Vex is blowing up my phone. Not in a bad way, but he's asking either or questions. The screen lights up again—*Do you like spicy or sweet?*

Each question is harmless, each one simple. *Tea or coffee. Dogs or cats. Sunrises or sunsets.* And I can feel my pulse racing anyway because I know what he's doing.

He's learning *me*.

And the scariest part? I think I want him to.

Neither, I send back to him. Though it's not exactly true, I love both, but it depends on where I'm at in my head.

My response must give him pause because he doesn't send me anything back for a while. So I get back to work. I am under a tight deadline to get four book covers to an artist that paid a pretty penny for a rush job.

I sit down at my desk and pull my tablet towards me. It doesn't take long for me to get lost in work. It's not until Harley is howling at the door that I realize that I've been at work for hours. There's a knock at the door.

I look through the peephole and step back. Vex is standing at the door, another bag of takeout in his hand. I look down at myself and grimace. I'm in my frumpiest muumuu and my hair is a rat's nest.

"Magpie, I know you're there. I don't care what you look like. Open the door, I'm starving."

I open the door with a groan and lean against it. "Could you have given me a bit of warning? I look like shit."

"First, you look gorgeous." He steps inside and presses a kiss to my temple as he passes. "Second, don't think that I'm not counting how many times you talk badly about yourself."

He heads to the kitchen and drops the takeout bag on the table. He bends down and starts loving on Harley. She rolls to her back and all her loose skin slides to the floor. She looks like she's melted.

He laughs at her open-air doggie paddle and stands back up. Harley sneezes her displeasure at no longer being the center of his attention and rolls over with a huff. He walks over to me and slowly wraps his arms around me.

I stand perfectly still, his scent wrapping around me. He smells of pine and bergamot with a hint of green soap. Normally, I would pull away quickly, but there is just something about him that makes me feel safe and seen.

I embrace him, barely able to get my arms all the way around him. I rest my head against his chest and just sit in the safety that he is providing. My entire life, I have braced for touch, no one understanding how painful it is for me.

"Sweet Magpie, I have been looking forward to this all day," he murmurs into my hair.

I don't understand. Why would he be looking forward to seeing me? "Did I miss the text that you were coming over?"

I pull away and pull my phone from my pocket. I scroll through our text thread and don't see anything saying that he would be coming over. I look back up at him and see him grinning at me.

"No, Sweet Magpie, I didn't tell you I was coming over. I didn't want you freaking out and panicking." He walks over to the kitchen table and starts pulling out containers of food. "I got a couple of different options, not knowing what you would like. I figured the chicken fingers and fries would be safe though."

He places the container on the table and slides it to me. I sit down and stare at the takeout container. "Why?" My voice is raspy and I'm trying like hell to hold back tears.

"Because you are worth it, Magpie." He sits down next to me and pulls a burger out of his container. He takes a massive bite of his burger and groans like he didn't just rock my entire world.

"Do you know what I love about sensations?"

I shake my head and nibble at one of the chicken fingers.

"There's predictability in the unpredictable. Metal is hard, right? But it can be hot or cold." He takes another bite of his burger and chews. "Water can be hot, cold, or frozen, but it is always wet."

"Then why are sensations so triggering for me?" I ask, the frustration building again.

"Because sensations haven't been safe for you, Magpie. No one stopped and thought about your reactions, your wants, or your feelings. You were expected to just deal with it."

Tears fill my eyes because he's right. My mom loves forcing me into situations that she knows I can't handle, then gets mad at me for having a meltdown. Now, it's people not thinking before giving me a hug or touching my arm.

"I want to teach you how to ground yourself, to lean into discomfort and know that you are safe, that you have a choice."

"Okay," I whisper. I pick up another chicken finger and start to eat. Vex and I continue to eat in silence, occasionally passing food to Harley.

"Which feels better to you: soft, light touches or firm, weighted touch?" Vex asks. He's finished eating and is putting the trash in the takeout bag.

I take a minute to really think about what he's asking. "Firm touches."

He looks up at me, a soft smile playing at his lips. "Do soft touches make your skin crawl or is it painful?"

Again, I have to think about the question he's asking. Nobody has ever cared enough to ask, and I haven't put a lot of thought into it. I've just avoided touch at all costs. "I don't know."

"Would you be open to an experiment?" My heart stalls for a second before taking off like a rocket.

"What kind of experiment?" I ask hesitantly.

"The kind where I blindfold you and touch you." His voice is low. "We won't go any further than you are ready, though."

"What if I can't do it?"

He leans forward, his soft smile turning wicked. "But, Magpie, what if you can?"

I nod.

"No, Magpie, I need the words. Are you open to an experiment where I blindfold you and then touch you?"

"Yes," I whisper.

Vex stands and walks over to me, pulling a long piece of black silk fabric out of his pocket. "You came prepared."

"No, I came hopeful." He places the blindfold over my eyes and I realize that I can just barely see shadows through it. He ties it behind my head and immediately my heart starts pounding. "Magpie, all you need to do is sit there and name whatever you are feeling. Focus on the sensations you are feeling."

"Okay." My voice is rough, a touch of fear bleeding through.

"What do you feel right now?" he asks.

It takes me a second to gather myself enough to answer him. "Fear...and arousal."

"Good girl." His voice has turned sultry.

I feel him step closer and put his hand on my elbow. I feel the rough callouses on his palm and his fingers are firm. But then I feel it—his thumb is softly stroking my inner elbow. My breathing picks up, and I can feel goosebumps rise on my arms.

"What do you feel now, Magpie?" His whisper is right next to my ear, his breath warm against my skin.

"Four," I blurt out. Vex's thumb stops stroking me for a second.

"Ten is full stop?" he asks.

I nod. I know my face and chest are burning red from embarrassment. I can't believe that I blurted out a number. My breathing picks up and my anxiety shoots up.

"Magpie, stay with me." His other hand grips my thigh firmly. The hand that was on my elbow disappears and comes to my face, softly tracing my jaw. "Breathe in for two, out for four."

I do as he says and focus on my breathing. It doesn't take long for the anxiety to go down and my embarrassment to fade. "Good girl, Magpie."

I don't know how long we continue with his experiment. But by the time we are done and he pulls the blindfold off, I am a puddle of arousal in my chair. I'm also touched and talked out.

"I know, Magpie. Where is your stuffy?" he asks like he already knows that my brain is mush.

"White dog on my bed," I manage to get out. Vex walks away, and Harley takes that moment to come over and press herself against my leg. Her soft ears rest on my knee.

He comes back in and places my stuffy in my arms. "Just one more touch, Magpie, and I'll stop, okay?"

I nod. He picks me up bridal-style and my head rolls against his shoulder. His scent envelops me, and I snuggle into him. He leans forward like he's going to place me on the couch, but I wrap my arms around his neck. "Please stay," I whisper.

"Okay." He sits down on the couch with me in his lap. Other than his arms wrapped around me, he doesn't continue to touch, just holds pressure against me. He doesn't talk, doesn't stroke. His stillness grounds me in a way that I have never felt before.

I must have dozed off in his arms because next thing I know, Harley is nudging me with her cold nose.

"Magpie, I think Harley needs to go outside," he whispers in my ear. I open my eyes and scramble off his lap.

"I'm so sorry. I didn't mean to fall asleep." My face is red and my anxiety is starting to crank up. Harley is nudging me with her nose and walking to the front door.

"Breathe, Magpie." He stands from the couch and walks to me. He puts his hand on my chest, applying just enough pressure. "In for two, out for four."

"I can't," I say. My brain is moving a million miles a minute and I can't catch my breath.

"Yes, you can." He takes my hand and places it on his chest. "In for two, out for four."

He takes a deep inhale before blowing the air out. I follow his breathing, feeling his chest expand under my hand. It takes a minute, but I can feel the anxiety melting away. "Where's her leash?"

"I'll take her out, you don't have to." I move to the front door before he can respond. But I feel out of sorts, like my brain isn't in control of my body. I try to get my flip-flops on but almost fall over.

I watch in awe as Vex drops to one knee. He helps me put one shoe on before helping me with the other. He stands, grabs Harley's leash, and clips it on her without another word. "Come on, Magpie."

He holds out his hand, and I take it without hesitation. I grab my keys as he leads Harley and I out the door. I lock up and we take the stairs down to the little dog park behind the building.

"I'm sorry for blurting out four," I say quietly. "My old therapist would ask for a number whenever I got overstimulated."

"Why would you be sorry, Magpie?" He looks up from where Harley is sniffing.

"Because you didn't ask for a number, you asked for a feeling or emotion."

"Yeah, I did. But if that doesn't work for you, that's okay too. You still answered my question." He patiently walks Harley around as she sniffs everything.

Harley must realize that I still exist because she hightails it over to me. She jumps up on my leg and I rub her long ears. He walks up to me and pulls me in for a hug.

"I just hate that my brain gets scrambled and I can't think. I hate that touch bothers me so much. I hate that I'm not normal," I mumble into his chest.

Vex reaches up and grabs the back of my neck. He pulls my head away from his chest and forces me to look at him. "You. Are. Normal."

I try to duck my gaze down, but he won't let me. "I told you that I am keeping track of how many times you talk badly about yourself, and I think I've discovered the perfect correction for that."

My heart pounds with dread, but also a touch of excitement.

"Every time you talk bad about yourself, you will look at me in the eyes for ten seconds." The grin on his face is menacing, like he knows how much I will hate this.

"Vex," I draw his name out. "That is torture."

"My Sweet Magpie." He laughs and brings his face down so that it is level with mine. "I know."

Overload Chapter 4

Vex

It's been almost a week since my experiment with Magpie. We haven't spent much time together because of our jobs. I've had back-to-back clients from open to close this week, and she's under a tight deadline for a rush job.

We've been texting each other, but it's not the same as being around her. I've thought about sneaking over there to make sure she's eating, but I don't have the time.

Instead, I've been asking her to send me pictures of what she's been eating. I started doing it to make sure that she was eating, but I am filing those pictures away so that I know what she likes to eat and what she finds comforting.

But tonight is the first night that we both have off with nothing to do tomorrow. I told her to be ready by eight with whatever she needs overnight. Initially, she was hesitant, but I told her to bring Harley, and she perked up.

I'm closing up my shop when my phone chirps with a text message. It's from Magpie.

I don't think I can do tonight.

I grin. Good, she should be nervous.

I'm on my way, Sweet Magpie. Be ready.

I finish locking up and make my way to her apartment. My phone starts chirping with incoming text messages, but I ignore them. I'm getting my Magpie tonight.

When I reach her apartment, I can hear her moving around. I knock on the door and hear a loud *fuck* and Harley start howling.

"Open the door, Magpie," I call out. I hear the pounding of footsteps and the scramble of Harley's nails on the floor. The door swings open and I see Magpie looking flushed and gorgeous.

I lean against the doorjam and take her in. Her messy bun is lopsided and her flyways are in her face. She's in a long black maxi dress and barefoot. "Did I interrupt?"

"I'm not ready, Vex. I thought I was, but I'm not sure I can do this." She backs away from the door, almost tripping on the hem of her long dress. She pushes one hand into her hair and starts chewing her thumbnail of her other.

I step inside and shut the door. "It's okay, Magpie." I step towards her and pull her hand away from her mouth. "It's okay to be nervous or scared."

I pull her into my arms, reaching for the hand that is in her hair and putting it on the back of my head, letting her feel soft skin there. I tuck her face against my neck, and I take a deep breath, and she follows. I take another and she deflates, her body relaxing.

"Your head is really soft," she whispers as she rubs the back of my head. I'm damn near a puddle of goo on the floor from her touch.

"Thank you." I laugh softly. "Feel better?"

"A little bit, yeah." She doesn't pull away, instead snuggling closer. "Sorry, I am freaking out because everything is a mess and I can't get my shit together."

"How about this? You go fix your makeup and hair. I'll finish gathering up your and Harley's things." Her head cocks to the side.

"What do you mean, fix my makeup?"

"Angel, you're missing an eye." I chuckle. She whirls around and races for her bedroom. I hear a screech followed by another *fuck*.

"Come on, Harley, tell me what to pack." I follow the path of destruction through her apartment and start to tidy up. She was getting Harley's dog food into a plastic bag and then moved on to something else. I put her food back and put the plastic bag in the tote bag that says "Harley."

I continue to tidy up when I see her come out of her bedroom. I'm stunned.

Her makeup is fixed, and her hair is down and curled. She's got a headband on to keep it out of her face. Her dark chocolate eyes are even now and lined with a thick kohl. She's painted her lips crimson.

"Damn, Angel." It's all I can get out before I have snatched her up and she wraps her legs around my waist. I bury my face in her neck and breathe in her scent.

"Uh, Vex?" I shake my head against her, loving the feel of her in my arms. "Vex?"

"Give me ten more seconds, please," I mumble against her. The last week is finally slipping from my shoulders and I feel like I can breathe better now.

"Vex, t's been ten seconds." I slowly release her, and she slides down my front. "Did you clean my apartment?"

"Yeah," I tell her. "I didn't know how much longer you needed and I knew you wouldn't want to leave until everything was picked up."

"Thank you," she whispers. She turns back into my chest. "That means a lot."

"I told you when we started this that I had you, Angel." I see her bag packed on the couch. "Is that all you need? Is your stuffy in there?"

She nods. I pull away from her and go grab the bag and Harley's tote. I clip Harley's leash onto her and open the door. "Let's go, Angel."

The walk from her apartment to my truck doesn't take long. I help her and Harley into the lifted rig and put her bags in the backseat. I don't live far from downtown Franklin, only about twenty minutes, but it's mostly back country roads.

I watch out of the corner of my eye as she pets Harley, stroking those long ears to keep from fidgeting. I press my hand to her thigh and watch as she relaxes in her seat.

When we pull up in front of my cabin, I kill the engine and hop out. I get Harley out first and then help Magpie down. I reach into the backseat for the bags and watch as Magpie looks around.

"It's so loud," she says in awe.

"It is, but it's soothing too. There's no honking horns, no people yelling or talking, just the sounds nature."

She picks up one edge of her dress, and we start towards the house. I unlock the door and let them inside. I'm nervous about having them in my space. Thankfully, Magpie and I have a similar minimalist style, but my cabin would probably be considered sparse. I don't need much, just a couch, TV, and bed.

"Where's your kitchen table?" she asks in confusion.

"I don't have one. Didn't make a lot of sense since it's just me." I set her bags on the couch next to Harley, who has already snuggled in for bed. I move into her. "Plus, the loft is where the fun is."

I take her hand and lead her towards the stairs that go to the loft. When we get to the top of the stairs, she freezes in front of me.

Along the back wall there are various toys, ropes, restraints, and more. But in the center of the room stands a St. Andrew's cross. That's where she will be tonight.

"Strip," I growl into her ear. I don't touch her, not yet. She needs to make this decision for herself. She pulls away from me and takes a tentative step towards the cross. She pauses, and for a second I think that she's going to say no. But I watch as she straightens her shoulders and grabs her dress. In one smooth motion she pulls the dress over her head and drops it on the floor.

I thank every star in the sky that she is still turned away from me because my jaw is on the floor and the blood rushes to my cock. She is stunning. Her skin is smooth and tan. There isn't a blemish on her. Her hips are wide and her ass is like a ripe peach.

While I am busy drooling over her, she has gotten to the cross and turns around to face me. I damn near swallow my tongue. Her large breasts are on full display, her nipples tight in the cool air of the loft. My gaze tracks lower and I see that her cunt is completely bare. I adjust my cock in my pants and walk over to her.

"Do you normally not wear a bra and panties under those dresses?" I ask as I start to secure her hands to the cross. "Because I'm a big fan."

"I don't like them, they're too constricting," she says breathlessly.

"Thank fuck for sensory issues." This woman is perfect.

I run my hands down her arms to her breasts and palm them. "Tonight is about you learning to ground yourself in sensations." I roll her nipples between my thumb and forefinger. "We will use the stoplight method and your anxiety scale."

I pinch her nipple, and she rises up on her toes. "Do you agree?"

She nods at me, but that isn't enough. "Your words, Angel."

"Yes," she pants. "I agree." I release her nipples, and she plants her feet.

I brush my lips against the shell of her ear, letting my breath move over her and whisper, "Good girl."

I step back and reach for the blindfold. "You won't be able to see through this one." I hold it up to her, letting her see the inky black fabric. "Do you agree?"

"Yes." Her voice is stronger this time. I fold the silk until it's thick enough that she can't see through it, but still wide enough to cover her eyes. I tie it behind her head and watch as she tenses up.

"Breathe, Angel. In for two, out for four." I move to the table that is set next to the cross. On it are all the potential toys that I can use to play with her. We'd negotiated quite a bit with what she was comfortable with and also things that she would like to try. But I think she is going to be surprised with what I use the most.

I start with pressure since she said it is how she prefers to be touched. Her nipple rolls between my fingers and she arches to thrust her breast into my hand. The first clamp clicks shut, then the second. Her entire body shudders when I let the thin chain drop.

I watch her for signs of tension or stress, at least the kind I don't want her to have. Her body is telling me that she is okay and that I can continue. "I want you to feel what I'm doing to you, but if it starts to get too much, I want you to focus on the pressure on your nipples. Color?"

"Green," she gasps.

I move to the ice cubes that are sitting in cold water on the table. I reach for one and rub it around her nipple. The sharp inhale is music to my ears. I reach over for the low temperature candle. I drizzle a bit of wax over the nipple that I just had the ice cube on. The moan she lets loose is sinful.

I lose track of time as I am play with her body, dragging every reaction out for as long as possible. It's not until after midnight that I see the first real sign of fatigue.

She has taken everything I have given her: the rope, the wax, the feather, only requiring my help to ground once. Every check-in is a green and her anxiety has stayed below a five.

"My sweet Angel, you did so good," I tell her. I reach up to release her arms and my chest brushes her nipples.

"Please, Vex," she moans. "I need you."

"I know, Angel, let's get you cleaned up first," I say as I release her arms and start rubbing them to get blood back into them. I rub her shoulders and neck. I remove the blindfold, and her beautiful eyes look up at me.

"Vex, I need you," she repeats. She's pushing away my hands. She reaches up and grabs my face, bringing my mouth to hers. "I need you."

"Okay." I bend down and lift her up, keeping our mouths fused. I take her to the small couch that I keep in the loft and sit down with her on my lap. She has allowed me to play with her body for hours—she can do whatever she wants to me.

She grinds against me, and I hiss in discomfort. I lift her up enough that I can free my cock from my jeans. She goes to drag herself along my length but freezes when she feels the cool metal. She raises her head and looks down at me.

"You're pierced?" she asks, and I just grin up at her. She drags her dripping cunt over my cock again, feeling every rung of my Jacob's ladder.

"Angel, if you keep grinding on me, this is going to be over a lot sooner than either of us want."

"Shut up and fuck me, Vex."

"Yes, Ma'am." I lift her hips and pull her down on my cock, slowly so that she feels every bar. Then I begin to move, pulling her forward and back, raising her just enough for her to get friction.

She takes over the rhythm, and it's not long before we are both at the edge.

"Take us over, Angel," I whisper in her ear. But she shakes her head. "Angel, we can do this again, as much as you want, but I can't hold out much longer."

She looks down at me and pouts. "Promise?"

"Anytime you want, Angel. Now come for me." I release the clamps on her nipples and she slams down on me with a scream. I pinch her clit and she comes, hard. It only takes another thrust and I am coming with her.

She continues to grind against me, drawing out her orgasm as I rub her nipples.

She finally stills and slumps against my chest. I wrap my arms around her and pull her tight against me. She snuggles in and within seconds she's asleep.

I startle awake when I feel a cold nose press against my arm. I look down and see Harley patiently waiting for us to go to bed. A quick glance at my watch shows that it's three in the morning.

"Angel?" I whisper. "We need to get to bed."

"Five more minutes," she says as she nuzzles deeper into my chest.

"Harley needs to go out and I can't feel my legs." That does the trick because she pulls back with a gasp. "There she is," I say as I brush her hair back from her face.

"I don't want to get up, you're comfy."

"I know, Angel, but we need to let Harley out and get you cleaned up. That wax isn't meant to be worn for hours."

She glances down at herself and sees the red and black wax all over her chest. "I look like a sacrifice." She giggles.

"That can be arranged," I growl as I lift her off me, and she stands on wobbly legs. I watch as our come drips down her leg. "Go shower, my bedroom is right off the kitchen. I'll let Harley out."

We stagger down the stairs and go our separate ways. I wait until I hear the shower cut on before I clip Harley's leash to her. I trail Harley through the yard, making sure that she does her business.

When we are done, I come back in and show Harley my bedroom. There's a brand new dog bed on the floor for her, but she's trying to get on the bed. "Baby girl, you won't be able to get up there, it's too high."

She gives me a disgruntled huff, and I hear my Angel come out of the bathroom. "She's slept on my bed since she was a puppy."

I look at her and then look at my bed. "She's not going to try and jump off in the middle of the night?"

She shakes her head. "She'll be out like a light and stay that way until at least noon."

I chuckle. "Alright, baby girl, let's get you on the bed." I lift her up onto the bed, and she plops down at the foot.

"Come here, Angel." I grab one of my t-shirts from the dresser. I pull it over her head and watch as it damn near swallows her. "Get in bed. I'm going to shower first."

When I get under the spray, I jerk back with a yelp. “Why do you shower in lava?” I yell out. I turn the temperature down. It’s not until I get out of the shower that I realize I never got an answer.

I peak into the bedroom and my heart melts. On my bed is my Angel spooning Harley, and they’ve left just enough room for me.

Overload Bonus Scene

Maggie

The last year has been the best of my life. I moved in with Vex a couple of months ago, and Harley and I have been slowly but surely taking over his space. He built me an office at our home and at his tattoo studio, allowing me to be comfortable in both places.

But that isn't the biggest change in the last year. Shortly after Vex and I started seeing each other, he took me to meet his parents and sister. I was coming out of my skin with stress and sensory issues.

His mother instantly noticed and, instead of making me feel bad, she led me over to a low, fuzzy couch. She placed a weighted blanket over me and handed me a pair of noise-canceling headphones. She told Vex to take care of me, and we would visit when I felt better.

No harsh words, no resentment, just acceptance.

It made me realize that this is what should have been done for me as a child and a teen. This is what Vex was raised with, and why he is so good for me. A small part of me is jealous that he got to grow up with parents that loved and cared about him and his sister. But the bigger part of me, the part that is still healing?

I'm grateful that he got to have that, because that means I get to have it now.

And I treasure it. Because shortly after, Vex and I go to my parents' house for dinner. I had a rough day at work, and nothing is fitting right.

I spend hours trying to get my makeup right, trying to get my outfit to stop driving me insane. Vex has to center me multiple times before we even leave the house. We have to leave Harley because my mother has a strict no dogs allowed rule.

The second I cross the threshold of my childhood home, my mask slips into place. I am the dutiful daughter. No aversions, no triggers, no mess.

I introduce Vex to my parents. My dad looks him over with a huff and goes back to building his latest model. But my mother? She looks like I've dragged home roadkill.

She doesn't show it obviously, just makes snide comments about what kind of work can he do if he's covered in tattoos. It can't be anything good. He tells her that he owns a tattoo shop in downtown Franklin, and she huffs again before turning her attention to me. She comments on my outfit, my makeup, my weight, and every other infraction. The cracks in my mask start to show.

Vex is vibrating with rage, but he's holding it together pretty well. I know he's trying to not make waves, he wants to protect me from my mother. But he also wants to let me handle this myself.

But it is dinner that breaks me. I knew the second I walked inside that my mother was going to cause a scene at dinner. She knew that I would be triggered...and she wanted Vex to witness it.

We're all sitting around the table getting ready to eat when she places the casserole dish on the table. The scent of hot tuna hits me like a fist. I try to hold back my gag, but I can't.

"Stop being dramatic, Margret," she says with a sneer. "Everyone loves tuna casserole."

She starts loading everyone's plate, and the sound of the metal spoon scraping against the glass dish gets the ringing in my ears started. But it's the wet plop of the slimy noodles on the plate that causes a shiver to run through me. Vex places his hand on my thigh and squeezes.

She serves Vex first, and he gives her a quick thanks before moving his fork through the pile of goop on his plate. He looks over at me and shakes his head. There's nothing in it that I can eat. I know that. I was forced to eat this meal every week until I moved out.

She serves my plate, and I turn my head to the side, breathing through my mouth in an effort not to vomit from the smell.

"Do you have something else she can eat?" Vex asks, his voice is carefully controlled, but I can hear the anger in it. "She can't eat this."

"No," my mother says as she finishes dishing out her and my dad's plates. "You eat what I cook in this family. Don't let her fool you with that *sensitivity* nonsense. She ate tuna casserole all through her childhood."

Vex looks at me with his eyebrow raised. His question is clear without him having to voice it. *Do you want me to handle this?*

I think back to how his parents are with him and his sister. Meals served buffet style with plenty of options for everyone. Alex's sensitivities acknowledged and worked around. Gentle pushes to try new things but no judgement or shame if you can't.

"I'm not doing this." I stand up and push my chair back. Vex stands with me and places his hand on my lower back.

"Sit down and eat your dinner, young lady." My mother points to my chair. "You are not going to throw a temper tantrum because you aren't getting your way."

Vex shifts slightly, bringing my mother's attention to him. Not as a threat, but as a reminder that he's there for me, not her.

"You don't get to rewrite my reality because it doesn't fit your narrative," I say firmly. I turn around and walk out of the house.

He's silent on the walk to the truck, hand on my lower back, offering comfort. But when we get to his truck, he presses me against it and wraps his hand around the back of my neck.

"You did so well, Angel." He presses a hot kiss to my mouth, grounding me, and my brain instantly quiets. "I'm so proud of you."

"I'm so sorry," I mumble against his mouth. He presses my face against his chest and wraps his arms around me. "I knew it would be like that. I knew that she would try to get me to have a meltdown so you could see how abnormal I am."

"Hey," he lifts my chin, forcing me to look into his eyes. "That's another ten seconds."

We stand there like that—me staring into his beautiful, almost white eyes. A year ago, this was torture, having to look someone in the eyes. But now, it's the easiest way to ground me, and he knows it.

"I love you," I murmur. The grin that takes his face is downright sinful.

"I love you too, Angel." He presses his lips against mine again. "Now, do we want real food or should I take you home and show you how much I love you?"

He opens the door to his truck and helps me inside. He buckles the seatbelt around me and gently shuts the door. I watch as he rounds the hood and climbs in. I look over at him as he cranks the engine, filling the cab with a low rumble.

"I want noodles and chicken fingers," I tell him with a grin. "Then I want you to show me how much you love me."

"Yes, Ma'am," he says with a grin.

Will he learn that submission isn't weakness?

Wild Obsidian: Ritual

Vic Raven

Trigger Warings

Ritual

Talk of war

Ritual Chapter 1

Grant

After months of work and classes, I am a full member of Obsidian and the newest bartender. I am off probation and can play with any member of the club that I decide as long as I am off the clock. I am excited, but also slightly terrified.

I'm not really sure what I want from Obsidian, from the community. I just know that something is missing.

Damien made the suggestion that I apply for the bartender opening at the club when I returned home after my retirement from the Army. I wasn't really interested in working. I had a full pension and my cabin was paid off.

But after a couple of months banging around that cabin all by myself, I realized that he was right. I needed something to do. So I applied for membership and the position.

I've learned a lot about the lifestyle and community in the last few months. It isn't always barked orders and pain, sometimes it's quiet disapproval and stillness. And honestly, the last part scares me the most.

I'm wiping down the bar when Casey walks in, her heels clicking on the old wooden floors. She's a tiny thing, only coming up to my collarbone with her heels on. Her bright red hair is in a messy, curly updo. She comes to a stop at the bar.

"Rook, I need you to finish setting up the rest of the bar before the doors open," she says before she continues to move through the club. "We open in ten minutes and you only have enough beer in the cooler for the first wave of people."

The quiet disapproval in her tone sets me on edge, but I can't figure out why. "Got it." I move to the end of the bar, to the storage area.

Casey stops dead in her tracks, her back turned to me. "Ma'am." She looks over her shoulder at me, a perfectly arched eyebrow raised. "The correct response is '*Yes, Ma'am*'."

"Yes, Ma'am," I echo her. Part of me wants to snap at her, to demand respect. I'm probably old enough to be her father. But the other part of me, a smaller part that has been smothered my entire life, exhales.

I watch as she continues through the club and into the back office. When she's out of sight, I grab more beers and start filling up the cooler the rest of the way. I shake my head and watch as more employees start filtering in.

I'm always early. After spending twenty years in the Army, I'll probably never break the habit. But that's fine with me. It's not like I have anything better to do at home.

Chris, the other bartender tonight, walks up and puts his stuff behind the bar. "You and me tonight?" he asks.

"You and me," I tell him as I finish stocking the beer cooler. Chris starts prepping and filling the various stations along the bar, making sure that everything was perfect before the night started.

I haven't worked with him before, but I had seen him around the club when I had a class or workshop. I'm not sure how to take him. He is a giant of a man, taller than my own six foot four by a lot. He is also built like a brick wall. But he wears a pair of silver cuffs that say *My Slut* on them.

I'm not trying to judge, but my confusion must be evident because he laughs. "My Domme gave them to me for my birthday a couple of months ago. She had them specially made for me. She likes to keep me on a short leash," he says with a grin.

I nod like I understand, but I really don't. My entire life, I grew up thinking and believing that the man is in charge. But my father's six divorces showed that to be a lie, and really my mother was no better.

Honestly, I'm not sure what to believe anymore when it comes to relationships. I watched as one by one the soldiers in my unit fell in love and got married. Then I watched as one by one they all divorced.

I had dated and even got engaged once while I was in the Army, but nothing ever really stuck. Nothing felt right.

I hear heels clicking on the floor again and look behind me after organizing the bottles on the shelves. I see Casey come out of the back office and walk towards the bar. Her electric blue corset pushes her breasts high and her short skirt makes her legs look a million miles long.

"Rook, you did a good job on prepping before opening, keep it up. Hey, Chris. Is Crystal here?"

My heart catches for a second at her praise.

"Yeah, she's over at the fire table getting set up." I watch as Casey nods and walks away. "Watch out, Rook, Casey is on the lookout for a new sub."

I turn and look at him.

"I'm not submissive," I tell him, but even to my own ears it sounds defensive. Chris just raises his eyebrow at me.

"If you say so, man. I'm just letting you know that the clench you felt in your chest and dick when she told you *good job*, says otherwise." He walks away with a grin and heads over to take an order from the first customers of the night.

The rest of the night passes in a blur of orders, cleaning, and more orders. By the time the club is closing down for the night, I'm exhausted.

I watch as Casey directs staff in closing tasks, and within an hour the club is ready to be locked up for the night.

I'm taking the last load of trash out to the dumpster when I hear those heels clicking behind me.

"You did good, Rook. Most bartenders cry their first night behind the bar." She leans against the open door and watches as I haul the trash into the dumpster. When I turn and look at her, I can see the open appraisal in her eyes.

I'm not conceited, but I know what I look like. I'm thirty-seven and in good shape, a little on the thicker side of muscled, but I can hold my own. Tonight, I'm wearing a simple black t-shirt, jeans and boots.

Nothing fancy. But the way she's looking at me makes me feel like I'm the most attractive man here.

"Thank you, Ma'am," I tell her. Her eyes sharpen as I walk towards the door that she's standing in the way of.

"You learn fast," she murmurs as she cranes her neck back to look at me. I have never had someone look up at me and make me feel small at the same time.

"You kind of have to when your life is on the line," I quip back. Her eyes darken and she frowns. I guess smartass isn't her favorite language. "Sorry," I mutter.

"Don't apologize if you're not sorry," she says firmly. "Do you have all your stuff? I'm going to lock up."

I check my pockets and nod. I didn't bring much with me.

"Good, I'm going to set the alarm and lock up. You can walk me to my car." She disappears back inside before I even have a chance to answer. I was going to walk her to her car anyway, but having her take control is hot.

I hear the alarm engage and hear those heels clicking on the floor as she walks out. With a twist of her wrist, the club is locked up, and she's walking to her car. I follow behind her, checking our surroundings and making sure that she's safe.

Casey walks up to an all white vintage Camaro and unlocks the car. She slides in and starts it to let it warm up. The rumble is loud in the still night air.

"There's an all night diner about five minutes from here. I'm starving." She looks at me expectantly. She's not asking me out, or demanding, but it's like it's a done deal.

"I'll follow you," I tell her. She grins up at me and closes the door to her car. She locks the doors and waits for me to get in my truck and pull in behind her.

When we were closing down the club, all I could think about was going home and going to bed. Now, I'm wired but hesitant. Chris' words are banging around in my head.

We pull up to the diner and I park next to her, secretly proud that she backs into her parking spot. I open her door and help her out. She's lost the heels and is now walking towards the diner in pink fluffy slippers.

I follow along behind her, and before I can say anything, she pauses at the door, letting me open it for her. The longer I'm around her, the more confused I become.

The diner is old school, with white and black checked floors, white and black vinyl booths, and even an old jukebox in the corner. The waitress tells us to seat ourselves, and Casey heads to the back corner booth. She sits with her back to the diner and lets me have the wall.

The waitress walks up and pours us two coffees from the carafe in her hand. "What can I get you guys?"

"I'll have your cheeseburger with no veg, fries, and a chocolate milkshake, no whip or cherry," she rattles off. The waitress nods and looks at me.

"I'll have the same with veg, a strawberry milkshake with whip and cherry," I tell the waitress. I don't normally eat greasy foods, but why not. I'm burning with curiosity over this woman.

I take a sip of my coffee as I look at Casey over the rim. She's a total stunner and from what I'm seeing, dynamite in a tiny package.

"You're probably wondering why I hijacked your night," she says with a chuckle.

"The thought crossed my mind," I tell her. And it has, but so have Chris' words. I'm not a submissive. I was in charge of making sure hundreds of soldiers stayed alive while I was in the military, there's no way I'm submissive.

"What do you know about the Dom/Sub lifestyle?" She jumps right in.

"If I'm being honest, just what I learned in the classes that Obsidian put on," I tell her, continuing to fidget with the coffee mug. "But before we go too far into this, I just want to point out that I'm not submissive."

She cocks her head to the side, those fiery curls catching the shitty lighting of the diner. I can see the wheels turning in her head, and it's making me nervous.

"The classes that the club puts on are very informative, but also lacking. The idea of those classes are to gloss over rules, roles, protocols, and skills. They aren't meant to give in-depth tutorials on how the lifestyle works. That's the mentor's job. Did you find a mentor?"

I shake my head. I haven't really found the time or even a particular kink that I wanted to explore.

"So I'm going to ask again, what do you know about the Dom/Sub lifestyle if you haven't found a mentor?" She grins at me like she's won, and I guess she has.

"Touché," I tell her. "Enlighten me." I lean back and wait for her explanation, fully intending to shut her down about me being submissive.

"The power exchange dynamic is probably the most fluid dynamic that exists in the kinky community because it looks so different for everyone. Primal play is the only other kink that comes to mind that is anywhere near as customizable."

"What do you mean *fluid*?"

"Power exchange can look like anything. For example, me telling you to restock the bar tonight places me in the power position. If you grab me by the throat, that puts you in power. Most people don't even track that they are in a power exchange dynamic until the label is put on it."

The waitress comes over and drops off our milkshakes and says it'll be another minute before our burgers are ready.

I watch as the waitress walks off, my brain going in a million directions. I continue to fidget with my coffee mug while Casey takes a sip of her milkshake.

"You know the interesting thing about Doms and Subs?" She asks softly. I bring my gaze back to her, and she has a thoughtful expression on her face. "Rarely, if ever, is the Sub a doormat. Rarely is the Dom always barking orders. I think you would be surprised at the amount of Subs that hold high-pressure, demanding jobs."

She reaches over and places her hand on mine, stopping me from fidgeting with the coffee mug. My stomach does a little flip. "Sometimes, a Dom's job is to create a safe place for a Sub to just exist without pressure or demands."

I look at our hands, her much smaller one over mine. But the power that tiny hand has to stop the whirlwind of thoughts floating through my head is staggering.

"Did you know that Chris is a captain at the police department? That Crystal is a stay at home mom?"

My shock must show on my face because I would never have guessed.

"I'll take that as a no," she says with a small laugh. The waitress drops our food off and walks away. "Chris isn't less of a man because he chooses to submit to Crystal. In fact, I would go so far as to say he's incredibly emotionally intelligent for knowing what he needs and asking for it. She offers him a safe place to release at the end of his shift. He's able to leave all the bullshit at the door and be who he really wants to be."

I take a minute to think about what she has told me.

"Here's what I propose: I will mentor you in the club. I will show you what it means to be both a Dom and a Sub. If at the end of sixty days, you continue to feel like you aren't a Sub, then I will show you how to be a proper Dom that doesn't bark orders and punish every infraction."

She takes a bite of her burger, moaning as the grease runs down her chin. She wipes it off with a napkin and looks up at me.

"You need to eat, Rook."

I look down at my food, a sense of calm washing over me. I pick up my burger and start to eat.

"Good boy."

Ritual Chapter 2

Grant

Working after club night is going to be a problem, at least for my sleep schedule. I'm usually a rise with the sun kind of guy and don't usually sleep late. But after my shift at the club and then dinner with Casey, my brain is scrambled.

I woke up after only a couple of hours of sleep, wired but ready to start my day.

Last night was wild, watching the various play stations and interactions between partners. I wasn't sure what I expected, but being approached by a five foot two Domme wasn't on my bingo card.

When we left the diner last night, I agreed to let Casey mentor me through the club. To figure out what I wanted and what I was comfortable giving. This morning when I woke up, there was a text waiting for me.

This morning, I want you to eat breakfast and put a call in to Chris.

I can guess why she wants me to call Chris, but breakfast is a no go. I don't eat this early in the morning, especially after a late night.

I shoot Chris a text, requesting a call when he is free, and go sit on my front porch with my coffee. It's not long before my phone is ringing.

"Hey, man. I wasn't expecting a call quite this early," I tell him. My nerves immediately start zinging and I start tapping my foot.

"I'll be honest, I wasn't expecting you to reach out this soon." He sounds like he's rushing around. "I figured it would take you at least a couple of days before you contacted me."

"If now is a bad time, you can call me later. I'm free most of the day."

"No, no. I'm just trying to get the kids to school. You're on my Bluetooth so they can't hear you. But I do want to hear your background, what brought you to Obsidian."

Chris and Crystal are founding members of Obsidian and have been in the lifestyle for over a decade.

"There's not much to tell. I'm thirty-seven, retired from the Army last year, and been drifting since. Damien brought me into the club when I had complained that I was bored and looking for something to do."

"How many deployments did you do?" he asks quietly.

"Six," I say it like a snap.

“They were that good, uh?” He says it sarcastically, but I can hear the gruffness in his voice. “I was in the Marines for eight years before I was medically discharged after an injury in Iraq. Hang on a second.” I hear the doors open and slam followed by a chorus of ‘*bye dad’s.*’

“Sorry about that, Crystal has a doctor’s appointment that we’ve been waiting on for months and couldn’t get them off to school."

"No need to apologize, family comes first," I tell him. That was one of the things I hated about the military. It was always mission first and family last. I had watched many families disintegrate because of that mindset. "Casey said to call you this morning."

"That actually explains a lot. She wants you to talk to an atypical Sub but I am going to talk to you vet to vet first." He pauses for a second, and I can hear the road noise of him driving. “Beyond the club, what are you doing to stay busy?”

“Uh, right now, nothing. My original plan was that I was going to take a year off, relax and reset.”

“How’s that working out for you, Grant?”

“Not well.” I sigh into the phone. And it hasn’t been going well. When I was in the service, I had a purpose, I knew exactly what I was supposed to do and how to do it. But now, I feel like I am adrift in an ocean.

"Unfortunately, vets have been trained for action. The longer a person stays in the military, the less they can mentally handle being alone and stagnant. What most people don’t realize, including ourselves, is that for some of us, the orders, the cadence, the discipline, it all becomes a mental safety net. It allows our brains to shut off and not spiral."

I stop and think about what he's saying. I feel like I am spiraling, but I don't know how to stop it. I don't even know what I want to do now that I'm out of the Army.

"Do you mind me asking how your dynamic works? Because I don't like what my brain is telling me."

"I don't mind at all. I mentor other men who are submissive or want to explore that dynamic. Crystal and I have a mostly *normal* relationship. The Domme/Sub thing doesn't really play a part in our daily life like you probably think. For us, she is my center, my true north. When flashbacks hit or the anxiety takes hold, I grab on to the ritual that she has set up for me."

I think about what he's saying—it's not anything like what I am thinking. "It doesn't sound any different than what a relationship should be like."

Chris laughs. "That's my point. I'm not less of a husband because I choose to submit to my wife. I am not less of a cop, veteran, or dad because I choose to submit to my wife. I am a better man because I learned, the hard way, that I need someone else to take the reins. But on club night or when the kids are out of the house, we can fully step into the dynamic," he adds. "That's when there are rules and protocols that we have set up that I follow. I find peace and love in her dominance."

"I guess I just don't understand the *how*. How does a Marine with eight years and deployments choose to submit to his wife? How does a police captain gain peace from letting someone else take the reins?" I know it sounds shitty, calling his manhood into question, but I am just trying to understand something that, for me, is confusing and terrifying.

"Ah, I got it. You want to know how a man, a man's man, became a Submissive. But I think you're still hung up on what you think submission means. If I had to guess, you are thinking that submission is bowing and scraping. That domination is punishments and demands, and sometimes that's exactly what it is. But the reality is much different."

He pauses, and I hear the road noise in the background cut out.

"Submission, at its core, is letting go of control, even if only for a brief time. It's letting someone you trust hold space for you to just exist, for them to keep the noise and static away. Let me ask you this, when you were in, did you like the structure, knowing what was going to happen day to day, and trust in your command to get you and your guys to safety?"

"Yeah," I tell him. "There was a certain comfort in knowing that my day was always the same. That if I did this, that would happen."

"And now?" he asks quietly.

"Now, I'm always anxious because my day isn't planned to the minute. I struggle to get to sleep because I don't have a set time to get up."

"A Domme would give you the structure that you crave and the safety to find yourself. As someone who really struggled with getting out of the Marines, being injured, and getting lost in my own head, having someone give me that structure has been better than any VA therapist."

"So you're saying that submitting to Casey could allow my brain to rest."

"I'm saying that for some men, the expectations to perform that society and we put on ourselves, are unnecessary. I'm saying that when you have someone that holds the line for you and allows you safety and security to let go and relax, is an intimacy that can't be beat."

We talk for a few more minutes before he goes in for work, and I am left to deal with the shift in my life that he has created.

I thought submission was more about control, about punishment. But hearing him say that submission is about letting go within a safe place has me thinking. That kind of submission is something that may not be too bad.

The rest of the day is spent cleaning my already clean cabin and thinking about what Chris said. Casey has been silent all day, and it's starting to make me feel itchy.

I've just finished cooking dinner when I hear my phone ring. My stomach clenches when I see it's Casey.

"Hello?" I answer. I'm not going to lie and say that I'm looking forward to this conversation, but at the same time, I want to talk to her.

"Hey, Rook." I can hear the road noise in the background. Does no one just drive? I can't stand talking on the phone when I'm driving. "I haven't heard from you today and I just wanted to see if you had eaten and called Chris."

"I'm getting ready to sit down and eat now, and yes, I called Chris this morning." I grab a beer out of the fridge and make my way to the couch.

"Is this the first time you're eating today?" There's an edge to her voice.

"Yeah, I don't eat breakfast." The silence on the other end of the line makes my stomach clench.

"Why?" The disappointment in her voice is obvious.

"Because it makes me sluggish through the rest of the day." I feel like I have to defend myself. "But I talked to Chris this morning, like you asked me to."

"First, those were tasks, not requests. Second, you have to eat in the morning. I don't care if it's a piece of toast or a five-course spread. And third, do not *yeah* me."

She never once raises her voice, but the reprimand is clear. "Yes, Ma'am."

"Good boy, you're a fast learner." I feel my face flush and I'm not sure how I feel about all this. "I just got off shift and planned on heading to get dinner and wanted to invite you, but since you're already eating, I'll just hit the sushi place on my way home."

"Uh, Ma'am..." I'm not really sure of the protocols and rules, but I feel like if I have to eat, she should get something more than take out sushi. "I've got a pan of shrimp alfredo that won't eat itself."

There's silence on the phone, and I think she's hung up on me. "Is it from scratch?"

"Of course, who uses jarred sauces?" I ask, genuinely confused. "That shit is nasty. Regardless of your taste in sauces, there is plenty if you want some."

"Text me your address."

I send her my address and she let's out a low laugh. "Oh, you are so fucked, Rook. If you can cook, you have just gained a dinner guest for life. I'll be there in five."

She hangs up, and I stare at my phone, dumbfounded and a little confused. She must live close by if she is on her way home and she's only five minutes out. I set to work cleaning up the mess I made while making dinner.

It's not long before there's a knock at the door. I holler for her that it's open and continue to work on cleaning up. It takes me a few minutes, but I realize that she's not in the house yet. Maybe I'm hearing things. I go to the door anyways to make sure.

When I open it, I see her standing there in a pair of light blue scrubs. She's got her hands on her hips and an eyebrow raised.

"Homemade alfredo sauce isn't going to save you if I have to open my own door, Rook." She saunters into the house and looks around.

My cabin isn't very big. I didn't need much space since it's just me. The open floor plan allows me to see all the doors and windows from any room downstairs.

I watch as she takes in my space, and I take her in. Her curly red hair is piled up in a messy bun, and she looks even smaller without those skyscraper heels on. But she's curvy and thick in all the right places.

"Food?" she asks. "I'm starving."

I lead her to the kitchen and hand her a bowl. "Beer or water? I don't have any soda."

"I'd love a beer," she says as she looks around. "Where do you eat?"

"The couch." I tilt my head in the direction of the living room. "It's just me and I don't have anyone to eat with. A table seemed redundant."

"I feel the same way." She laughs as she heads to the couch. "It's just me and the dog at my house. But I splurged last year and got a table. You'd be surprised how much a fucking kitchen table can ground you, though."

She kicks off her sneakers and curls up on the couch. She waits for me to sit down before she tucks in. The moan she let's loose is far too erotic for alfredo. I raise my eyebrow at her and she giggles.

"I haven't had a home cooked meal since I left foster care when I turned eighteen." She says it off-handed, but I can see the hurt in her eyes. I decide not to touch that one just yet.

"What do you do?" I ask as I motion at her outfit.

"I'm a pediatric trauma doctor in Atlanta," she says as she scoops another forkful of pasta into her mouth.

I stare at her. "You don't look old enough to be a doctor," I blurt out.

Casey laughs. "I get that a lot, but I'm thirty-four. It's challenging, but I love every minute of it. The drive is brutal, but until the pediatric wing here in Franklin opens up, I'm kind of stuck."

I sit back, stunned. "I thought you were in your early twenties." I shake my head and fork up a bite of pasta, spearing a shrimp as I do. I can't imagine seeing kids that have been hurt day in and day out. "How do you do it?"

"It's hard," she says quietly. "But I want to help kids. I didn't have anyone there for me when I was growing up. I want to be that for kids that need it."

"That's the second time you've brought up being in foster care. Do you want to talk about what happened?"

I watch as she finishes her bowl. I stand up and take the bowl from her and head back to the kitchen and get her a second helping. When I bring it back, she has her head cocked.

"Not yet." She takes another bite of her pasta. "I want to talk about you."

Ritual Chapter 3

Casey

I watch as Rook squirms in his seat. He's gorgeous. Normally, I'm not one to go for the giants, since I'm so damn short. But there was something about him when I watched him move behind the bar last night at the bar.

The quiet confidence he carried told me that he moved with purpose and chose not to waste time or energy.

He was still mostly clean cut from his time in the military. He didn't sport the typical military high and tight, instead letting the top of his black hair grow a little longer but like most military men, he kept the sides short.

His eyes were stunning, the lightest brown I had ever seen. They were damn near gold, but there was an exhaustion in them that I didn't expect. Almost like he was defeated.

I have learned a lot about him in the last forty-eight hours since I approached him.

Before I agreed to take him on as a student, I asked around the club about him. Bear is his sponsor, and I called him when I couldn't find him at the club. According to Bear, Rook had just gotten out of the Army about six months ago.

He had been high-ranking enlisted and had six deployments under his belt before he retired. When I asked Bear what kind of play Rook was into, Bear said he didn't know, but if he had to guess, a Service Sub would probably be right up Rook's alley.

That was interesting because I got the same vibe. But when I approached Rook, he bucked against being called a Sub.

"Rook, what did you think after talking to Chris today?" I'm not the type to beat around the bush. My job has taught me that life is too damn short.

"To be honest, I'm really confused. I don't really understand the dynamic, and I don't understand why you or Chris think I'm submissive."

"Let me stop you there. We don't think you're submissive. At least not the way you are thinking. When you have been in the lifestyle for a long time, you pick up on things that people in the vanilla world don't really see. You are looking at being submissive as being a doormat or as a bad thing. You're not seeing what we see."

I watch as this man starts to fidget with his fork, gently clicking it on the side of the bowl. I take the bowl from him and put it on the coffee table next to my bowl. I hand him his beer and pick up my own.

"How about I tell you what I'm looking for in a Submissive so that you have some context in what you would be getting into?"

Rook nods and picks at the label on the beer bottle. He's so anxious that if I don't give him something to fidget with, he's going to shut down. I place my feet in his lap, and he just looks at me.

"Being my Sub isn't about lavishing me with attention or being wrapped around my finger. That's not something that I'm really interested in. In the past, my Subs had various tasks that they were expected to complete within a certain time frame. If they didn't, their correction was dictated by what we had agreed upon. But some of the common corrections were self-care for them, explaining to me in detail why they were unable to complete the tasks, and so on."

I pause and watch as he stops fidgeting and starts rubbing my feet. It feels fucking divine, but the more important thing is that he is no longer anxious. Instead, he is using me to ground himself. But I hold on to that tidbit for another minute.

"For you specifically, some of your tasks would include eating more than one meal a day, learning a new skill, and creating a support system."

He pauses his heavenly foot rub and stares at me. I wiggle my foot in his lap and he starts rubbing again.

"As our Domme/Sub relationship progresses, if it continues to progress, more tasks or protocols would be introduced. We would always agree to them beforehand, and if one is a hard limit, we will adjust or not do it."

"Can you give me an example?" he asks softly, his voice gruff. He is continuing to massage me but has moved to my calves, and I feel like I'm going to melt into the couch.

I clear my throat. "Okay, this morning I texted you and told you to eat breakfast and call Chris. You didn't eat breakfast. Your correction could be to wake up fifteen minutes early tomorrow and make yourself breakfast. You would send me a picture of not only your breakfast, but of you eating it. The correction isn't about punishment or shame. It's about follow through."

Rook is lost in thought and has moved from my calf to my knee. "And if I don't agree?" he asks.

"Then negotiations stop. I'm still willing to mentor you as a Dom, but I don't think it will be a good fit. The best Doms learned how to submit first before they asked for submission from someone else. If you can't submit, if you can't follow, you can't lead."

"Why do you think I'm submissive? I don't see it. My entire career—"

"You submitted," I interrupt him. "You are looking at submission from an alpha male perspective, not from a power exchange perspective. Really think about your military career. When you went through basic training and AIT, you gave the drill sergeants the power. When you went to your unit, you gave your sergeant power. As you rose through the ranks, your power shifted, but at the end, you had people in charge of you."

I pull my feet away from him and sit up. He reaches for his beer and takes a sip before going back to picking at the label.

"But that's not what I see when I look at you, Rook. What I see when I look at you is a man who is anxious, who isn't taking care of himself, who gave everything to the military before they said they were done with him. I see a man that has minimal support and, if I'm being honest, has a need to serve."

"How do you figure I have a need to serve?" He's skeptical, and I can't blame him.

"Just tonight, you fed me, got me seconds, and rubbed my feet, all without me asking," I tell him with a grin.

"That is called hospitality."

"And the feet?" I ask. The look on his face is priceless.

"I'm not interested in convincing you about what you are or aren't. That's for you to decide. I told you that if you chose to submit to me for sixty days, and it didn't work out, I would mentor you in being a Dom. The rest is up to you to decide." I stand up and put our bowls in the sink.

"Text me when you get up in the morning and I'll give you your tasks for the day. If I don't hear from you, I'll assume that you aren't interested in mentoring."

He gets up and walks me to the door, opening it before I have a chance. He walks me to my car and waits until I pull away.

I really hope he texts me in the morning.

The last couple of weeks have passed in a blur, and I have to admit, I love being right. Not because it strokes my ego, but because Rook is getting what he needs.

Rook is a natural service Sub. Every morning when he gets up, which is almost the same time I do, he sends me a picture of his workout and then his breakfast. Every night, he makes us dinner when I get off shift. When we are done eating, he rubs my legs as we talk about our day.

He started working with Jordan, learning how to work with metal and silver. He's learning a lot and has started to talk more about what he wants to do with these new skills. He's already mentioned building a forge on his property and making knives.

But the thing I'm most proud of him for, is that he has found a support system beyond me. He is having lunch with Chris at least once a week and he hangs out with Bear regularly as well. He's engaging at club night and we have even changed some of our rules and protocols when we go to the club.

But tonight is the real test. The club is hosting a small gathering for a collaring ceremony. It's a high protocol night and while Chris, Crystal, and I have explained in great detail what it entails, Rook feels like he is ready.

I'm waiting for Rook to arrive to take us to the club and I'm not going to lie, I'm nervous as fuck. Not because I don't think Rook can handle it. No, I'm nervous because high protocol is a huge turn on for me.

I've been a part of these nights for years, and it has only gotten hotter. Some would see what happens at these events and think that it's about humiliation and degradation, but if you asked the Submissive, they would tell you that they love every second of it. They love that they get to show their love and commitment to their Dom.

I hear his truck pull up and wait for him to come up to the door. I hear his footsteps on the deck and then the knock. When I open the door, my cunt clenches.

He's beautiful.

Rook is on his knees, his weight shifted back so that he is sitting on his heels. His hands are resting on his thighs with his palms up, and his head is down.

He's wearing black leather pants that mold his thighs and a leather harness with no shirt. His stacked muscles are on full display. His jaw is clean shaven and his hair is slicked back.

"Look at me," I say softly. When he raises his eyes to meet mine, those gold iris' are nearly swallowed whole by his pupils. He is as turned on as I am. "Good boy."

A blush stains his cheeks, and I can tell that he wants to fidget, but he holds himself still. I place my hand on his jaw, and he immediately relaxes. "You are perfect."

I step inside and put on my heels and grab my purse that is on the table next to the door. When I step back out, he is still on his knees, head still up and looking at me. I lock the door and hold my hand out for him. He stands smoothly, taking my hand and tucking it through the crook of his arm and he walks us towards his truck.

He helps me inside and buckles my seatbelt for me. I can see the desire burning in his eyes, and I give him a short nod. Rook leans forward and presses his lips to my temple. He breathes deep, as if my scent calms him.

He shuts the door and rounds the hood. I watch as he reaches for the driver's side door and takes a deep breath. He opens the door and slides in. "Are you ready for tonight?"

"Yes, Ma'am." His tone is a quiet calm that a few weeks ago, I didn't think he would achieve. But the transformation in him is unbelievable.

He puts the truck in gear, and we start the short drive to Obsidian. I reach over and tug his hand from his lap and place it on my thigh. One of the things I have noticed about Rook is his need for constant movement. Tonight will be the true test in all the things he has learned.

The radio hums in the background and, to my surprise, he doesn't fidget once. He keeps his hand on my thigh and expertly maneuvers his truck through traffic. When we get to Obsidian, he parks and waits until I release his hand. He gets out and opens my door for me, helping me out of the truck.

"Remember what I told you about tonight. If anything feels off or you get uncomfortable, all you have to do is give me a color. If we need to leave, then we leave."

"Yes, Ma'am."

I turn and start walking towards the club. Rook stays exactly one pace behind me and to the left. I hand my invitation to security, and he allows Rook and me to enter. Inside, the club has been transformed.

The play stations have been moved to the storage rooms in the back, and the tables have been set up banquet style. Tonight, socializing is held off until after the ceremony, and we have been asked to find our seats quickly. Next to each chair is a pillow on the ground for our Submissive.

Rook waits until I sit down before he kneels on the pillow and gets into position. He is practically vibrating with nerves, but he is holding himself perfectly still. I place my hand on his jaw and tilt his head so that he is looking at me.

He closes his eyes and leans into my hand, his body instantly relaxing. I press a light kiss to his forehead. "Would you like to put your head in my lap, Rook?"

He nods and adjusts until his temple rests on my thigh. I place my hand on the back of his neck and watch as the officiant and Domme start walking to the front. From his position, he'll still be able to watch the ceremony, which is the most important reason I wanted him to come with me.

"Rook, you need to get into whatever position you are most comfortable in. The ceremony is about to start and you can't move unless you have a problem," I whisper to him.

Rook doesn't move. "You want to stay like this?" He nods his head against my thigh.

"You are doing so well, Darling." The name just slipped out, but it fits.

I keep my hand on the back of his neck to keep him grounded, so he doesn't fidget during the ceremony. I watch as the Submissive is led in by his mentor and kneels in front of the Domme. The ceremony starts without fanfare.

It's not a long ceremony. The Submissive promises to trust in his Domme and the Domme promises love and safety. She clips the silver collar around his throat, stepping around him to lock it, and helps him to stand. The officiant finishes the ceremony by presenting the couple to the community.

I feel a tremble run through Rook and I'm hoping it's because he's moved and he isn't about to start fidgeting. I place my other hand on his shoulder, hoping to offer him comfort either way.

"It's almost done, Darling. You're doing so good," I murmur to him.

Ritual Chapter 4

Grant

My feet are asleep and my back is killing me, but there is nowhere else I would rather be. Less than a month ago, I would never have thought I would be here. Kneeling next to a Domme, with my head in her lap, and loving every minute of it.

But that's exactly where I find myself. I was skeptical at first, thinking that submission was a weakness. But now I see the difference. It's not about weakness and strength. It's not about shame and degradation.

It's about peace, at least for me.

In the last three weeks, I have given myself over to the process, to the power exchange. And the difference I see in myself is night and day.

Before, I didn't eat breakfast, hadn't worked out in months, felt like I was a waste of space and time. I didn't realize how anxious I had become. In short, I was miserable.

Now, I have energy that I haven't felt since I was in my early twenties. I am learning a new skill and have hope for the future. And the most important change, I have people that actually care about me. Not what I can contribute or how well my soldiers do their job. Just me.

The ceremony is almost over and I watch as the Domme places a collar on her Sub. I didn't really understand the significance of a collar when Casey brought up the invitation to the ceremony. And I didn't really understand what high protocol meant.

She explained that there would be a lot of kneeling, standing, and serving. That tonight isn't a test of my obedience or her control, but that it *is* expected that I do exactly what I am told. She also warned me that high protocol situations are a huge turn-on for her.

She explained that while she receives pleasure from my submission, it's not necessarily a turn-on sexually. She said there was just something about high protocol that set her on fire. She placed no expectations on me and said that we would not have sex or other intimacy beyond my submission until we were both ready.

And still I didn't understand.

As I was getting ready for tonight, I realized that the leather pants and harness that she had me buy for tonight was another act of submission. When I put them on, I felt grounded because I was doing what she told me.

When I got to her house and knelt on her porch, it all clicked. And when she called me a *good boy*, I felt a wave of calm wash over me. Every text, every meal I cooked for her, every foot rub, finally meant more when I looked at it with new eyes.

I'm not weak for offering her my submission. I am stronger. With her guidance and patience, I have learned that it is okay to feel things. It's okay to want to protect and provide but also to serve. And it's okay to want protection in return.

I'm drawn back to the ceremony and watch as the Domme places the collar on her Sub. It's beautiful because I finally understand what he is feeling. A tremor courses through me, and I feel Casey put her hand on my shoulder. I want to tell her that I'm okay, but I can't. Instead, I do the only thing I know how. I still completely and take a deep breath.

The scent of her arousal, so close to my face, is making my mouth water. All I want to do is tackle her to the ground and take her. But I don't. Instead, I think of all the things I would let her do to me.

My cock is thick and hard in my pants. Leather doesn't allow for much movement, and the increasing pressure is getting harder to ignore.

The ceremony ends as I am trying to regain control of myself. The Doms are asked to rise as the couple walks to their table. I lift my head from Casey's lap and sit back on my heels again. I keep my palms up on my thighs, but the friction of my cock against the leather almost has me coming in my pants.

Casey stands and watches as the couple makes their way to the table. She looks down at me, and her gaze turns heavy. She leans down to whisper in my ear. "Oh, Darling, are you aroused?"

I swallow hard. Her scent surrounds me, and I feel lightheaded. "Yes, Ma'am."

"If you can be good for the next hour and maintain your composure, I will make sure you are rewarded." She straightens back up and places her hand on the back of my neck.

The rest of the evening passes in a blur. There are toasts and conversation, but I take none of it in. Instead, I stay kneeling, my gaze focused on Casey. She takes a look at her watch, and there's a small smile on her face.

"You did perfect, Darling." She places her napkin on the table. "It's time to go."

She releases me from kneeling, and I stand slowly. The blood rushes back into my feet, and for a second, a wave of dizziness overwhelms me. Casey puts her hand on my chest, grounding me in the moment, and soon the dizziness is gone. When she sees that I'm okay, she steps away and starts walking towards the door.

I fall into step behind her and follow her to my truck. I help her in and get behind the wheel.

"Take me home, Darling," is all she says before she leans back in her seat and slips her heels off.

I reach behind the seat and pull out a pair of pink fuzzy slippers. I gently pull her feet towards me and slip them onto her. When I look up at her, I see her eyes are glistening.

"Thank you." She pulls my hand into her lap and runs her thumb over the back of my hand.

I nod and put the truck in gear before heading back to her house. The ride is quiet, just the radio in the background and the road noise to keep us company.

When I pull into her driveway, I am calm but excited. I work through the ritual she has requested: opening her door, helping her out of the truck, walking her to the door. But this time, it is with new eyes.

I watch as she pulls her keys from her purse and hands them to me. I unlock her door and let her inside.

"Rook." She stands just inside the doorway and looks up at me. "I want you to shower and get on the bed, naked."

She pauses and looks at me with her head cocked. She is offering me an out, I realize. I can say no, and that would be that. But I don't want to say no. I want all of her.

I walk in the direction of her bedroom and get undressed. I place my harness on the chair next to her bed, my boots below it. I start the process of extracting myself from the tight leather pants and fold those and put them on top of the harness.

I walk into her bathroom and start the shower, waiting until steam is billowing out before I climb in. I don't take long in the shower, too impatient to have her. A quick wash with her body wash gets all the sweat from the leather off me.

I step out of the shower and quickly dry off before I go back into the bedroom. I stop in my tracks when I see her standing at the end of the bed. She has removed her black dress but left on the black lace teddy.

"On the bed, Darling." I climb onto the bed and lay on my back, keeping her in my sights. She climbs up on the bed and crawls over to me.

"I knew you would be a good boy for me," she whispers in my ear as she straddles me, and I feel that her teddy is crotchless. "What do you want as a reward for such good behavior?"

My eyes damn near roll into the back of my head as her hot cunt rubs against my cock. I place my hands on her hips and drag her against my cock again. She lets out a moan and rocks against me again. I lean up and whisper in her ear, "I want to taste the cunt I have been smelling all night."

I lay back down on the bed. I lift her hips and bring her to my face. "Please, Ma'am, let me taste you."

The moan that leaves her is sexy as sin, and before I know it, she is sitting on my face and riding it. I nibble, lap, and lick before sucking her clit into my mouth. I reach behind her back and gently lean her back so that she is more reclined, giving me all the access I need to have her ready to come in seconds.

"Fuck, Darling," she says on a gasp. "I'm going to come if you keep that up."

I unseal my mouth from her dripping cunt. “Isn’t that the point?” I go back to her cunt and keep licking, her arousal sliding down my throat.

“I want to come on your cock, Darling.” I release her reluctantly. She drags her cunt down my chest and over my stomach before palming my cock. She smears the pre-cum that is dripping off the tip around the crown with her thumb.

“So big and thick." She moans, and I groan. I wasn’t much for talking during sex, but I could get behind this. "You’re a big boy, aren’t you, Darling?”

“Yes, Ma’am,” I murmur. She lines up my cock at her entrance and slowly starts to work herself onto it. I run my hands up her hips and sides before palming her large breasts in my hands, my thumbs stroking her nipples.

She gasps and slides the rest of the way down my cock, seating me completely. We both groan, and then she starts to move.

Up and down, back and forth, the rhythm she sets is smooth and methodical. I was close to coming before, but now, I’m about to blow.

“Please, Ma’am, please come,” I beg her. I can’t last much longer with the pace she’s set. I reach forward and press my thumb to her clit, applying just enough pressure, and I watch as her world detonates.

She falls over the edge of her orgasm with a scream. I slam her down on me one last time before I empty myself into her. She collapses on top of me, and I wrap my arms around her. Her slight weight grounds me back in my body.

I brush her curly red hair back from her face and watch as she comes down from her orgasm. Pride fills my chest that I am the one that took her there. That my obedience, given freely, is what made her happy.

"Thank you, Ma'am," I whisper in her hair. I feel the whole body shiver that takes her.

"You were such a good boy tonight, Rook. I'm so proud of you and everything you've accomplished in such a short time." Her voice is thick with emotion.

"Thank you, Ma'am. For everything." And I mean it. "But I like Darling better."

Her laugh is like balm to my soul.

Ritual Bonus Scene

Grant

I watch as Casey gets ready for tonight, inspecting herself in the mirror. Her curly red hair is piled up on her head in an elaborate style that uses the entire pack of pins. Her makeup is flawless. But all I can think about is how badly I want to smear those crimson-painted lips.

I don't. Not tonight.

I'm sitting on the edge of our bed, waiting for her. And I would wait for a hundred years if that is what she asked of me. She shuts off the lights and walks towards me. The black gown she is wearing swishes around her legs. She stops in front of me and hands me her heels.

I get down on my knees in a fluid motion, my knees popping. She places her hand on my shoulder for balance, and I pick up her tiny foot. I put the heel on and secure the strap around her ankle, kissing the top of her foot before placing it back on the floor.

I repeat this with the other foot before sitting back on my heels, palms up on my thighs and my head bowed.

“Are you ready for tonight, Darling?” she asks softly. The hand on my shoulder moves to the back of my neck and rubs gently.

My entire body relaxes and yet awakens at the same time. I nod my head but keep looking down. She hasn’t given me permission to look at her yet.

She moves her hand to my jaw and tilts my head till I’m looking at her. She gazes into my eyes for a minute before she steps back. “Then let’s go.”

It takes me a second to get off my knees, but once I am up, I follow her out of the bedroom. She pauses at the door and allows me to open it before gathering her purse and the black box that is next to it.

I usher her out of the house and lock the door. I help her down the stairs and into my truck. The same ritual that we have been doing for the last eight years. The same calming awareness washes over me.

When I get in the truck and start towards Obsidian, my nerves start to show. But before I can start fidgeting, she grabs my hand and places it on her thigh. The act instantly calms me, grounding me.

As usual, the only noises in the truck are the low radio and the road noise. Neither one of us likes to talk when we are driving, preferring the silence over more noise.

When I pull the truck into Obsidian, it's a packed house. It's not a club night, but a collaring ceremony for one of the founding members.

I turn off the truck and get out. I help her out of the truck and walk one step behind her and to the left, taking comfort in the protocols that we have established over the years. Casey hands our invitation to security, who immediately lets us into the club.

The club looks much like it did that night when everything clicked into place for me. The tables are set up banquet style, and a platform is set up for the ceremony. Everyone is already seated, and I look around at everyone.

Chris is kneeling next to Crystal. Bear has Jordan tucked into his chest, his hand resting on her pregnant belly. Those closest to us are here...for us.

Casey walks to the front of the room, her chin high and shoulders back. I watch as the officiant steps up onto the platform.

It's my turn to go to the front, and I watch as Crystal gives Chris permission to stand. He comes over and gives me a hug. We have become close over the last eight years. He took me under his wing and mentored me, not just as a Service Sub, but as a man.

He walks me to Casey, and when I reach the platform, I kneel on the pillow that she made sure was in place. But this time, instead of bowing my head, I look her in the eyes as the officiant starts the ceremony.

I think back over the last eight years with this woman. It wasn't long after I learned what submission meant to me that she moved in with me. The pediatric floor opened in Franklin, and she was able to work there instead of driving to Atlanta.

We had our ups and downs, when the world chaffed and rocked, but I still texted her every morning that I had worked out and eaten breakfast. I continued my weekly lunches with Chris, and I am now a renowned knife maker.

Despite everything that could have torn us apart, we stuck it out. Her quiet confidence and commands. My absolute trust and devotion to her.

This ceremony has been a long time coming, but neither of us were in a rush. We were content to just be.

But Jordan contacted her about a collar she was working on and wanted Casey's medical input. It wasn't long after that we started discussing our own collaring. We were both ready.

As I kneel in front of Casey, there is no part of me that isn't one hundred percent sure that I want to be this Domme's Submissive. She pulled me back from a brink that neither of us realized I was on.

She opens the black box that she brought from the house and shows it to me. I recognize Jordan's work immediately. It is stunning. A simple, thick silver choker with *Darling* stamped across the front. She hands the box to the officiant and pulls it out of the box.

I bow my head, and she steps behind me, placing the thick choker around my neck. It's snug but not tight, forcing me to drop my shoulders so that it doesn't dig into my jaw. I hear the snick of the lock and watch as she steps back in front of me. She pulls a second chain from the box and slips the key onto the chain.

I watch as she places the chain around her neck, and the small key rests between her breasts.

She steps forward and places her hand on my jaw. I nuzzle my head into her hand and take a deep breath.

"I promise to spend the rest of my life holding a space for you to be at peace," she says, her voice breaking at the end.

"I promise to spend the rest of my life being the man and Submissive you deserve."

She presses her lips to mine, and instantly heat burns through me. When she pulls away, her pupils dilate, and she grins. "You've got to be good for at least an hour."

Nothing stops them from the hunt

Wild Obsidian: Run

Vic Raven

Trigger Warnings

RUN

ACCIDENT (BONUS SCENE)

Primal Kink

Knife Play

Injured Hunter

Run Chapter 1

Tristian

Tonight is shaping up to be a disaster. Brent is running late and I'm not doing any better. He was supposed to be home an hour ago, but like most people in public safety, he's going to be late.

I can't say much. I got off late this morning and my entire day has been fucked ever since. Between the late call, cleaning up the med unit and then getting back to the station, I was three hours late getting home.

On a normal day, it isn't a big deal. But today isn't a normal day. It's pack weekend at the Wilds, and it's one of the few nights a year that Brent and I get to unleash, to be wild.

But there is prep work that has to be done for us to leave the boys home alone for the weekend. Not only do I need to make sure that they don't burn down the house, I have to make sure that they have meals prepped, the animals are taken care of, and phones are charged.

I've got to make sure that people are on standby, us included, if something goes wrong. It's a lot of work. But the boys are fifteen and seventeen and are mostly well-behaved. I'm not worried about them throwing a party or trashing the house.

No, I'm more worried that they will spend the next two days glued to their video games and forget to let the dogs out and eat. But that's what cell phones are for...if they're charged.

I've just finished pulling my uniform from the washer when I hear the front door open.

"Honey, I'm home," Brent calls from the door. I roll my eyes but can't stop the grin that forms.

"Bout damn time, you slacker," I quip back from the laundry room. I hear his laugh and his boots *thunking* back to the laundry room. "I know you aren't wearing your work boots in my house!"

The *thunking* stops immediately, followed by a few grunts and groans. I hear the front door open again, and this time when I hear his footsteps, they are much quieter. "Thank you."

He appears in the doorway, sans boots, and I'm instantly filled with love and longing. This man has held my heart for over twenty years. We had been through so much in that time: love, loss, moves, and so much more. But we clung to each other the whole time, through the good and bad. And now, with our boys moving into the next stage of their lives, we are even closer than before.

"Thank you, Stud," I tell him as I lean up for a quick kiss. He goes to grab for me. "Nope. You need to take that nasty uniform off before you start trying to love on me."

As an arson investigator, he climbs around in the soot and ash of burned-out buildings. Normally, he doesn't come home without showering at the station, but today he was rushing to get home.

I watch as he pulls the polo over his head and chucks it in the washer, followed by the t-shirt underneath. By the time he gets his pants and socks off, I am a panting mess. It doesn't matter how much this man has changed since he was twenty-two—each version of him is hotter than the last.

Brent is standing in his black boxer briefs with surfing squirrels on them, his body heavily tattooed and muscled. His long, brown hair is tied back, and he needs to trim the sides of his mohawk before we leave tonight. I can see the gray coming in at his temples.

I scan him for injuries, like I have everyday day since I got the call that he had been hurt on the job. He had been working a wreck on the highway when a distracted driver plowed into him. That night had taken his leg and his job, and gave us the reminder that life is short.

There are no new injuries, but there is soot covering every inch of him. "Go shower, I've got to keep getting ready."

He leans forward and presses a kiss to my forehead. I swear my brain short-circuits, and all I want to do is join him in the shower, but I don't have time and neither does he.

I get the washer going and head into our bedroom to start packing our bags. We don't need much, most of our weekend will be spent naked, but there are other things that we need to have on hand. Things like bug spray, calamine lotion, sunscreen, and the like.

No one wanted an itchy asshole from falling into poison ivy. The Wilds is good about keeping the grounds clear and safe, but last year a woman fell into a pile of poison ivy...lets just say it wasn't pretty for anyone.

I manage to get most of our stuff packed up before Brent comes out of the shower, but I stall out when I see him standing in the doorway. He's got a towel wrapped around his tight waist and water is still dripping down his chest. His long hair is damp like he had barely taken the time to towel dry it. He trimmed the sides of his Mohawk to the skin, and I want to touch it.

I know I'm standing there staring at him, but fuck me, he is delicious. Between the muscles, tattoos, and his hair flipped to one side, I am a mess. And he knows it.

"Do you want to play early, Darlin'?" he asks, his voice scratchy and gruff.

I shake myself out of my hormone-induced lust. Damn these hormone patches, they seemed like a good idea because of perimenopause. Now, I'm hornier than I was when I was a teenager.

"No, we are already running late. Do you have everything you need?" I have the accessories that we have learned that he needs for these weekends: small fans, extra liners, lotions, wipes, and even a small multi-tool. But sometimes he surprises me with wanting something extra or different.

"No, I've got an extra shell and blade for the leg and the toolkit to switch them out," he tells me, and I'm once again flabbergasted.

How the hell does he do it? How the hell does he go into the woods for two days with an above the knee amputation, with just a tool kit and an extra foot shell and blade?

"You take care of me," he says simply, like he knew exactly what I was thinking. "Darlin', you have been taking care of me and this family for two decades. I know you. I know how you operate. You aren't going to let me forget anything. So yes, I have everything I need. I have you."

My heart damn near bursts with love for this man. We had our fair share of bumps in the road. Years where we both took advantage of each other's strengths, and sometimes weaknesses. But we always held one thing above all else—me and him against the world.

Yes, I could get upset that I do everything. But I learned something really valuable over the last couple of years—I enjoy doing everything. I enjoy taking care of my family. And I know that if I drop the ball on something, the only one that cares is me. My boys don't care if they have enough underwear. Brent doesn't care if I forgot to bring him enough pants.

They care about me, and that's pretty damn special.

"Alright, enough with the mushy stuff," I quip back at him. "You need to get dressed, we're already running late."

With that, I start taking our bags to the living room. I am beyond excited for this weekend. I've been running ragged over the last couple of months. Between working full-time as a medic, teaching, and running the house, I've started to feel really overwhelmed.

Pack night, or in this case weekend, only happens twice a year; usually the beginning and end of summer. Being in the mountains of North Carolina, it isn't really safe to have pack hunts in the fall and winter, but some of the pack are willing to brave the elements.

Brent and I used to love hunting in the fall, but after his amputation, we had to adapt to life with him only having one good leg.

The first real hunt after his amputation was comical, but taking care of his stump after was a pain in the ass. We learned a lot, and each hunt has gotten better and better.

I've got the last of the bags by the door when I hear Brent come out of the bedroom. "You ready, Stud?"

He comes up behind me and wraps his arms around my waist. He buries his face in the curve of my neck, and I lean back against him and just take a minute. It's like he knows that I need a reset.

"I didn't get my hug today," he says with a grumble, and it almost sounds like he's pouting.

I reach behind me and gently scratch the back of his neck, running my fingers through the long hairs there. "You were dirty when you came home," I murmur back to him.

"And? Our shower is big enough for two." He's definitely pouting.

"We tried that one time, remember? We both almost ended up in the hospital." I laugh. I try to pull away, but he holds me tightly. "You okay?"

"Yeah, it was a house fire. The family didn't make it," he says quietly. "It looks like the ex-husband may have set the fire."

I stiffen. No wonder he's been so quiet. I move to turn in his arms, to give him a proper hug, but he won't let me. "Stud…"

"Nope, I just need a minute."

"Okay," I say, continuing to scratch the back of his neck with one hand and grip his arm with the other. I hold him like that, offering him comfort, but he pulls away after a few minutes.

"Where are the boys?" he asks.

"Hopefully finishing up their homework." I sigh.

"Boys!" Brent hollers up the stairs and bends down to take a couple of bags to the truck. I bend down to grab a few others, and he clears his throat at me.

"For fuck's sake, I can carry bags to the truck," I snap at him.

"Yeah, but what's the point of having boys if we can't turn them into pack mules." The boys appear at the top of the stairs. "Good, you're still alive. Grab the rest of these bags and bring them out."

"Nice to see you too, Dad," Michael quips at us.

Between the three of them, they get all the bags loaded into the bed of Brent's truck and secured. I'm getting the last bit of stuff squared away when everyone walks back in.

"We're burning daylight, Darlin'," Brent tells me.

"I know, I just want to make sure everything's good for them." I load the fridge with drinks and snacks.

"Mom, we're good. It's only two days," Michael says as he comes into the kitchen.

"Yeah, well, my babies are going to be home for two days with you two. I want to make sure that at least someone will be fed," I snark back.

"I love how you're more worried about the dogs than us," Patrick sasses as he walks in.

I'm about to say something when Brent steps in. "Darlin', they're not going to starve, I promise."

"Boys, make sure your phones are on and on you," I say as Brent starts pulling me towards the door. "And don't forget to give the dogs their treats."

Brent is actively pushing me out the door now. "I love you guys!"

"Be good. Don't set the house on fire," Brent says as he closes the door. He opens it back up and says, "Oh and love you."

I'm laughing as we head to the truck. Brent opens the door for me, and I climb in. He presses a kiss to my forehead and shuts the door. I watch as he rounds the hood of the truck.

His limp is more of a swagger now, and it's good to see. There was a time I was worried that the amputation would take more from him than just his leg. It would take his confidence, his swagger, his charm.

"You ready, Darlin'?" he asks as he starts the truck. His deep southern drawl wreaking havoc on my hormones.

"Oh, you have no idea, Stud."

Run Chapter 2

Brent

My brain is still scrambled from the house fire investigation. I thought I was okay, but I can barely focus on what Tristian is saying. All I see is the victims buried in ash and wreckage.

I hit the blinker to get off the highway, and Tristian asks, "What's wrong?"

"I need a minute." I get us safely off the highway, and I pull into a gas station. "I'm not as okay as I thought."

Tristian leans over the center console and places her hand on my chest, pressing into it slightly. She rests her head on my shoulder as she does it, grounding me. She doesn't demand to know what's going on or for me to spill my guts. She doesn't have to. She knows how hard the job is. How hard it can be to clean up the mental aftermath.

Some men probably won't open up about needing a minute. About not being okay. But I'm not most men. I have learned a lot about what it means to be a man in the years since I lost my leg.

I learned that the man I was before the amputation was a man that thought he had to be in complete control of himself at all times, to show no emotions, to protect and provide. That couldn't let the job get to him, I was a firefighter after all. I grew up in firehouses that said *if you can't hack it, get the fuck out.*

But what I really learned was how toxic I had been to my wife, my boys, and my rookies. I learned that I am not invincible, and that it's okay to lean on those that love you.

It's crazy how losing a limb can change your entire perspective on life.

I put the truck in park and lean my head back against the headrest and just stare at the ceiling, gathering myself.

"The youngest was four," I whisper into the truck. "The fire started in the mother's bedroom, and gas was the accelerant. The gas trailed into each of the bedrooms, but I guess he ran out when he got to her bedroom. That little girl died of smoke inhalation."

I turn my head to look at Tristian, her beautiful blue eyes staring back at me. "The crews couldn't get in to save any of them. I'm still waiting on the scene reports, but it sounds like the ex barricaded the doors and windows so no one could get in…or out."

Her head is still on my shoulder, and I rest mine against hers. Her hand is still pressing against my chest. I reach up and place my hand over hers.

"The crews have already been debriefed and the counselors have already been brought in, but I'm not one of the crew anymore. Now they see me as someone who is critiquing their work. Not the firefighter that went into those houses with them."

I sit in the silence of the truck for another minute or two before I get out. I don't need gas, but I need something to do with my hands.

"Let's go get dinner," Tristian says. She must have gotten out of the truck without me noticing.

"No, it's pack night, and you have been looking forward to this for months. I'm not ruining this for you." She comes to stand next to me. I look down at her and barely manage to hold my grin in. She's adorable when she's like this, like a pissed off pixie.

"Stud, I don't give two flying fucks about pack night, we can go home for all I care. I care about *you*. And if you're not okay, then I don't want to go."

I'll be damned if she doesn't stomp her little foot to prove her point. "No. We're going, I just needed a minute to get my mind right."

She doesn't believe me, and really she shouldn't, because I would do anything for this woman. Even ignoring my mental health.

“Brent, I swear to fuck, if you are going to be stubborn about this, we are going to fight.” She crosses her arms over her chest, and it raises her small breasts up. I am momentarily distracted from what we are arguing about. “Eyes up here, you big oaf.”

I bring my eyes up to her face and realize that I must have really pissed her off. “Sorry, you’re adorable when you get mad at me.”

I put the gas nozzle back on the hook and wipe my hands on my jeans. “Darlin', I’m okay. I just needed to get that out.”

She doesn’t look convinced. “I promise, I’m okay now,” I tell her.

“Well, now I want dinner.” She pouts. I chuckle because I know exactly what she’s doing. Yes, she’s probably hungry because in her rush to get ready, she didn’t eat today. But this is for me. She’s giving me an out to reset before we head to pack night.

“Okay, you little gremlin, what do you want to eat?” I help her into the truck and wait until she’s got her seatbelt on.

“Noodles.” She looks up at me with those big blue eyes, and I can’t help but laugh.

“Alright, let’s get you fed.” I shut her door and head back to the driver's side. After I get in and settled, I lean over to her and kiss her on the temple. “Thank you.”

“You never have to thank me, Stud. You matter to me more than anything, including pack night.” She places her hand on my arm and says, “Now, noodles.”

How this woman knows that a good meal and her presence is the reset I need, I'll never know. It's probably the same place in her brain that houses her GPS for all the shit I lose.

Over dinner we talked about everything under the sun: work, the boys, upcoming house projects, the full marathon we are running in October. The reminder that the world still spins is enough to get my head unscrambled.

Those that aren't in public safety don't understand—the return to normal is exactly what we need. Wallowing in the chaos of our work doesn't help. If anything, it makes doing the job harder. But the gentle touches shared through dinner, the quick check-ins, the silence that says *I'm here*, is sometimes all that really matters.

We are getting ready to pull into the Wilds when she turns and looks at me.

"Stud, do you remember what I told you when you lost your leg?"

"That it was unfair that I dropped twenty pounds overnight while you struggled for years to lose ten?" That earns me a swat on the shoulder.

"No, you big oaf! I told you that if you grew six inches or shrunk six inches, it didn't matter to me. If you cut off all your hair or grew it out, it didn't matter to me. That all I want is you. Do you remember that?"

"Yeah," I tell her, suddenly choked up. I remember that conversation well. I was in the hospital and had just come out of surgery. I was going up against a lot of physical therapy, pain, and loss.

I was struggling with the idea that I wouldn't be able to protect or provide for my family. I was struggling with the idea that I wouldn't be able to walk or lift weights, or do any of the things I wanted to do. And I was terrified that we wouldn't be able to hunt anymore. That she wouldn't want me anymore.

And through it all, I remember this little spitfire sitting next to me telling me that none of that mattered. That as long as I didn't give up, she wouldn't give up either.

"Good. The things you do or don't do aren't what makes you valuable. You are valuable all on your own."

"Fucking hell, Babe," I mutter. I'm already trying to hold back the emotions clogging my throat. "You couldn't have laid that on me two miles back."

"Nope." She pops the *p* and turns her head to look out the window.

I pull into the Wilds and see the cars and trucks parked in the gravel lot. It's going to be a busy weekend, but man, it's going to be worth it. I love this shit. Everything about the hunt is exciting and arousing.

I park the truck in front of the cabin we will be using, thankful and irritated that we have to have one. I would love to go camping in the woods with Tristian, but the first hunt after my amputation was eye-opening. I ended up with a pretty severe infection that just about sidelined me.

Now we get a cabin. I hate to sound ungrateful because I'm not. But sometimes it's frustrating seeing all the ways my life has changed because someone didn't think a road block applied to them.

I hop out of the truck and carefully make my way to Tristian's door. Gravel and prosthetics don't play well together. Fuck, I'd probably have to use my cane getting around this weekend.

I open her door and help her down. She raises up on her tiptoes and plants a kiss on my mouth. She probably meant for it to be a quick kiss, but I am having none of that.

I keep hold of the door with one hand for balance and bring her body closer to mine with the other. Once she is pressed against me, I run my hand up her back and grip the long blond hairs at the back of her neck. With a pull on her hair, I crank her head back.

I run my tongue along the seam of her lips, and she slowly opens for me. I feel her tongue brush against mine and the switch in my brain flips. I let out a growl and push into her body further. Her back hits the side of the truck and a whimper hits the air.

I grind against her and she moans louder.

"Save it for tomorrow, you two," a voice calls out. My head snaps up, and a growl leaves my throat. I look around for who'd interrupted me.

"Lucas, you asshole!" Tristian yells at him. I'm ready to tear him apart, but he's right. Some of this pent-up lust needs to hold...at least until I get her inside the cabin.

"What took y'all so long?" he asks as he lowers the tailgate to the truck.

"He had to stop and feed me. That late call this morning put me behind and I forgot to eat." She looks around him. "Where's Lana?"

This woman is amazing, protecting me from unwanted attention and pulling it towards herself.

"We got a cabin this year. I'm getting too old to be sleeping in a tent. She's unpacking her nine million bags," he says with a laugh.

"It's three bags, you pain in the ass. And two of them are your hair products," Lana sasses as she walks up.

Lucas jumps up into the truck like he's twenty, not forty-three, and starts moving bags to the edge for us to get. He holds up my cane and wiggles it at me. I nod and take it from him.

That's the thing about Lucas, he just does shit. He doesn't make a big deal out of anything. He saw me holding on to the truck and realized that the gravel was going to be a pain in the ass for me. So he fixed it.

Tristian goes to grab a bag and I growl at her. It doesn't matter if it takes me a hundred trips, she doesn't touch the bags when I'm around.

"Ease up, tiger, you really think I'm going to let her carry a bag inside? Please." With that, Lucas grabs all the bags and starts towards the cabin. "What did y'all pack? Cinder blocks?"

He doesn't even strain as he lugs all the bags into the cabin.

"Ya know, I'll never get used to him," Lana says as she leans against the truck next to Tristian. "I've been with him for eight years now, and known him for damn near thirty, and I still can't believe how he just knows what needs to be done and does it."

"It's just who he is," I say as I lean against the truck next to her. I pull Tristian back against me and wrap an arm around her. "He was like that in the fire academy too."

"Oh, I know. Do you know how hard it was to go through academy with him and Lex? They wouldn't let me do shit. Hell, the instructors threatened to flunk me if they didn't leave me the fuck alone."

"I remember." I laugh. "How's the farm going?"

"Same shit, different day. Lucas threw a fit when he saw the number of tomatoes we have to can this year."

"I bet he did. Did you remind him that your tomato sauce is fucking fantastic?" Tristian asked. "Because that should change his tune real quick."

"Oh, it doesn't matter. He's going to throw a fit and then help me lug in all those tomatoes."

"Y'all want to head to the bonfire?" Lucas asks when he comes out of the cabin. "I put all your stuff in the living room for y'all to go through later."

"Thanks, man," I tell him and I am grateful. It would have been a bitch to get all that stuff inside.

"Of course. So… bonfire?" He grabs Lana's hand and starts walking towards the main lodge.

"I guess we're going to the bonfire." Tristian laughs. She puts her hand through my arm and we slowly make our way to the main lodge. There's a big group of people around the bonfire already.

As we get closer, I can make out who's here. Rhett, Maris, and Cam are talking with Becca and Derrick. I see Cam and Rhett palm Maris' belly. The last time I saw them, she was only a couple of months along.

I make my way over to one of the chairs set up and sit down. I rest my cane against the chair and lean back. My leg is starting to throb and I need to get off it. I'm getting ready to pull Tristian into my lap when she stops me.

"I'm going to go grab a cider. Do you want something?" I know what she's actually asking. *Am I going to take a pain pill for my leg*?

"I would love a beer," I tell her. My leg isn't so bad that I need a pill just yet. Just being off of it will help a lot.

"Okay." She nods like I answered her question. She looks over at Lana and Lucas. "Do y'all want something?"

"I'll go with you," Lana says, and they start heading towards the lodge.

Run Chapter 3

Tristian

Lana and I walk through the doors of the lodge where the open bar already has a line forming.

"How are you liking the hunts?" I ask as we get in line. Because Lana and I are on different shifts, we don't get to catch up as much as I'd like.

"Oh, I fucking love them. The ability to let go of the responsibilities, the mom and medic load? I didn't realize how much I was drowning until Lucas made his move."

"I'm really glad. I knew you were struggling, but I didn't know how to help you," I tell her as we move up with the line.

"I didn't know how to help myself. But Lucas wouldn't let me drown, and when he made his move, I guess I was ready to let him in."

We continue to talk about life, work, kids, and everything else as we wait in line. When we finally get our drinks, we head back to the guys. Brent tugs me down to sit on his lap. I hand him his drink and cuddle in.

Normally, I hate being short. At five foot two, life is not built for me. But when I get to snuggle into Brent and feel his arms wrap around me and his chin on my head, there isn't much better than being short.

I watch with a smile on my face as Lana gets comfortable on Lucas' lap. Lucas is a big man, but Lana is super tall too.

Lana catches my smile and shoots me a look. "Shut it, pixie."

I start laughing and snuggle into Brent further. "You're just mad because you can't live in Lucas' pocket," I tease.

"Yeah, but I can reach the top shelf," she sasses back.

God, I love this woman. "Yeah, well, I can grab a chair, Goliath. Can you duck without hitting a ceiling fan?"

She starts laughing.

"Alright, killer, I think you won that one." Brent laughs. I feel the rumble of his laugh through my cheek.

We watch as the pack starts gathering around the bonfire for tonight's run. Brent stiffens and looks down at me. I just smile at him. "This is way better."

Tonight's coordinator, Megan, starts going over the rules. Chem lights for safety and consent. Green means go, and they are open to any member hunting them. Yellow means they are in negotiations with someone, and if you are not their yellow, you do not engage.

Red means do not touch. Normally, the reds have an additional chem light so that there isn't confusion as to who belongs to whom. It was a disaster the first couple of years of the hunt. People would start chasing someone, catch them, and realize that wasn't who they were supposed to go after.

Megan also reminds everyone that greens must use the stoplight method if they are caught and need to signal that they are not okay. She mentions that the moon is full tonight and that the visibility throughout the Wilds is good, but to please be careful.

With that, she tells the sacrifices to line up next to her. These are the prey that have negotiated a different kind of scene with their partner. Every one of them has a red chem light on them. I watch as Maris walks up to Megan, her pregnant belly leading the way. I was wondering if she was going to run this weekend, but I guess this is much safer for her.

Becca walks up as well, and Jordan isn't far behind her. When no one else walks up, the sacrifices are released into the woods.

Next up is the prey, those that want to be chased down by their partner or the pack. I glance over at Lana and Lucas. Lana should be getting up, but when she sees me looking at her, she gently shakes her head.

Lucas wraps his arms tighter around her and starts talking softly to Brent. Brent's voice is low, but I can hear him just fine from my perch.

Megan releases the prey, and they take off running through the woods. Some strip down before entering the treeline. Others leave their clothes on, choosing to fight to the bitter end. I am one of the latter. I make Brent earn every article of clothing he manages to get off.

The prey gets a five minute head start before Megan releases the predators, and you can tell that every one of them is ready to maul their prey.

"Do you want another beer, Stud?" I ask Brent. He nods and loosens his hold on me. I stand and see that Lana is untangling herself from Lucas.

"I can bring you another," I tell her.

"Nah, I need to stretch these long legs," she sasses.

"Fucker."

We make our way back to the lodge. It's quieter now that most of the pack is gone.

"How's Brent after the fire last night?" Lana asks once we are out of earshot of the guys. "Lucas said it was brutal inside."

"I heard it go out over the radio last night but didn't really think anything about it. But Brent texted early this morning and said that he would probably be late getting off. I didn't put two and two together until he got home and looked bomb blasted."

"I was with Marshall on the med unit so we were running recovery, but yeah..." Her sentence hovers between us.

"He's okay," I tell her. "Are you?" Lana has been through a lot in her life, and after losing her first husband in the line of duty, she was really closed off. She's opened up again, but this job tends to take more than it gives.

"I'm fine. Lucas is doing okay too. Some of the other rookies aren't doing so well, but we are getting them through it."

We continue to make small talk on our way back to the guys. Brent has pulled his leg up and crossed it over his knee and is rubbing right above the prosthetic. I know he's hurting, but I also know that he won't say that he's hurting.

"Hey, Stud. I'm getting tired. You mind if we head to bed?" I tell him. The look he sends me is nurturing, but under that, I can see the relief.

"Yeah." He maneuvers himself to standing and pulls me in close. "Y'all have a good night, and try to keep the noise to a minimum."

Lucas and Lana laugh and say their goodbyes.

Brent is careful as he walks with me to the cabin, making sure that his good leg and cane are planted before taking a step. I walk on his bad side to make sure that I can help if he stumbles. But he doesn't. He's slow and methodical as we walk to the cabin.

When we get inside, I see that Lucas has set up our bags so that I can get everything unpacked with ease. Bless that man.

"Your bag is here if you want to take it to the bedroom." I point to the bag that I packed for him earlier today. "Do you want help?"

"No, I got it." He lifts the bag and slowly starts making his way to the bedroom. I bring his beer in to him and start helping him unload the bag. "Thank you, Darlin'."

He goes back into the living room and brings the other two bags we brought, putting them on the bed.

"I've got this, Stud. The fan for your sleeve is in that bag." I point to the bag next to him, silently trying to get him to sit the fuck down and take his prosthetic off.

After rifling through the bag, he finally finds the fan and his other supplies. I lean against the door frame, watching as he goes through his nightly ritual. The first six months or so, I would help him, especially checking the stump for infection. But as we both grew more confident in his amputation and prosthetic, he wouldn't let me help.

I had to be okay with it. This was his body, and really his mind, at stake here. He had to come to terms with what this meant for him and us. But I never wanted him to think he was alone. I am always there, ready to help whenever he needs it.

The faint hiss of the vacuum seal breaking comes first before he eases the carbon-fiber prosthetic off. Next, he rolls off the black silicone liner underneath. He checks it for wear spots and wipes it out with an antibacterial wipe before putting the fan on it for the night.

Brent checks every bolt and screw before propping it up on the nightstand. Finally, he checks the stump, making sure that every inch of skin is clean and there aren't any pressure spots. Once that's done, he puts on the lidocaine lotion on his stump to help with nerve pain.

When he's done, he tugs on the compression sleeve, the color worn after hundreds washes. He looks around for his elbow crutches. I hold them up and he just grins at me.

"I love you, Stud."

"Come here, Darlin'," he murmurs that deep drawl doing wicked things to me. He holds out his arms for me to come snuggle into him. I walk over to him and lie down on the bed next to him. He wraps his arms around me and pulls me closer. "You are the most amazing person I have ever met."

"Nah, I just love you." I snuggle deeper, reveling in his scent and the feel of his muscled arms around me.

We stay like that for a while, and I'm about to nod off when there's a knock at the door. I get up to answer it, but Brent beats me to the door. How that man moves faster than me when he's on one leg and crutches, I'll never know.

Megan is at the door. "Hey, guys. Sorry to bother you, but it looks like one of the couples may have hurt themselves while running tonight. Can you come check them out?"

Brent looks over his shoulder at me. "Come on, Cruiz. A medic's job is never done."

Megan hands me the med bag that the Wilds keeps on standby for pack night. I pause and look at Brent. "Do you want to put your leg back on?"

"No, I'll be fine." Brent takes the bag and throws it over his shoulder. He heads out the door, his crutches making a *tink tink* sound on the steps. "I can probably move faster with these, anyways."

And with that, we head back towards the bonfire. The couple in question is one of the pack that usually hunts on their own. Jesse is laying on her back with her knee to her chest.

"What happened, Jesse?" I ask her.

"I was running from Cash when I tripped on a log. My knee twisted and then popped," she tells me. Her voice is hoarse like she's been crying.

I look over at Cash, and he nods. "I carried her back here, and we came to get help."

"How bad is the pain?" I ask as I check her knee. It's swollen, but she's got full range of motion.

"As long as I'm not on it, probably a four, but as soon as I move, it's a solid eight."

"You need to get this checked out, but I think you can wait until morning to go to the urgent care. I'm going to wrap it up for you for tonight. Make sure to take something for pain, though," I tell her as I wrap up her knee.

Brent stands behind me as I work, handing me things from the med bag without me having to ask for them.

“Thank you, guys,” Megan gushes. “I’m so glad you guys made it tonight. I promise, next time I’ll bother Lana and Lucas.”

I laugh as I pack my supplies back into the bag. “Don’t worry about it.”

With that, Brent hands the bag back over to Megan, and we start walking back to the cabin. His crutches crunching against the gravel as he moves slowly and deliberately.

We get inside and head towards the bedroom. Brent leans his crutches against the nightstand next to his leg and sits down on the edge of the bed.

“It’s pretty rare now, but sometimes, I still get angry about that twat hitting me on the highway.” He rarely talks about the night that our lives changed forever. “I know that we’ve come out the other side mostly intact, but the fact that I lost the career I loved, mobility, and autonomy still chafes my ass.”

He pulls the band out of hair and all that glorious soft brown hair tumbles around his shoulders. He pulls his shirt over his head and tosses it towards the empty bag in the corner. I watch as he finishes stripping down to his boxer briefs.

“You never have to pretend that you’re over it, Stud. It’s okay to be pissed off that she took those things from you.” I walk towards him, moving to stand between his legs.

Brent runs his hands through his hair, his frustration obvious. “But I don’t want to wallow in it either. I just miss the chase, being able to move without thinking, lift without adjusting.”

I pull his hands away from his hair and run my nails along his scalp. Loving the feeling of his skin against my fingertips and the long hairs against my forearms.

“And all of that is fair. But you still chase, you still move without thinking and lift without adjusting. You have figured out how to live with your injury, and it no longer defines you.”

“You make it sound like I’ve coped with it,” he jokes.

“You have. We have,” I tell him. He buries his face against my chest, just breathing. I continue to run my fingers through his hair.

“Let’s get you to bed, Darlin'.” He leans back and gets under the covers. I head to the bathroom to do my nightly routine and get changed.

When I come back, he’s laying on his side waiting for me to bury myself in his arms.

“You are my favorite person, Stud.”

“You are my only person, Darlin'.”

Run Chapter 4

Brent

The next morning at the Wilds is full of chaos and excitement. Those that couldn't make it the night before start trickling in. Those who choose to come in the night before, like us, are making our way out of our cabins, the main lodge and camp sites.

It's organized chaos at its finest.

Tristian and I have already completed our eight mile morning run, dodging sleepy campers, lost shoes, and discarded clothes.

When we get back to our cabin, we enjoy a hot shower together, thank fuck for handicap accessible showers. The bench allows for a different kind of hot shower. After we are clean, dressed, and sated, we head to the main lodge for breakfast.

The dining room at the Wilds is filled to the brim with the pack, and trying to pick our way through is like running an obstacle course. When we finally make it to the table, I lean back and let out a breath. The excitement is catching, listening to everyone talk over each other, pack mates catching up and seeing people we haven't seen in months.

Jesse comes hobbling over and sits with us. She's already been to urgent care and is in a brace. They want her to see an orthopedic specialist because they think she tore her ACL. After asking her if she wants to see my sports medicine doc, I send a quick text to the after-hours nurse.

Within minutes, she's got an appointment for the following day. We chat for a few minutes before our attention is called to the front of the room.

Megan's partner is making introductions to new pack members and letting us know of today's activities. There are classes in the main lodge, survival training in the woods, and a couple of others that I don't have much interest in.

Megan comes up to the front and tells us about tonight's hunt. It's going to be a full one, with over fifty people running tonight. The good thing is that there are a fair amount of sacrifices, so that cuts the number of runners down.

I look over at Tristian, knowing that we don't hunt the same way as we used to, or the way that others in the pack do. Instead, we use stealth and cunning, a fight for dominance. It's not about the run anymore—it's about the catch.

We are both predators. We both hunt each other. And it's a fight to get every piece of clothing off. A fight for the upper hand. But in the end, I always win.

She's leaned back in her chair, her legs kicked back, and she's running her foot along my prosthetic. I can't feel it, but knowing that she wants the connection has me leaning over and picking up her leg. I place it on my lap and start rubbing her calf. She damn near melts into her chair.

As I'm working my way up her calf, I lean over and press a kiss to her knee. These small moments are what I live for, the connection I crave. Mentally, I am much better than I was yesterday.

I know that I've got a mountain of paperwork waiting on me when I get back to the office, but for today, I'm just a man that is going to chase his wife through the woods and fuck her until she screams.

We spent the rest of the day attending classes and demos before helping Megan repack first aid bags. It doesn't take long and then we are back at the cabin, snuggled in the hammock.

As soon as dusk settles, we go through our go bags. Mine is quite a bit heavier since I need to have crutches, tools, and other shit for my leg. But hers is equally as important, it carries our own first aid kit, clothes, and various other things.

I head to the counter and grab our chem lights. Red for no touching. Blue because she's mine. I add them to my bag so that they don't hinder my movement being around my neck.

I walk towards Tristian after she gets her pack settled on her shoulders. It's the one and only time she's allowed to carry a bag. I place the chem lights on the shoulder straps before taking her throat in my hand. I tilt her head back so I can look into those blue eyes.

"Are you going to run from me, Darlin'?" I growl, thickening my drawl because I know what it does to her.

Her smile is bright and wide. Pure happiness and excitement rolls off her in waves. "I'll never run from you. But I will fight you to the bitter end."

She leans forward into my hand, her cheeks starting to stain red. She will never willingly give an inch, never surrender. "Good girl."

She pulls away from me and heads towards the door. Tristian looks back at me. There's a question in her eyes. I can't help but grin as I walk towards her. "You're mine, Darlin'. And I am going to make you beg."

I walk past her and open the door, waiting for her to get her bearings after that bombshell.

She snaps out of her daze and walks out the door, waiting on me to lock the cabin. She puts her arm through mine and together we walk to the bonfire in the clearing.

Lana and Lucas are already there, standing to the side. Jesse is helping Megan get everyone lined up and ready.

Megan calls our attention to the front. It's the same as last night. The sacrifices go first. When she calls for the prey or hunted, I walk up to the front. I need more time to get into position since I need more time than everyone else.

I watch as Tristian stands there, her chin high and a look of desire painted on her face. Like she can't wait for the sexiest and feral game of hide and seek to start.

Megan releases us, and I start towards the trail with the least amount of obstacles. The trail is packed dirt instead of soft moss, perfect for my bad leg to actually get traction on.

I take my allotted five-minute head start to find a good spot to tuck into. There's a group of trees right off the trail that have all grown together tightly. I can see down the trail in all directions, and she won't be able to sneak up on me.

I place my pack on the ground, hiding the chem lights so that she won't be able to see them. I'm dressed in all black and even made sure that my prosthetic doesn't have any shiny pieces to give away my position.

I check my watch—my time is up.

I slow my breathing until it's barely a whisper and wait. I have become my inner panther, lying in wait for my prey to come within striking distance. As I wait, my senses come alive. I can hear every snapped twig, the pounding feet of other hunters. I can smell the smoke from the bonfire and ozone from the incoming storm.

Still, I hold steady, waiting on her to come through the woods. She isn't sleek like a panther. Instead, she is fire and ice, a storm of her own making. I check my watch again, only ten minutes has passed since I came into the woods.

I scan the woods, watching for movement. I know I won't see her chem lights, she's too smart for that. But the moon is full, and it allows me to see her before she sees me. I hold perfectly still, waiting for her to get closer.

She's wary, stopping when she hears a sound. I ease back onto my good leg, the one that will allow me to use every ounce of strength to leap out and grab her. I hold still again, waiting.

Just then, my prosthetic lets out a small noise, almost a sigh as it recalibrates to my new position. I freeze, and so does Tristian. She heard it, but it's too late.

Before she can process that what she heard was me, I'm on her. I slam her against the tree, digging my prosthetic into the ground for balance. She turns wild fighting, kicking, and pushing.

I grab her hands and force them over her head, pushing my hips into hers. She manages to buck her hips enough that she can slide between me and the tree. And she's off and running.

I take off after her, my long legs eating up the ground, and I tackle her to the ground. I roll at the last second to take the impact off of her. I band my arms around her and she is clawing at me, ripping my shirt. She turns absolutely feral.

She manages to grab a handful of my hair and pulls. I release a growl that has her pausing, but instead of stopping, she looks down at me and grins. She pulls the knife that she had in her pocket and holds it to my throat.

I lay perfectly still and look up at her. Her grin is triumphant as she cuts the collar of my shirt. She traces the knife down my chest, cutting the shirt but careful not to cut me. With a flick of her thumb, the blade is secured, and she rips the shirt off me.

With the knife put away, I flip her over onto her stomach. I grab her braid and push her face into the soft moss that we landed on. She goes wild, bucking and fighting, trying to get her hands and knees under her to flip me off.

I flick my own knife open, the sound freezing her instantly. "If the knives come out, I'm going to win. Just remember, you started it," I growl into her ear.

I run it along her back, cutting her shirt and bra in one go. I flip the edge of the knife and run the dull edge along her back. She stays perfectly still, the trust she has in me causing my heart to flutter.

Her leggings are no match for my knife, and within seconds she is naked beneath me. She's panting, but I know as soon as I let up, even a fraction, she will be up and running.

"Do you submit?" I already know the answer, but it never hurts to ask.

"Never." Her answer is muffled by the moss. But she's still not moving, the knife is still in play.

"Good girl," I growl into her ear. I can feel her muscles coiling, bunching like she's ready to flee. But I don't let her.

I lean forward and with a snarl I clamp my teeth on the curve where her shoulder and neck meet. It's our unspoken acknowledgement of surrender.

She goes limp and starts moaning, rocking her hips back into me as much as she can while still pinned down.

I work to free my cock from my pants. I keep my hand on her braid, and use my other to line up my cock at her entrance. With one smooth stroke, I am fully sheathed inside her.

Her cunt spasms around my cock. I release my teeth from her shoulder and pull her hips up so that I can pound into her.

"Please," she cries out. "Harder, Stud." I reach down and pull her up so that her back is flush with my front. Her small breasts arch up, the nipples hard.

I wrap my hand around her throat, and my other hand finds her clit. I apply pressure to both and within seconds she's soaking my cock.

"Are going to come for me, Darlin'?" I growl into her ear. There's an answering gush that soaks my cock.

She pants and moans, but I can tell that she's holding back. She doesn't like to be told what to do, instead wanting it taken from her.

I push her back down onto her hands and drag my thumb through her slick cunt. I continue to pound into her and when she's least expecting it, I sink my thumb into her ass. I feel her cunt and ass clamp down on me, the growl she lets out raises the hair on my arms.

She starts moaning and grinding back against me, but she still won't let herself come. "Someone is being a Brat," I tell her. But I am close to coming and I need her to come with me.

I pick up my pace, keeping my thumb in her ass, and I can feel her cunt clenching, dragging me further in. I push my thumb down and rub the front wall of her anus and watch as she goes perfectly still.

Her entire body tenses up, and she stays like that for just a few seconds before I slam into her one more time.

Her scream lights up the woods, and she is coming. I continue to pound into her, chasing my own orgasm and drawing hers out. I feel my balls draw up as her orgasm comes to an end and mine rips through me like a punch to the gut.

She collapses on the ground, and I follow behind her.

I pull her into my chest and just breathe with her. I don't know how long we stay like that. It could have been minutes or hours. I run my hand up and down her back, into her hair, giving her comfort and taking some for my own.

It's not long before I hear a beep. I let out a sigh. "Come on, Darlin', bionic Brent needs to recharge."

Tristian starts laughing. It's one of the few things that she laughs about when it comes to the prosthetic. I help her up and set my clothes to rights before I hobble over to my pack. I didn't realize that the battery in my leg was that low.

I grab one of the elbow crutches out of my back, extending it. I watch Tristian pull clothes from her pack as I put my own pack on. This woman is my life. Even when I was at my lowest, she was there.

She catches me watching her get dressed and smiles. "Come on, bionic Brent, let's get you charged up."

Run Bonus Scene

Tristian

I have been sitting in the waiting room for the last three hours as the surgeons do emergency surgery on my husband... I'm not okay.

I'm barely holding myself together, and if it weren't for a waiting room full of firefighters at three in the morning, I would be a sobbing mess. But I won't crumble in front of them. That can wait until I'm alone.

I still can't believe that it happened to us, and definitely not like this.

I got the call around midnight that Brent had been in an accident, and my heart stopped. His chief said that Lucas and a couple of deputies were on their way to the house to come get me. They were less than five minutes out. He said he would give me the details when I got to the hospital but that Brent was going to be okay.

Lucas came screaming into the driveway, lights flashing. My 4Runner was running, and I was on the phone with my mom, trying to explain a situation I couldn't explain. One of the sheriffs said they would stay at the house with the boys until she could get there.

I was given a police escort to the hospital, and when I reached the emergency room, they had already taken Brent to surgery. Chief pulled me in for a hug and then sat me down to tell me what happened.

They were working a wreck on the highway. Brent had gone around the back of the engine to grab something out of a side compartment when a car sped around cop cars and lost control. Her car slammed into Brent, then into the side of the engine, pinning him.

The guys were able to get him extricated quickly and got a tourniquet on his leg, but the med unit on scene already had a critical patient. It would have been another fifteen minutes until another unit could get on scene.

So they did what they do best, they loaded him into the squad on scene and hauled ass to the hospital. Chief called Lucas to get him headed to my house, and the rest I knew.

Thankfully, Mick was on the squad that day, and they were able to give him care and give him pain meds before they got him to the hospital.

I'm still working through everything when the doctor comes out. "Family for Brent Cruiz."

Every firefighter stands up, and my eyes prick with tears.

Chief, Lucas, and I walk to the front of the room and stand in front of the doctor. "He's my husband."

The doctor looks out over all the guys and then back at the three of us. "Let's go into the family room."

My heart stalls. That's where they go to give bad news to the family.

"No, they're family, too," I tell the doctor. He looks at me for a long second then nods.

"Brent is lucky. The quick thinking of his family with the tourniquet and getting him to the hospital saved his life. When the car hit him, it shattered his tib/fib and tore all the muscles in his calf. His posterior tibial artery was severed when the car pinned him."

I hear someone swear behind me. I feel the same way.

The doctor pauses and takes a deep breath before continuing. "The amputation itself was clean, surgically, but we will have to do a second surgery in a couple of days to finish closing the stump. He's got a long road ahead of him, but he's young, strong, and healthy."

"Thanks, Doc," Chief says when I don't respond. "When can she see him?"

"She can go to his room now. He'll be coming up from surgery in the next hour or so." He looks out over the guys. "But for the rest of tonight, y'all can't go in there. You can visit with him over the next couple of days, but there are other patients in the hospital."

Chief thanks the doctor and motions for Lucas to take me up to the room. As Lucas and I leave the waiting room, I hear him giving out orders for watch rotations, who can take care of the house for us, and other details I hadn't even thought of.

But this is what public safety does. I know that if I were to go home at any point while Brent is recovering, there will be a squad car parked in front of the house. There will be a twenty-four-hour watch here at the hospital until he goes home.

Everything will be taken care of so that I can take care of Brent and he can heal.

Lucas wraps his arm around my shoulder and pulls me into his side as we wait for the elevator. He doesn't say anything—he doesn't need to. We are all reliving what happened to Lex and Lana. And unbelievably grateful that a missing leg isn't a missing husband and friend.

I open the door to Brent's room and look around. He's going to be miserable for the next couple of days as he heals and gets used to his new normal. But the doctor is right—he's strong, young, and healthy. And I have to keep reminding myself that he's alive.

"How are you doing, Tris?" Lucas asks as he folds his massive frame onto the bench by the window.

"All over the place." I sit on the chair by the empty bed. "I'm reliving getting the news about Lex, and the terror that it happened to us hits. Then the gut-wrenching relief that he's going to be okay. Then the guilt that you and Lana weren't that lucky. You?"

Lucas nods, but his eyes are haunted. "About the same."

There's a knock at the door, and we stand up. They wheel Brent in on the stretcher. He's still groggy, but I've never been more relieved to see his gorgeous brown eyes. The nurses get him moved over to his hospital bed and get him set up on the monitors and pumps.

"Hey, Stud," I whisper as I push his hair back from his face. "I heard you needed a little extra attention tonight. You couldn't wait until you got home?"

His chuckle ends in a grimace as he shifts in bed. "You know me, always flirting with the nurses."

The nurses laugh and murmur something about getting him more pain meds. They leave the room, and I press a kiss to his forehead before resting my head against his. "You scared me tonight, Stud."

"I scared *me* tonight, Darlin'." He wraps his arms around me and pulls me closer.

The nurses come in and give him another dose of pain medicine, and I watch as his eyes unfocus and he falls asleep. I climb into the bed next to Brent, thankful again for being so small.

I look over my shoulder at Lucas, who hasn't moved since helping get Brent settled in bed. Lucas places a blanket over me, making sure that all the IV lines and tubes are clear of me and Brent.

"I'm not going anywhere," he says quietly. "Get some sleep, Tris."

Will she rise like a phoenix or let her fire go out?

Wild Obsidian: Recover

Vic Raven

Trigger Warnings

Please do not try without proper education, enthusiastic consent AND mentorship!

Fire play

Narcissism

Recover Chapter 1

Brin

Divorce is messy. Especially when you poured everything you had into your marriage and they walked away. Like it was the easiest thing to do, like you didn't matter, like you were at fault.

Divorce is even harder when you are both members of the same club, with the same friends. No one knows what to do, how to act, and no one is sure how to play. At least with me. He has come through this messy situation mostly unscathed.

I'm sitting at the bar watching the crowd and trying my hardest not to watch as Clint works over a pretty little Sub. I'm not jealous. She can have him for all I care.

But I am frustrated. I gave him everything; my body, my mind, my voice.

But it wasn't enough. I wasn't enough.

I turn back to the bartender and pretend to be unbothered as I order my drink. Rook slides my glass over to me with practiced ease, and I nod my thanks.

I don't even know why I'm still here tonight. It's demo night at Obsidian, and I already gave my demo on fire play. The Bottom and I work well together, and everyone loves watching the danger and safety of fire play.

Something that Clint initially loved about me, my love of fire. But once he got his hooks in me, my choices stopped mattering, my dominance was smothered, my demos became less and less.

At first, I didn't realize what was happening. It was a slow burn over the five years we were together. He would plant seeds when I was tired or drained. *Do you really want to demo tonight*? Then as time went on, it was, *look how well your students are doing, you can sit back and relax.* Finally, *they don't need you to demo, they've got plenty of people who teach better than you*.

Then the gaslighting started. *Brin, you are a submissive. Brin, let me take control for a while. Brin, you love it when I dominate you.*

I didn't realize what was happening at first. He wasn't obvious about his need for attention, his need for the spotlight. But looking back, it was classic narcissistic behavior.

And I fell right into it.

I thought I knew better. My father was a narcissist, and I swore that I would never allow anyone to treat me the way that my father treated my mother–and then I married one.

It's been six months since the divorce, and I am slowly coming back to my old self. It's been an amazing process if I'm being honest with myself. I feel like I've been transformed.

But I also realize how far I fell and how much further I have to go to climb back to the surface.

I really should take advantage of the offerings tonight. I've wallowed long enough in my stupidity. I grab my drink and start wandering through the club, careful to avoid Clint's station.

I've stopped at a rope demo, and I watch as Jason ties up a new student. She looks like she's in heaven. I watch as he lays down rope after rope, turning her from a gorgeous woman into a masterpiece.

"Like what you see?" a voice whispers in my ear. It's heavy on the Scottish brogue and it's panty-melting.

I turn my head slightly, just enough to see who came up behind me. Though there aren't many Scotsmen at Obsidian, it's always a good idea to check.

"I'm not interested in playing tonight, Lock," I tell him. And I'm not. At least not his kind of play.

"I wasn't suggesting that we play, Firebug. I am simply asking if you like what you see."

That's the thing about Lock. His favorite type of play is the mindfuck, the psychological dominance. Something that I don't really need after coming out of a five year relationship where I was mindfucked every day.

"Yes, I like what I see," I say as I turn back to look at Jason. "But I'm not one for rope."

"Why is that?" he asks. I feel like he's gotten closer, but he's still not actually touching me.

"The loss of control isn't something I'm interested in." I keep looking at Jason and his student, watching as he ties a knot right at her clit. "No matter how erotic it can be, it's never been a thing for me."

"Yet you gave him your submission, unearned." He steps back, his warmth leaving with him.

"You know nothing about what happened," I snarl at him. I turn to face him fully now, and I really wish I hadn't. Shaggy black hair is swept back from his face, showing the silver at his temples. His dark grey eyes speak of thunderstorms at sea.

"I know that you turned yourself into something that should never have existed. I know that you took yourself apart, piece by piece, until you fit who he wanted you to be." He steps in closer to me, still not touching. "And I know that he left you high and dry when he was done breaking you apart."

His words land like blows on my already shattered heart.

He steps back again. "Did I leave anything out?"

I want to hit him. I want to yell and rage. But I can't. He's right.

"When you are ready to take those pieces back, ready to be the Firebug you were before, call me."

Lock steps back and disappears into the crowd, leaving me fuming. He's not wrong, but fuck if I need the reminder of everything I gave up for what I thought was love.

I continue to watch the rest of Jason's demo, watching his Sub slip into subspace as she swings in the harness that he's made for her.

That should have been my first warning that I wasn't a Sub, that never once did I slip into subspace for Clint. That I never willingly settled into submission. But I thought there was something wrong with me, that I wasn't doing it right.

Lock is right. I let him break me into something that shouldn't have been in the first place.

It's been a couple of days since demo night at Obsidian, and Lock's words are still banging around my head. I wish I could be mad at him, but I can't. He's right.

I let Clint tear me apart, even going so far as to hand him the tools to do so.

But something that Lock said is screaming at me the loudest. Do I want to be the Firebug I was before? Or do I want to be a fucking Phoenix?

Thankfully, I've been in my shop all morning, cataloging inventory, filing orders, and doing general shop work. The busywork is a great distraction, and it's easy enough to do so that I don't get bogged down in the shit of my brain.

I'm getting ready to break for lunch before I take over the forge from Jordan.

I still can't believe how lucky I got when I moved here seven years ago. The shop behind Jordan's forge was leaving because it was too hot, and I was looking for a place that I could run my glassblowing shop.

A match made in heaven or, with how hot it got in the forge, hell.

Jordan and I split the fuel bill, and I didn't have to buy or build a forge. It was a win-win for both of us. The only part that sucks is that we have to split the forge. Not a deal breaker for me, I'm a night owl by nature, so I have no problem coming in later and working into the night.

I text Jordan that I will be back after lunch. I don't wait for a response. That woman will work until Damien pulls her away from the forge and forces her to eat. The three of us became fast friends, and they sponsored my membership to Obsidian when I asked if there was a kinky club in the area.

A couple of years ago, when Jordan was pregnant, she had to step away from the forge. It was quiet on the other side of the wall when she took a couple of months off to finish out her pregnancy and have Chance.

Now, though Damien takes care of Chance when Jordan is in the forge. He gets his estimates and work done for his logging company in the afternoon while Jordan mans the front of her shop. It works out perfectly for all of us. There are even times when I take Chance for the morning so Jordan can get some work done and Damien can do what he needs to do.

It wasn't always like this, though. Clint hated that Jordan, Damien, and I helped each other out. Looking back, I can see it was abuse. That he was trying to keep me isolated. But at the time, I thought he was worried that they were taking advantage of me.

Just another reason I am glad he's gone.

I step out of my shop and walk over to the little diner down the block. It's got the best milkshakes in town, and the burgers are perfectly greasy. I place my order to go, and the waitress wastes no time in making my milkshake for me to have while I wait for my order.

She told me that dessert should always come first, and I happen to agree.

It's not long until I've got my order and I head back to the shop. I'm eating my lunch as I wait for the forge to heat up to my operating temps. I look over and see Jordan standing in the doorway.

I hold out the other half of my burger for her.

"You're a lifesaver," she says before taking a massive bite of the burger. "Damien is running late, and I haven't had a chance to eat since this morning."

"I never eat the whole thing, you're welcome to it." I push the rest of my fries towards her as well and watch as she dives into those too.

"I saw you talking to Lock last night," she says with her mouth full. "Going to try something new?"

She laughs at the look I send her. "Not likely. I'm not interested in a psychological sadist, thank you very much. Been there, done that, got the divorce to prove it."

She stops eating, her head cocked to the side. "Have you ever played with him?"

"I don't need to. I know what I can and can't handle. That's not something I can handle right now. Not so soon after Clint." I toss my milkshake cup into the trash can in the corner.

"Brin, he's not like that. Not at all." She throws the takeout container in the trash as well. "I know you're still raw from Clint, and I don't blame you one bit. But Lock isn't that type of sadist. He's not a narcissist."

My doubts must show on my face because she continues. "Do you remember Alyse? How she went through that really shitty breakup with her ex?"

I nod. What happened to Alyse was terrible and made my divorce look like child's play.

"Lock helped her regain her confidence. He isn't into degradation or shame. He's about building people back up."

"Why?" I ask in disbelief.

"That's his story to tell. But I can tell you this, I think he would be good for you. I think it would bring you back to who you were before you met Clint."

"Maybe." I don't really believe her. "Now, go home. You need to see your boys."

She gives me a knowing grin and waves, locking her side of the forge up for the day.

I begin gathering my supplies and pull out the sketches of the latest piece I'm going to start working on. It's not long before I'm lost in the heat and glass.

The rhythm of pulling glass, turning and molding, breathing life into this piece, is soothing in a way that I didn't realize I needed. It's a piece that I've been thinking about for a while, but never really had a reason to make. If I'm being honest with myself, I didn't really have the confidence to make it.

But as the golden phoenix takes shape on my stand, I realize that I don't want to be a firebug anymore. I want to be a fucking phoenix.

Recover Chapter 2

Lock

I have been watching Brin for the last hour as she shapes this beautiful golden phoenix. How that idiot ever got her to submit, I don't know.

Her t-shirt is stained with sweat. Her thick canvas pants mold to her curves. Her dark auburn hair is pulled back in a messy bun with a bandana tied around her head to keep the sweat out of her eyes.

I watch as she continues to craft her phoenix. Plucking, pulling, and moving the molten glass until it's exactly how she wants it.

The way she pulls and molds the glass into the feathers is breathtaking. But I'm starting to get a little worried about her. When I walked in, she was sweating in rivers. But now, her face is flush, but dry.

She's getting ready to gather more glass when I've had enough. I step into the forge, and her head snaps up. "You need to drink some water, Firebug."

She places the tool that she is using down and puts her hands on her hips. "I'll drink water when I'm done."

"Now, Firebug." I hand her a bottle of water that is sitting on the table by her phone. "We can't have you dropping from heatstroke before you finish her."

The phoenix is cooling on the stand, and the colors are deepening. I walk around her, noting the details.

"She's not done yet," she says, inspecting her work. "I've still got a long way to go with her."

"Her or you?" I ask as I take another pass around the phoenix.

"Both." She downs the rest of the water. "What can I do for you, Lock?"

"Well, I just got off work and finished grading about a hundred papers. And I wanted to check in on you when I didn't hear from you." I lean against the counter, but I can still feel the heat coming off the phoenix. "Did you lose my number?"

"No." She mirrors my pose, leaning against her work chair. "Just weighing my options. I'm not interested in jumping into another dynamic."

"Who said I was offering a dynamic?" I stalk over to her, forcing her to lean her head back to look at me. "What if I just want to see you rise, Little Phoenix?"

She straightens up, still tiny compared to my six foot two frame. But the fire in her eyes is a welcome sight. “What makes you think I haven’t already risen, Lock?”

“Because you don’t play anymore. Maybe a demo here or there. But I remember when you would close the club out every night, with any Bottom. Pulling a release from them like it was flame from the air, stripping both of you clean.”

I push off the counter and walk around the phoenix again. “But you haven’t played, with the exception of last night, in the six months since your divorce. I want to see you rise again, better than before.”

“What’s in it for you, huh?" Her stance is pure defiance; arms crossed over her chest, pushing those big breasts high. Her chin is tilted up, showing the curve of her jaw and the line of her throat. "Why do you care so much?”

It’s impressive until my stare is all it takes to break her defiance. I watch in silence as her shoulders slump in defeat. “What do you know of mythology and the gods?”

“It’s been a while since I opened a textbook, teach.” She starts moving to shut down the forge.

“Funny.” I watch as she goes about her closing duties. Shutting off fuel lines, putting tools away, gathering up trash. “A better question would be what do you know about Hecate?”

That gets her attention. “Not a lot, just that she was the one who lit the way for Persephone to find her way out of the Underworld.”

I'm impressed. Most people have no idea who Hecate even is. "You would be mostly right, but depending on the mythology would depend on if Demeter asked for Hecate's help in rescuing her daughter or if Hecate simply lit the way for Persephone to find herself."

"I'll be really honest, Lock, I don't know what that has to do with what you want from me." Her tone is irritated, and I can't blame her.

"I'll get to the point," I tell her, taking the trash bag from her hand. "Much like Hecate, I have no desire in dragging you kicking and screaming into your power. What I want is to light the way for you to find your power. I want to watch as you rediscover your backbone, your strength, and your own fucking autonomy."

I turn towards the back door. "I believe that Demeter didn't want Persephone back because she was abducted by Hades. I believe that Persephone ran away from her controlling mother, into the arms of someone who taught her that she was strong enough to stand for herself."

"And you fancy yourself Hades?"

"No, Little Phoenix, I fancy myself Hecate." I walk out of her shop and out into the cool night. I take the trash to the dumpster, and when I turn around, she is holding the door open for me.

"If I come back inside, I will take it as an invitation. That you are open to my brand of mind-fuckery." I walk up to the door, giving her plenty of time to block my way through. But the defiance is back now, and she lifts her chin as she walks back inside, holding the door open for me to follow.

"This is going to be fun, Little Phoenix." I step past her into the shop. "To clarify, I don't want your submission. I don't want you to change anything for me."

"Then what *do* you want, Lock?"

"I want a partner. I don't, and have never wanted, a submissive partner. I want someone who will call me on my shit, and I'll call them on theirs. I want someone who will fill my life with…life."

I stand in front of her, watching her as she takes in what I said. "And you think I can do that for you?"

"Maybe, maybe not. You asked what I wanted, and I told you. I'm not willing to settle for less than that. Instead, I'll keep lighting the way for those that need it until I find the person that sets my soul on fire."

"I don't know if I can be that for you, Lock. I can barely fill my own life." She crosses her arms over her chest. "I lost my fire a couple of years ago."

"I know. I watched as it happened. I'm not looking for you to be my partner. I'm looking to help you find your fire."

She grabs her bag from under the counter and locks the door from Jordan's shop to the forge. She walks into her own shop, closing down and locking up.

"Let me make sure I've got this straight," she says as she walks towards her 4Runner. "You want to be my Hecate, lighting the way for me to find my own fire. You aren't interested in a submissive partner. And you don't want that partner to be me."

I chuckle. "Almost, Little Phoenix. I think that you would make a great partner, but that is not why you caught my attention. I hate that a vibrant, passionate Firebug rolled over for a pissant of a boy. And I want you to find your fire again."

"And what if I want to play with you? To Top you?" She puts her bag in the back of her SUV before leaning against the rig.

"I would be honored to be your Bottom." I step into her space, forcing her to look up at me. "Be warned, I will Top from the Bottom though. I will make you earn every lick of flame against my skin."

"Alright, Lock." Her pupils dilate and she tilts her chin up, defiance and lust written on her face. "Then let's negotiate."

"Next club night is in two weeks. You agree to my brand of psychological play, and I will gladly lay on your table."

She climbs into her rig, and I stand watch until she pulls away. I've never been pulled to the edgy side of kink. I prefer to use my mind to dominate my partners or Bottoms. But the thought of Brin learning to stand on her own and using my body to do so makes me hard as fuck.

I climb into my old Bronco and head to the school's ball fields for practice.

I am mentally and physically exhausted when I get home after practice. I'm not the kind of coach that tells players to run the field and not run along with them. My kids respect me because I'm out there with them, running the balls and doing the work.

I love every second of it.

When we were in Scotland, I started playing football at five and never looked back. I excelled at it, and it wasn't long before I was on travel teams, my dad at every game cheering me on.

When my dad took a job in the States when I was in high school, I reluctantly went along with it. But it turned out to be one of the best things that ever happened to me. I got a full-ride scholarship to the University of North Carolina and was even picked up by scouts. That would never have happened in Scotland.

But going pro never sat well with me.

It wasn't that I didn't *want* to go pro, I just couldn't stand the idea of selling pieces of myself. The politics, cronyism, and generally shitty behavior were not only accepted, but encouraged. That's not who I am or who I wanted to be.

Instead, I chose a career that would allow me to stay in the game but out of the politics. Teaching has been a boon I didn't realize I needed. I get to keep my mind and my body sharp, but I also get to shape the next generation. Teaching values that get lost in a digital world.

Grabbing my bookbag and lunch box from the passenger seat, I drag my exhausted body out of my Bronco. I don't bother unloading the gear from the back. I'll need it tomorrow night.

As I approach my house, I hear Rus going nuts inside. He's raising holy hell because I left them inside today. In my defense, it was supposed to rain all day, but, true to North Carolina weather, it didn't rain a drop.

Rus was going to be a beast for the rest of the night. But Cerb? He doesn't give a flying fuck as long as his dinner is on time.

I get the front door open, and Rus launches himself out of the house. He gives me a huff of annoyance before he bounds down the steps and into the yard, sniffing and marking his territory.

Cerb is much more sedate, slowly climbing off the couch and stretching before walking over to me. He sits down and places his head against my hip. “I love you too, ya big lug. Now go do your business.”

With a pat to his head, Cerb is out the door and following his brother. I put my stuff down on the kitchen island and start pulling out our meals. It’s nights like these I am incredibly glad that I meal prep.

While I’m serious about my diet, meal prepping is for convenience during football season. I put my food in the oven to heat up and get the dog’s food ready, thinking about how these two knuckleheads ended up with me.

I had just gone through a pretty rough breakup with a Sub and saw that the shelter had a litter of puppies. All but two had died, and these two were the only ones left.

They were two tiny black things, all legs and ears, and skin and bones. The shelter said they were lab mixes and would be forty-five to fifty pounds max.

I couldn't separate them, so I took them both. Thankfully, the school was good about letting me bring them to work when they were little, especially when test scores started to climb. But when they were a year old and already seventy-five pounds, I realized I might be in trouble.

The vet said they could be mixed with lab, but more than likely, they were Mastiff mixes.

Now, they were three years old and tipping the scales at a hundred and twenty pounds each. Forty-five pounds my ass.

Cerb and Rus come inside right as my food is ready, and I get them fed. As I sit down to eat I think about Brin, about what I want to do with her.

She's already done a lot of the hard work. She got away from Clint, but that is only the beginning. If she isn't careful, she will end up caged again.

I pick up my phone and send her a text. *If you want me on your fire table, meet me at the ball field tomorrow at 6pm.*

I'm not thrilled with the idea of being a Bottom, especially with fire play, but I don't mind it either. If it means that she will get what she needs, then I will gladly climb on that table.

I finish eating and clean up. The dogs are back outside, and I head up to take a shower. I hear my phone chirp, and I see that she has texted back.

Do I get to watch you chase a ball for hours on end?

I feel a grin spread across my face. *I wish that was the case. No, I want to see you, and I don't have much time until the season is over. You get to watch me coach the JV team.*

Her text comes through before I even have a chance to get to the shower. *You planning on making me run laps, Coach?*

I bark out a laugh, startling Cerb and Rus. They look at me with their heads cocked. "Fucking hell, Phoenix," I mumble.

Only if you start running your mouth. I send back.

Then I guess I'll have to stretch before I get there because I've got plenty to say.

The grin hasn't left my face.

I don't think she realizes it yet, but that exchange, it's not just flirting. It's a spark of her old self shining through. It's a piece of herself long buried.

I guess we'll see if she can keep up with me.

Recover Chapter 3

Brin

To say that the last two weeks have been easy would be a lie. It's been a battle of wills with Lock, but I actually feel better, like my old self again. With Lock's direct communication and my competitive drive, I've learned to communicate directly and say exactly what I need to. I have learned to calm my temper but keep the fire behind it.

And I'm not magically cured either. I know I still have a long way to go, but fuck, it's nice to not feel so damn small.

Tonight is the first night that Lock has had off since we started talking. We are going to go to dinner and discuss tomorrow night's scene. We both know I've earned the right to work him over.

I'm closing up the shop when I hear the unmistakable rumble of his old Bronco. He told me that his dad bought it for him when they moved to the States when he was in high school.

I'm locking up to head out when I hear Rus going ballistic. When I turn around, I can't help but laugh at the scene in front of me. Lock is trying to keep Rus in the truck, and Rus is trying to jump out the window to get to me. Cerb is in the back with his head out the window, not a care in the world.

I am a dog person, but I love big dogs, the goofier the better.

The first time I met Lock's crazy mutts was that first night at the ball fields. Watching Lock run with his dogs and kids was hysterical. There were so many times the dogs would chase down the ball and take it from the kids. No one minded, and Lock would just shrug and tell the kids to be faster.

Lock finally parks the Bronco at the base of the stairs to my shop, and I walk down them. "Who's the goodest boy?" I call to Rus.

"This dog is a fucking menace," Lock says in his thick Scottish accent, but the grin on his face tells a different story. He loves Rus' crazy.

"Rus." I gasp playfully. "Do you hear how your daddy talks about you? He's so mean to you." Rus starts trying to get to me through the window.

"Rus, if you break that window again, you're grounded from car rides!" Lock growls at Rus.

Rus immediately stops trying to get out and plops his big butt on the seat. Cerb takes this as his cue to try and climb out the window.

"Cerb," Lock growls at Cerb, and he immediately plops his butt down. "I take it back, they're both fucking menaces."

I can't help the grin that splits my face. Cerb and Rus are both trying to sit on the front seat, and with Lock in the background, they look like the real three-headed Cerberus.

"Back," I tell the dogs and,, much to Lock's surprise, they listen.

I climb in and we drive off. It's not long before we are at one of my favorite restaurants and settled on the patio with the dogs. Initially, Lock was struggling to get Rus to chill out and lay down next to the table. But one look and a pointed finger from me had him laying down with his head in my lap.

After we've placed our order, and our drinks have arrived, I get down to business. "How many times have you Bottomed?"

"Not many." Lock takes a sip of his drink before putting it back down with a solid thunk. "I experimented when I first got into the scene, but nothing ever really felt right."

"Were any of them edge play?" Rus lets out a groan when I find a good spot behind his ear.

"No. You are the first Fire Top that I've ever had the pleasure of being under." The waitress takes that time to drop off our food, and we both tuck in.

I look up at Lock between bites, and a different type of hunger starts to grow. He's got a rebellious Clark Kent thing going on, and it's delicious.

You can tell that he just came from school and is at the end of his day. His normally smooth, thick black hair is disheveled, like he's been running his hands through it all day. A lock of hair keeps falling onto his forehead, giving him an air of youth which is completely at odds with the grey at his temples. His grey eyes are hidden behind thick, black-framed glasses.

His black button-down shirt is untucked, and the sleeves are rolled up to his elbows, showcasing not only the thick muscles there, but also the tattoos that wind up his forearms. The silver tunnels in his ears are giving him that rebellious streak. I know the girls, and women, at his school eat him up.

"How many times a day do you have to tell your class to stop drooling and draft the curve instead of staring at yours?"

Lock chokes a bit on the bite he just took. "Depends on the day. Some of them learn faster than others," he says with a smirk.

We finish our meal and start passing out bites to the dogs, but it's not long before we circle back to the reason for our dinner.

"I've never been into edge play because I've found that the mind is where I thrive." He hands off another fry to Rus, barely keeping the fingers on his hand. "I can bring about more change and catharsis with my mind and a conversation than I ever could with fear."

"It's not always about fear and catharsis, though. Sometimes, it just feels good to dance on the edge of danger, knowing that the person trusts you enough to not truly hurt them." I hand off a piece of my sandwich to Cerb, murmuring a *nice* to him. He takes it like a perfect gentleman.

"How do you get them to listen to you?" He sounds amused, but the look of adoration on his face has me sitting back.

"I just set my expectations for them," I tell him as both dogs sit in front of me, patiently waiting for more food. "I don't tolerate their bad behavior."

"Do you think that you will tolerate bad behavior from your next partner?" He asks it quietly, like he didn't just break apart my world with that one. He looks at me, that damn lock of hair in his face.

But I sit with it for a second.

That's the thing about Lock—the questions, the tasks, the conversation isn't just habit or without thought. He doesn't want an immediate response, he wants you to think and then answer truthfully.

"I would like to say, *oh, no, never*. But the reality is I can't say that I won't. I will say that the last seven months since my divorce have been eye-opening. But the last two weeks have been a mental transformation that I can't describe."

The look of pride on his face makes me feel like I hung the moon. "And that's why I'll gladly get on your table, Phoenix."

Tonight is the night, and I am on the verge of panicking.

After Lock and I ate dinner, we walked to the park with the dogs. We talked about what tonight would entail, and how far Lock was willing to go. What he should expect, what he should wear, and all the other little details.

I also told him that there was a chance that he could become highly aroused if he hadn't ever tried edge play. It's pretty normal, and I don't expect any sort of intimacy from him. The look he gave me was downright sinful, and I can't help but expect that our relationship is about to change.

And if it doesn't, I have to be okay with that too.

I've already packed my bag for the night; fuel, torches, aloe, and a first aid kit. Now, I'm trying to get myself into my favorite corset. Normally, I wear one of my bodysuits with my hair pulled back in a bun for safety.

But tonight, I wanted to dress up. Not just for Lock, but for myself. Jordan helped braid my hair back in Viking braids today at the shop. But now I have to finish getting ready, and I'm alone in my apartment.

I've just about got my corset figured out when there is a knock on my door. I check the peephole and see Casey and Rook on the other side.

"Oh, thank fuck you're here," I tell Casey and just about fall into her arms. She gives me a squeeze, and I mutter, "I can't do this."

"Darling, will you grab her a glass of water?" she asks Rook, then sits with me on the couch. I can hear Rook banging around in my kitchen. "Why can't you do this?"

Rook kneels next to Casey on the floor and hands her the glass of water. She hands it to me. "Take a sip."

I take a sip of the water, letting it cool the burn in my gut. "What if I hurt him?"

"Then you will help him through it and then get him medical help if it's significant." She rubs her hand on my thigh.

"But what if he doesn't trust me again after this?" I'm babbling and I know it, but the panic that I've been keeping inside for the last twenty four hours is hitting.

"Brin, you are one of the most skilled Fire Tops at the club. I would go so far as to say the most skilled. Yes, accidents happen, and he knows that. He understood the risks when he agreed to play."

"I don't want to hurt him, Casey," I mumble. "I really like him."

"You're not going to hurt him, Brin," she says as she stands and holds out her hand for me. "Now, let's finish getting you ready so that you can knock his socks off."

I take a deep breath and let it center me. "Okay."

I head towards the bedroom but turn and watch as Casey releases Rook from his kneel. He just shakes his head at her, choosing to stay in his kneel. The love those two have for each other is what I want one day.

Casey walks towards me with a soft smile on her face.

"How is married life treating you?" I ask with a nudge to her shoulder. I was at their collaring ceremony, despite Clint's efforts to keep me away.

"It's amazing. We had been together for a long time before doing it and neither of us thought it would change anything. But it did. It's only gotten better and better." We've made it into my bathroom, and she looks over the disaster.

"I was too occupied trying to get my corset latched," I say with a shrug.

"Well, let's get your corset fixed before we get to work on your makeup."

It doesn't take Casey long to turn my halfhearted and panicked attempts into a masterpiece. I'm stunned by my image in the mirror. I can feel my old instincts rising up inside me. The confidence that I know what I'm doing, and the quiet reassurance that I'm not going to hurt him.

"He won't know what hit him," Casey says from her perch on the counter.

When I arrive at the club, I've officially slipped back into my role as a Fire Top. I show my ID to security at the door and walk over to my favorite play station. It is dead center of the room and already has all the equipment set up on the table.

I put my bags down and call over one of the club staff to help me get set up. We get the thick canvas tarp laid down on the floor and move the table back over it. He gets the stanchions and ropes set up to keep the crowd back while I start laying out my tools.

I begin my ritual of placing fuel on a metal rolling table, clearly marked and away from fire. I have another table that will hold my flame and torches, wet towels next to that. A small fire extinguisher is on the floor next to my bag, tucked away but still easily reachable. On and on I work until my station is set up exactly how I want it.

Fire scenes are always popular with the crowd. Even now, at the beginning of the night, people are lining up and asking questions. It feels good to answer every one of them and not feel like a fraud.

The energy of the club is humming, the bass thumping and the low murmur of voices setting the stage for club night. I check the clock over the bar and realize that Lock should be here any minute.

I step back from my table. Nerves threaten to take over, but I take a deep breath and count to four before slowly exhaling. I close my eyes and imagine the scene that will happen tonight.

The rhythm, the coolness of the alcohol before the heat of the flame. Lock's tall, muscled body on my table, finally seeing all that beautiful artwork he's kept hidden with workout gear or button-down shirts.

I reach into the pocket of my leather pants for my lucky zippo. I strike the flint, and when I open my eyes, Lock is staring at me from the other side of my table. My heart stalls for just a second before it takes off at a gallop.

He's gorgeous. Gone is the soccer coach running with his kids. Gone is the math teacher with glasses and button-downs.

Instead, Lock the Dom is in his place. His damp hair is curling at the ends that touch the collar of his black t-shirt. Leather pants encase thick thighs. His posture is relaxed, arms by his sides, shoulders back. His eyes are dark in the club lights.

But I'm not the only one affected. The way his eyes roam over me, catching on the swell of my breasts, the curve of my hips, is enough to have me ready to launch myself at him.

I light the small lamp next to my wands before placing my zippo next to it.

"Whenever you're ready, you can get on the table," I tell him. My voice is calm and controlled, not once conveying the nerves in my chest.

I watch as Lock smirks and pulls his shirt over his head. I'm momentarily stunned. I have never seen him without a shirt on. I knew that he had tattoos, but I didn't know that he is covered in runes, ravens, and wolves. I didn't know that his nipples are pierced.

And now, I am not sure I want to play with him. I think I'd rather fuck him first.

But I don't. Instead, I wait for him to get on my table.

Recover Chapter 4

Lock

The Domme in Brin has come out to play. The leather pants show the curve of her ass perfectly. The leather corset pushes her breasts high. Her thick auburn hair is braided back from her face, and the rest is pulled back into a high messy bun. She looks like a shield maiden from a legend.

When she tells me to get on the table, my cock twitches at the dominance in her low voice. I pull my shirt off and watch her eyes dilate and her lips part. A flush heats her cheeks, and I smirk.

I climb up onto the table and lay on my back. The leather of the massage table is cool on my skin. I watch as the crowd grows larger, being held back by the rope. I'm not necessarily a voyeur, but I won't lie and say I'm not getting aroused by the entire scene. We haven't even gotten to the good part yet.

As Brin finishes getting ready, I think back to last night. We had gone over safety and protocols, safe words and other details.

I had felt pretty confident that I could handle what I had signed up for until I was getting ready to get in the shower for tonight. Brin had said that if I had chest hair, I needed to shave it, along with my stomach and arms, before we played, all the way to the skin. She said that while the flame never really stayed on the skin long enough to ignite the hair, it was better to be safe than sorry. Plus, burned hair smells really bad.

I'm not necessarily attached to my body hair, but it did get me thinking about the dangers of what I had signed up for. I was hesitant, but a deal is a deal, and I took a set of clippers to myself before shaving in the shower. It is weird to be this smooth, but I kind of like it.

"Are you ready?" Brin asks as she steps up to the table.

"If you are controlling the flame, Phoenix, I am ready for anything." She adjusts the table so it's to her liking, moving the arms until they are stretched out like a T.

"It will feel even more intense if you close your eyes," she says as she dips a cotton ball in what I'm assuming is alcohol.

I close my eyes and take a deep breath. I hear the hiss of the torch ignite, and I wait. The anticipation builds as my senses come alive. I feel the cool dampness of the alcohol-soaked cotton ball as it teases my stomach.

The shock of heat causes me to take a sharp breath in, but before there is any pain, her cool hand is putting out the fire.

"Color," Brin says.

"Green, Phoenix," I tell her, my voice low and raspy. I didn't realize that I had been holding my breath. I keep my eyes closed and wait for the next place that she will put her fire.

This time, she places the cool cotton on my arm and I feel the heat a second later. Like before, there is a flare of heat, but it's replaced by the coolness of her palm before it can burn.

The pattern continues, and I've lost track of time, reveling in the sensations of cool and heat, her hand always following quickly behind. Not knowing where she will go next has me a ball of nerves and anticipation...and arousal.

I stay perfectly still, not wanting to distract her, but my cock is thick and hard in my leather pants.

"Color," she asks quietly against my ear.

"Phoenix, I will stay on this table as long as you want me to. But the longer you touch me, the more I want to fuck you," I whisper to her.

I hear her sharp inhale before she leans even closer to me. "Then I guess we are done here."

I open my eyes and blink a couple of times, seeing the crowd we have gathered. Casey and Rook are standing next to Cam and Maris. Jordan and Bear are looking on with pride in their eyes as Brin dabs aloe on the tender spots on my skin.

A staff member has come over to help break down Brin's station while she continues to glide aloe over my skin. I sit up and pull her between my legs, keeping my back to the crowd of onlookers.

I run my hands up from her hips to her jaw and tilt her head back. Her pupils are blown, and her lips part. I lean down and press my lips against hers. She opens for me, and I deepen the kiss, pulling her body closer to mine. She pulls away just a bit.

"I have to pack the rest of my stuff, Lock," she whispers against my mouth.

I look over my shoulder to Jordan. "Can you put this away for her?"

Jordan shoots me a grin and nods, untangling herself from Bear.

I look back at Brin. "Any other objections?"

Brin shakes her head. "Good. Because now it's my turn."

I hop off the table and pick Brin up in one smooth movement. I throw her over my shoulder and stalk towards the back stairs to the hoots and hollers from the crowd that gathered around her station.

Being a founding member of Obsidian has a lot of perks, the main one being the private suites. I don't use mine much, but the staff keeps it ready for me. I dig the keys out of my pocket and unlock the door.

I enter my space and place Brin down next to the bed. I'm still reeling from the sensations of our fire scene. Arousal, desire, and the need to dominate her course through my veins. She looks up at me, and I pull her close. "I'm going to fuck you, Phoenix. Tell me now if it's not something you want."

"I want this, Lock." She pulls my head down and presses her mouth to mine in a demanding kiss. I open for her and let her make her demands.

It's not long before I take over. I press against her, pulling at the strings of her corset. She reaches up and moves her fingers gently over my nipples. A shudder works through my body.

"If you're going to touch them, you better mean it, Phoenix." She rolls my nipple between her fingers. "Harder, Phoenix."

Her grip tightens, and I feel like a bolt of electricity runs from my nipple to my cock. I unlace my leather pants to give myself some space. She pushes my hands away and finishes unlacing them, tugging the flaps to the side and pulling my thick cock out.

She runs her hand over me, and I groan. Her hands are cool against the heat of my cock. I start working to get her corset off, and when it finally opens for me, I get my first glimpse of her.

High, full breasts with dusky nipples begging to be sucked. A trim waist that flares to full hips. I unbutton her leather pants and start working them down her legs, taking her underwear with them.

I kneel down and slide off her boots, taking her pants with them. She's standing in front of me, naked and glowing. I bring my face to her pussy, inhaling deeply and smelling her desire. I push her back until her thighs hit the huge bed behind her. She sits with a huff, and I push her back until she is laying down.

I shoulder my way between her thighs and see a glint at the apex of her cunt. I spread her legs wider and run my hand over her soaking cunt.

"Are you pierced?" I ask her.

"Yes." She gasps as I run my thumb over her piercing. She jerks and moans as I continue to roll her piercing with my thumb.

"Oh, naughty Phoenix." I replace my thumb with my mouth and suckle her clit, rolling the piercing with my tongue.

Her hands grasp my head, and she starts to grind herself on my face. I thrust a finger inside her, thrusting in time with my tongue against her clit. I add a second and then third finger, stretching her.

It's not long until I feel her thigh muscles quiver and tighten against my head. Her little gasps and moans grow louder as she stretches towards her climax. I pull her clit and piercing into my mouth and suck hard. Brin comes with the ferocity of a storm, full of fire.

The walls of her cunt pulse around my fingers, damn near drowning me with her arousal. I continue to suckle and thrust, drawing out every last wave of her orgasm, until she is pushing me away.

I stand up from between her legs, taking in the image of her laying on my bed. Her eyes are glassy, hair a mess, thighs slick with her arousal. I peel my leather pants down my thighs and kick off my boots.

I palm my cock in my hand and squeeze before running my hand from root to tip. I reach into the nightstand and grab a condom, rolling it on as I watch her.

Her eyes are still dazed but tracking the movement of my hand. She licks her lips, and I can't help the image of her kneeling in front of me that pops into my head. But that's not what tonight is about. We'll get there eventually.

I lean down and pick her up, moving until my back is against the headboard and she is straddling me. I kiss her neck and then work my way down to those lovely breasts.

I take one nipple in my mouth, rolling the other between my fingers. She arches into my hand and mouth, grinding herself on my cock. I feel the metal of her piercing rub against my shaft.

She lifts herself up, and I notch my cock at her entrance. She starts to sink down slowly, taking only a couple of inches before bringing herself back up, working me into her. The ecstasy that flashes over her face is downright sinful.

When I am fully seated, she begins to rock and grind against me. I palm her breasts and tweak her nipples, grinning when she gasps and pushes her breasts into my hands again.

Every tug on her nipples causes her pussy to clench, making me damn near feral with need. I grab her hips and start to move her harder and faster against me. I feel the drag of her piercing against my cock when she grinds and I am about to come undone.

"I need you to get there faster, Phoenix," I groan into her ear. I pull her to my chest, her breasts rubbing against the bars in my nipples. We both groan, and I feel the first spasms of orgasm rolling through her.

She stills above me, her orgasm taking hold. She lets out a guttural groan before she slams down on me again, grinding as the orgasm rips through her.

My rhythm falters, and I slam into her twice more before I come with a shout. I hold her close, rocking into her as I come into the condom. We stay like that for another minute, catching our breath.

"Such a good Phoenix," I say as I run my hands up and down her back. I lean back against the headboard, bringing her with me. I wrap my arms around her, cradling her head against my chest.

Brin runs her hands across my chest, feeling the smooth skin. "Do you have any sore spots I need to know about?"

"No, Phoenix," I murmur into her hair. "It didn't even hurt. There was a flash of heat and the expectation of pain, but the fire was gone before my brain could register the pain."

"Good, I was worried I would hurt you, even unintentionally." Her voice is muffled, like she is trying to hide herself.

"You're not going to do that, Phoenix. You did exactly what you said you would do, and it didn't hurt, exactly like you said it wouldn't." There is still work to do with her and her confidence, but watching the Fire Top come out to play tonight is a good first step.

"I like you smooth," she whispers to me. She trails her fingers over my chest and arms.

"My bathroom looked like I fought a fucking bear when I was done. I didn't realize I was so hairy," I joke.

"It's why I wax. I learned early that fire and hair don't play well, and shaving is a pain in the ass."

"Waxing isn't a bad idea, actually. Then I don't have to worry about breaking a set of clippers trying to get ready for your table again." I toss the statement out causally, but internally, I'm hoping there will be a next time.

"Again?" she asks as her head snaps up to look at me. "You want to do it again?"

"Phoenix, the only person that is going to keep me off that table is you." I press a kiss to her lips. "I'd like to try out being your partner. You are smart, loyal, strong, and take no shit. You care about those around you, but you are willing to hold your boundaries. I want that in my life, but only if you are ready."

She stares at me for a moment, thinking about what I said. A grin splits her face, and I can see the joy in her eyes. "You only want me because I can get Rus to behave."

A laugh barks out before I can hold it in. "You got me, Phoenix. I only like you because of my dog."

Recover Bonus Scene

Brin

It's the state championship game in Asheville today, and I am in the stands with the parents, raising hell every time our boys get near the goal. Lock and his boys have worked their asses off all year to get here. They went undefeated this year and are up against a bigger school with deeper pockets.

It's been a nail-biter since the start. Now, it's the final ten minutes, and the score is tied. Everyone is exhausted, and it shows on every player's face. But this game is an important one for our school, for Lock. It determines how much funding the school will allocate for the upcoming year.

He has been begging for more funding for the soccer program for years. But the school continued to spout the same bullshit every year: *soccer isn't football*.

Until this year, when the principal told him, *if you win state, I'll increase your budget.*

Lock has been stressing for weeks about this game. He's been watching past games, both theirs and the other teams, studying formations until late in the night, and I've been having to drag him to bed.

I'm worried about him, but I also know that if this game doesn't go how he needs it to, the program at the school could be scrapped completely.

I've had him on my fire table damn near every night this week, working on a different spot, hoping to get him to release some of this tension and stress. But he can't, not with this looming over him.

This game means everything to him and these boys. It's not just funding for the program, though. For some of these kids, it's the only ticket to college...or the pros.

I watch as Lock stalks up and down the sidelines, barking orders, accent getting thicker and thicker as the end of the game comes closer. The parents can't barely understand him, but those kids do.

When the game started, he was decked out in his coaching gear. Tight navy joggers, black sneakers, hair combed back, and hat with the school logo. But no amount of polish was going to change the rebellious Clark Kent look. The tattoos and gauged ears wouldn't let him be too polished.

As the game went on, the sweatshirt came off, the shirt came untucked, and his hat went backwards. I was struggling to maintain my composure and thankful that we are at a school event where I can't jump his bones. Because if we weren't? I'd already have dragged him under the bleachers.

I'm snapped out of my daydream when the other team calls a time-out and our team comes to the sidelines to get water. I can hear Lock talking to them, telling them that he's so proud of them. I look over when a scout from UNC comes to stand next to me. He's standing there with his hands in his pockets, watching the huddle.

The players take the field again, and Lock looks over at me, noticing the scout standing next to me. His eyes widen briefly before his eyes lock with mine. I give him a shit-eating grin and a thumbs up.

We're down to the final five minutes. We're still tied up, and the other team has the ball.

The next four minutes are a fight over the ball, and I think I'm going to be sick. No one wants this game to go into extra time.

Then the break we needed comes—our midfielder manages to steal the ball and starts taking it down the field. Every parent and spectator is on their feet, screaming at the top of their lungs.

Our kid that stole the ball, launches it to our forward. He does a scissor kick, and the ball flies past the goalie just as the buzzer calls time.

There is a split second of complete silence before the entire stadium erupts. Parents and spectators take the field, and the boys are engulfed by people.

Lock just stands there, frozen. I scramble down the stairs and push my way to him. When I reach him, I reach up and pull his face down to mine. "Look at me, Baby."

When he finally looks down at me, there are tears running down his face. "They did it," he whispers. "They fucking did it."

He picks me up with a laugh, and I am crushed against him. His team swarms us, grabbing at him and shouting.

"You did it," I tell him and place a kiss on his mouth.

The scout that was standing next to me walks up. "I've been hearing good things about your players, and I'd like to talk to you about a couple of them. If they want a ride to UNC, give me a call."

He holds out his business card, and Lock is too shocked to take it.

"Thank you," I tell the scout as I take the card. "I'll make sure he gives you a call."

A couple of the seniors look down at me with hope in their eyes.

"Well, let's go celebrate!" I call out. The boys head to the locker room, and Lock is still standing next to me, his arms wrapped around me.

"Baby, you need to go talk to them. I'll be here waiting. Always."

Will the knife finally let her feel?

Wild Obsidian: Knife

Vic Raven

Trigger Warnings

Please do not try without proper education, enthusiastic consent AND mentorship!

Sacrifice play scene

Off page abuse (not by MC's)

Injuries from war

Knife Chapter 1

Jordan

Tonight is club night at Obsidian. A night that is for pleasure, pain, and debauchery. I have been a member of Obsidian since it opened, hoping beyond hope that something here could help me.

I have been a Top and a Bottom. I have played with rope, whips, fire, and done primal play. I am one of the most well-rounded mentors in the club. But I still haven't found my purpose, my drive, the thing that I look forward to the most.

Sure, I have fun. I have learned what my body likes and doesn't. And I am a resource to new members who are learning their way around the scene and community. But under it all, I am numb.

The numbness started when I was a kid. I didn't react the way that I was "supposed" to. I didn't feel things like everyone else around me.

Family member died? No reaction. Father couldn't be bothered? Whatever.

But if I even thought that I had done something wrong? Complete and total panic. Boyfriend mad at me? Groveling mess.

Initially, my mother had me tested for sociopathic and psychopathic tendencies after my grandfather died, and I showed no reaction to it. But the therapist said I showed none of those qualities.

I was just a fucked up kid who didn't feel like anyone actually cared about her. According to the therapist, this was my brain's way of coping with stress and dysregulation. My mother didn't want to hear it and said I was emotionally stunted.

Instead of letting my therapist help me, my mother just berated me until I graduated high school and moved out. Since then, my therapist has made a lot of money off me in my attempt to figure out what is wrong with me.

The official diagnosis would make the alphabet soup company jealous. AuDHD, ODD, OCD, C-PTSD, all sprinkled with anxiety, paranoia, and people-pleasing. But I'm not depressed, just numb. So I've got that going for me.

Tonight, as I walk through the club, I take in all the play partners at the various stations. Rhett is tying up Maris, Cam is whipping Henley, Becca is chatting with Beth, who is watching Henley. Derrick leans against the back wall, watching Becca, hunting her.

I've thought about playing with Cam or Cody tonight, seeing if a whip or flogger could get me out of my head enough to feel something. But I can't gather up the enthusiasm. Instead, I walk over to the bar and order a vodka cranberry.

The bar is situated at the back of the old textile mill. It's on a platform that allows the people at the bar to look out over the stations and dance floor. I sit at a stool, order my drink, and start people watching.

A few people come up and talk to me. Some are past students from silver smithing, some are people that I mentored in the club. Others are looking for a good time. But none of them stick around for long.

Story of my life.

I notice Damien swaggering through the club. He's walking like a man on a mission. His large body cuts through the crowd like a tank. I take a second to take him in. He's tall, probably around six four or more and he's built like a linebacker.

Damien is not one to watch his carbs. In fact, he needs them for the work he does. He owns his own logging company, but he's not one to sit behind a desk. Nope. He's out there with his crews running equipment and doing the work.

A couple of years ago, he came into my shop looking for a custom piece for his student that was graduating from his mentorship at the club. I got to know him pretty well in that time and in the years since.

But like everything in my life, our relationship is only surface level.

I watch as he cuts through the crowd to the bar. His gaze lands on me, and I see the spark of recognition in his eyes.

I run my thumb over my bottom lip, making sure there's not any drool forming there. He comes to a stop before me, his weight resting on his back leg. He looks pissed, and I can't tell if that's just his face or if he's actually mad.

"What can I do for you, Bear?" I ask him. His dark brown eyes are warm despite the look of menace on his bearded face. His long, brown hair is pulled back in a bun, and I hope it's as soft as it looks.

"Nothing, Little One. Just need a beer to wipe away this shit day." He gestures to the bartender and sits down next to me.

His scent is strong but not overpowering: diesel, pine, and outdoors. He's in his signature look: jeans, boots, and a button-down black shirt with a black leather vest.

"Sounds like a normal day at the office," I quip back sarcastically.

He laughs into his beer, showing off straight, white teeth hidden beneath his beard.

"You're right about that." He takes another swallow of his beer. "What have you been up to recently?"

"Same shit, different day. Customer backed out of a commission at the last minute, so I have a super specific choker with no one to sell it to. Not unless they want *Goat Slut* front and center on their throat."

Damien starts laughing and almost shoots beer out of his nose. I land a couple of wallops to his back, doing nothing to actually help him.

Once he gets himself under control, he looks over at me. "*Goat Slut*?"

"Yup. The unfortunate part isn't just the name, it's absolutely gorgeous. Emerald and onyx stones, hex lock clasps, and four inch wide solid sterling silver." I shake my head.

"It sounds stunning. Did you at least get a deposit for it?" He's been running his own business for a long time. He knows how people can be.

"You bet your ass I did. And thank fuck. I'll be able to tear everything apart and reuse most of it with minimal loss. It's just frustrating."

"The perks of being a small business owner," he says sarcastically. "But it sure beats punching a clock, doesn't it?" He clinks his beer against my glass in mock salute.

"Damn straight." I take a sip of my drink and survey the crowd again. "Aren't you supposed to be playing with Sam tonight?"

"She bailed on me again. It's the third time this month. I'm done with it. If she wants to play, she'll need to find someone else. I don't like my time being wasted."

"Ah, that explains the mean mug you were rocking when you came over here."

"What about you?" He asks it easily, but I can feel the deeper question under it. *Do I want to play with him?*

Damien the logger is a great, funny guy. But Bear the Dominant? Demanding, aggressive, painful are just a few words that come to mind. His specialty is knife play, and I have never been brave enough to get into that.

"What do you have in mind, Bear?" I ask tentatively.

"Well..." His smile sharpens, slow and deliberate, the change subtle but unmistakable. "I need to let out some frustration, and it sounds like you do, too."

I think about his offer. I could use a bit of catharsis right now. But my brain isn't there tonight.

"Normally, I would jump at the opportunity to play with you, Bear. But rule one of Obsidian is *enthusiastic consent, always*. And I can't be enthusiastic right now."

I watch as his face morphs from savage Dom about to play to worried friend.

"Is everything okay?" he asks. "We don't have to play for you to talk to me."

"Yeah, everything is fine, just in a bit of a funk tonight. I thought coming here would help ease it a bit, but clearly it's not working."

He nods and looks out over the crowd. "Can I ask you something?"

"Of course, Bear."

"How about just aftercare?"

"What do you mean?" I'm not a fan of aftercare in general. I know it's important, not just for the Bottom, but also for the Top.

"I've been in the community for the better part of a decade, and one thing that I have seen over and over is that sometimes you don't need the shit beat out of you. You don't need to beat the shit out of someone. Sometimes, the aftercare is what is really needed. Someone to take care of you for just a few minutes, until your world is set to rights again. And sometimes, a Top just needs to care for someone."

He gestures over to Cam, Henley, and Beth. The three are cuddled up, and Beth is taking care of both of them.

"She has very little to do with the scene that Cam and Henley just had, right? But her role at the end is to care for both of them. That's what she gets out of it. Beth isn't kinky in the traditional sense. She's not a Top, Bottom, or Switch. She's not into pain. But she is a natural caretaker. That is her kink. That's where she gets her pleasure."

I watch as Beth hovers over both Cam and Henley, tucking blankets, rubbing Cam's neck, and just...taking care of them.

"I think you've become numb to everything around you for so long that nothing is working. Pain, pleasure, the risk, it's not getting you where you want to be. It's taking more and more to get you to feel something. That's why you haven't been playing for the last couple of months."

I look at him then. I didn't think anyone had noticed my lack of involvement in the play scenes. I just wasn't interested if I wasn't getting what I needed. But him nailing the numbness is more of a shock. I haven't told him about the numbness. Hell, the only one that knows how numb I have become is me.

"And what would aftercare look like?" I ask, my skepticism obvious.

"Well, for starters, we would find a couch and a blanket. We would cuddle, talk, or just be silent. Or you could tell me why you aren't playing and I could tell you why I need a new knife."

I think about what he's saying. And I realize something very important about myself. Something I haven't even thought about.

I'm not ready. I'm not ready to be taken care of.

It's why I don't like aftercare. Why I don't really offer it when I enter negotiations as a Top. I'm not comfortable with taking on more responsibility when I can barely take care of myself. It's why my walls are so high.

"You already said no. That's a full and complete sentence." He finishes his beer and places it on the bar top behind him.

I stare into my drink and nod absently.

"Do you want to stay here or go home?" he asks gently.

I place my half empty drink on the bar top and nod to the bartender. I gather up my things and head towards the front of the club. Damien follows me, his hand a reassuring presence on my lower back.

When we make it to my truck, he opens my door. I climb in and shut the door. He continues to stand there, so I roll down the window.

"Would it be okay if I text you? Make sure you make it home okay?"

I just nod, and with a tap to the window frame, he steps away from the truck. I put the truck in gear and start towards home.

For the first time in a long time, I feel something. I feel seen. And I'm not sure I like it.

Knife Chapter 2

Damien

I watch as Jordan drives away, my mind still sitting at the bar where I saw a woman that is miserable.

I have seen that bomb blasted look before, usually on soldiers who had just gone through some shit. Hell, I'm sure I had that same look on my face after my unit had been hit in Afghanistan. That look is why I made a beeline for Jordan tonight.

Jordan isn't okay, and I'm not really qualified to help her. Not really. I'm not a therapist. I'm not a professional. I'm just someone who has been in the trenches and knows what that feels like.

I head to my truck and get in, letting the old girl warm up before I head home. I don't have a long drive, only about fifteen miles, but it's straight up a mountain, so it takes forever. I pull out of Obsidian's lot and start towards my house.

My mind is full of Jordan as I navigate the switchbacks up to my home. I want to help her, and I think I might know how.

When I pull into the drive, I take in my home.

The cabin sits on seventy acres of mountains and has been in my family for generations. The original cabin was for weekend hunting trips and was rustic at best. No running water, no electricity, nothing.

I tore down the old cabin and built my home by hand about six or seven years ago with Cam's help. All the lumber came from the land that I had cut by hand. Cam helped bring my vision to reality, but the labor was all mine.

I kill the engine and climb out of my rig. Gunner comes out from around the house and barrels into me. He's a huge Cane Corso, probably topping out at a hundred and thirty pounds. He jumps up and plants his paws on my chest. I rub his sides and nuzzle my face into his.

"You hungry, bud?" I whisper to him. Gunner goes nuts and races towards the house. I follow behind him at a much slower pace. My hip catching with every step.

I feed Gunner and head back outside to the hot tub. Every night after work, and again if I've played at club night, I soak in the tub. The last deployment, before my contract was up, was brutal.

My unit had been hit by rockets, and while we all made it out alive, most of us were pretty fucked up. I made it out with all my limbs, but my back is a patchwork of burns and scars from shrapnel and my hip is on its last leg…literally.

At twenty-eight, I came back stateside with a Purple Heart, PTSD, and enough scars to make Frankenstein proud. And when I built this house, I knew I would get a hot tub big enough to fit my ass into it.

I strip my clothes and climb in the hot tub, not bothering to hide the wince as my hip catches when I step over the side. Gunner comes out and lays down on the porch next to the hot tub. He's chewing on the deer femur I gave him from my last hunting trip.

As I let my body settle back against the side of the tub and the jets do their work, I think back to my time at Obsidian.

When I found Obsidian, I had only been out of the Army and home for a couple of months. I was struggling to get my footing and my business off the ground. A buddy told me about Obsidian and I finally found what I was looking for.

I applied for membership, attended the classes, and within a year had a steady, experienced play partner. I figured out what I liked and didn't. I learned how to bring forth pleasure and pain. And I figured out that aftercare helped me more than it helped my Bottom.

After a couple of years, I learned the fine art of knife play. I learned that it wasn't necessarily the bite of cold steel into soft flesh that got a Bottom off. It wasn't the blood that welled up or the scars left behind. Though sometimes, that's exactly what a Bottom needs.

It is the mental aspect. The forced stillness that allows someone to fly. It is the forced presence that breaks through the numbness that allows even the most repressed to break free. You can't hide from the blade of a knife.

And that's what I think Jordan needs.

I've watched Jordan play over the years, both as a Top and a Bottom, and one thing is perfectly clear: she can take whatever is dished out. It is impressive, and depressing, to watch her get worked over by a Top.

Jordan's body goes through the motions and reacts to pain the way it *should*. But if you look at her, really look at her, she isn't really there. She locks herself away in her mind where nothing can touch her.

As I continue to soak in the tub, my muscles finally relaxing in my back and hip, I start formulating a plan. I want to play with Jordan, but not if she won't let me in. I don't want her to hide behind her walls.

I want to take a nuclear bomb to them. Then, I want to help her rebuild them. Walls that protect her but don't keep her contained. Walls that allow her to actually feel things when it's safe to feel them, instead of not at all.

My phone goes off with a quick chirp. I reach over to the porch rail where I left it when I got in the tub. It's Jordan.

Home.

I take a minute to think about my reply. I want to play with her. I want to help her. But I don't want to run her off either.

Thank you, Little One. Are you at your shop tomorrow?

I see the read receipt, and the three dots start and then stop. Finally, after what seems like hours but is probably only a few minutes, I get my response.

Yeah, I have a commission to finish up. I'll probably be available after two.

That's perfect. I've got a couple quotes on her side of the mountain and I should wrap up around then.

I'll see you then, Little One. Get some sleep.

I climb out of the tub, my hip and back already feeling significantly better. I don't bother getting dressed, shaking myself off like a dog. I'm the only one out here for miles. Gunner grumbles, but grabs his bone and follows me into the house.

I throw on a pair of boxer briefs and then crawl into bed. Gunner abandons his bone, jumps up, and snuggles into my side.

Tomorrow, I'm going to go see her and see if she's willing to be my new plaything.

Dawn breaks over the mountains of North Carolina. I've already been up for a couple of hours at this point.

You can take the soldier out of the Army, but not out of the man. I've already walked four miles on the treadmill to warm up my hip for the day and I'm just starting my workout.

Logging keeps me in good shape, but the workout is for my mind. It didn't take long after coming home for good for me to figure out that I needed to keep working out to keep my mind sharp.

My therapist suggested it after I complained that I felt like a part of me was missing, that I felt like I was not meeting my goals despite how hard I worked. He said that a lot of veterans, especially injured male vets, struggle with feeling inadequate after injuries. And he was right.

My mind makes me think I am weak because I can't do things the way I used to. While I know it's a lie, my mind doesn't actually care. I found that if I don't sling around steel in the gym a couple times a week, my mind takes control.

But I've been able to keep working out and avoid injuring myself further. The plus side is that I've actually made the muscles and tendons around my hip even stronger. I've had to make adjustments to how much weight I move and how I do it, but for the most part, I've still kept my pre-discharge maxes.

I'm just finishing up with my last set of deadlifts when I hear my phone ring. I set down the bar and head over to where my phone is.

It's Sam.

"Hey, Sam." I answer on the third ring, but my tone is distant. I am serious about what I said last night. "What can I do for you?"

"What happened last night?" Her tone is indigent. "I waited for you to come back in after you took off with Jordan, but you never showed up."

"Sam, I waited for you at my station for over an hour. You didn't show up at our agreed time."

"So? It's not like I wasn't coming." Sam is known for being a Brat, but the difference between a Brat and a brat is intent. And her intent was to be disrespectful.

"I'm not doing this with you, Sam. We agreed that you would be at my station by seven. I waited until almost eight thirty. If you saw me leave with Jordan and that's when you showed up, that puts you at least two and a half hours late. That's not being a Brat, that's disrespectful."

"But Bear, you know how I am," she whines. I fucking hate whiners.

"I'm not doing this with you, Sam. I told you the last time you stood me up that I'm not interested in that kind of Bratting. I told you to either be on time or find someone else to play with. Do you remember what you told me?"

"Yes, Sir," she whispers.

"What was that?" I bark into the phone.

"Yes, Sir!" This time, she yells into the phone.

"What did you tell me?" I growl into the phone.

"That I would be on time," she says, just above a whisper.

"Right. And while you may not value my time, I do. You can find someone else to play with from now on. It won't be me." With that, I hang up. I should have listened to others at the club who told me I wouldn't enjoy playing with her.

Some Tops and Dom/mes enjoy that type of Brat, but I don't. I don't mind Brats, in fact, I love them. I've been known to be a Brat right back. But not when it turns disrespectful, and that's what Sam is. She hides her disrespect behind her Brat persona. Regardless, I'm done with her.

I walk out of the gym in my shop and start heading towards the house. Gunner takes off and starts running around like a complete spaz. I watch as he grabs up a stick and damn near breaks his neck when it gets stuck in the dirt.

With a laugh, I call him into the house to feed him while I go hop in the shower. As I wash up, I begin to lay out my day. I've got two estimates to run before I can get to Jordan's shop. One is commercial and one is residential—both stand to make my business a ton of money.

But that's not my biggest concern. Jordan is.

Last night, I came up with a plan to enter into negotiations with Jordan. I know exactly what I want, and I'm really hoping she's game.

Knife Chapter 3

Jordan

I watch as Damien pulls his work truck into the lot behind my shop. I've got a sweet location in the art district of downtown Franklin. The front of my shop houses my store, office, and classroom, and the back is my smithing shop.

My rent is high, but being right on the main drag makes it worth every penny. Currently, I'm boxing up my latest commission, a pair of silver cuffs with *My* stamped on the right cuff and *Slut* stamped on the left. This very Bratty Submissive is well loved by his Domme.

The customer, a busty six foot tall bombshell, watches me box up the cuffs. "Thank you, Jordan. These are gorgeous. Your attention to detail is absolutely stunning."

"Thank you. I'm sure he will love them, Crystal," I tell her. And he will, if only because she bought them for him.

I hand over the box and process her payment when Damien swaggers in.

"Hey, Damien. I haven't seen you around in a hot minute." Crystal gives Damien a side hug.

"Just been busy with work. How have you been?" He glances at me before turning his attention back to Crystal. His face is hard to read with that thick beard.

"Good. Just getting Chris his birthday present." She holds up the box. "Jordan, it is a pleasure as always. I'll be back for that *Goat Slut* piece if your client doesn't come back for it."

"I won't break it down until I hear from you," I tell her. When she walked in and saw the choker, she about died laughing. Her sense of humor is totally warped, and she decided right then and there that she wanted it for Chris. Why? Because Chris is terrified of farm animals of any kind.

Damien looks at me with his eyebrow raised but doesn't say anything as Crystal walks out the door.

"She thinks it's hysterical and wants it. I had to tell her that I have a sixty-day hold policy, but I think Chris will end up with a new choker for Christmas." I shake my head. "I'm not sure that it'll fit around his neck, though. I'll have to make a spacer or add some links to it."

Damien looks like he's about to lose it. "I don't want to yuck someone's yum, but why *Goat Slut*?"

"I don't ask. This person is from out of state and was visiting when they placed the order. I'm damn near burning with curiosity, but at the same time, I really don't want to know."

I finish with all the paperwork and log Crystal's transaction into my system. I'm just about finished when Damien steps up to the counter. He must not have been logging today. His clothes are mostly clean.

"What can I do for you, Damien?" I ask with an air of nonchalance, but inside, I'm praying he doesn't ask me to play with him. Not because I don't want to, I would love to. No, I'm afraid that if I play with him, my world will never be the same again.

"What do you know about Edge play?" He doesn't play around and he doesn't beat around the bush. He looks me dead in the eye as he knocks my world off its axis.

"I know that Edge play is pretty risky. There needs to be complete trust between both parties and that more often than not, it ends in the Bottom needing significant aftercare."

"That's the gist, but have you ever experienced it?"

"No. It's not something I've ever really been interested in," I tell him with complete honesty.

"This is an incredibly personal question and you don't have to answer it, but I've seen the look in your eyes when you're at the club. I've seen you pulling away from mentoring and playing." He pauses. "Would you be open to negotiating a scene with me? Would you let me help you feel something?"

I take a deep breath. He's right. It is an incredibly personal question. "I don't think that's the question you need to be asking. The question is, do I *want* to feel something?"

I take a step back from the counter, from him, and head back to my shop. I hear the *thunk* of his boots on the worn hardwood floors before it transitions into the worn concrete of my shop.

I start working to set my shop to rights, giving myself time and a distraction to think about not only his question but my own.

Damien starts walking around the shop, careful not to touch anything. It's always weird having someone in my space. I've been alone since I turned eighteen. Everyone that should have given a shit about me bailed.

My father was never around. My mother had done her "duty" and got me through high school. I had no siblings and no real friends. I mentor new people at the club and help teach, I occasionally have silversmithing students, but that's about where my ability to socialize ends.

I have had a couple of partners over the years, both men and women, but I am so closed off that they just didn't last.

I turn to look over at him. "Before I answer your question, I have one of my own. The same rules apply, you don't have to answer. Why does it matter to you? We are acquaintances at best."

It's Damien's turn to take a minute to respond. He looks around the shop. His gaze stops at the *Goat Slut* choker sitting on the shelf and lets out a chuckle. He turns his gaze back to me. "It matters to me because I saw that look in the mirror every damn day while I was deployed in Afghanistan."

He leans back against the workbench. "It matters to me because while you may think we are acquaintances, I feel like you're a friend. Numbness shouldn't be a way of life. It has its place, and it's there to protect us. But we are supposed to *feel*. We are supposed to have a support system that actually supports us. I want to be that for you. I want to help you learn to feel again."

"But again, why would I want to feel? Every day of my life has been a struggle. Every relationship I've had has ended with me being too much or not enough. I wasn't good enough for my father. I was too much for my mother. I poured into my students, but once they had what they needed, they were gone too. My past partners couldn't be bothered. Why the fuck would I want to feel any of that?"

Damien looks baffled by that. "What do you mean, everyone has bailed on you? Like, I heard what you said, but how?"

"I don't know. I guess they thought I didn't want or need them. It's the curse of being a *strong woman*. People think you have your shit together on the outside while you're drowning inside. So I learned how to swim."

“So for the last, what, ten years you’ve been alone?”

“Something like that,” I say. I turn around and wipe down my workspace, getting ready to close up for the day. “It’s not so bad now, though.”

Damien doesn't say much, just watches me putter around the shop.

I shut the lights off in the shop and move back into the front of the store. Damien follows me and takes my hand as I shut off the last of the lights and grab my bag from behind the counter.

“I’m not going to ask if you are okay with that, because clearly you’re not. Nor should you be. But I am going to ask if I can be your friend. If you don’t want a scene with me, that’s fine and I won’t be offended. But I *do* want to be your friend.”

I think about his words as I let go of his hand and usher him out of the shop, and I set the alarm and lock the doors. I start walking towards the parking lot. I’m still working through what it could mean to be his friend when I stop next to my truck.

I turn and look at him. Really look at him. His work clothes are similar to mine: thick pants, T-shirt, and boots. His beard is long enough to grab on to, but not so long that it gets in the way. He's got his hair pulled up in a messy bun, and it should look out of place on a man, but on Damien, it looks good. There's nothing fancy about him, and that's just the way I like it.

“How about we go to dinner and finish this conversation?" I ask him. "There’s a noodle place down the road about half a mile if you’re good to walk it.”

Damien has a shit-eating grin on his face. "I'm game."

With that, he takes my hand and places it through the crook of his arm. We start walking in the direction I pointed, and I am surprised by a few things right off.

First, I am not walking on the road side of the sidewalk. Anytime we have to walk through traffic or a crosswalk, he tugs me behind him. Second, I feel dainty next to him. At six feet tall and a solid hundred and eighty pounds of curves, I'm not a small woman. And third, regardless of whether or not I decide to play with Damien, there's a very real chance that I could actually have a friend at the end of this.

And I'm not really sure how to feel about that.

We are about to walk into the restaurant when Damien's gait suddenly changes. It goes from a swagger to a limp. "Are you okay?"

"Old injury is bothering me," he says shortly.

I just *hmm* him and keep walking. I'm used to being shut down, but I didn't think it would happen so quickly after an offer of friendship.

"I'm sorry, that was really shitty. I don't talk about it much because it makes people uncomfortable. I was hurt in Afghanistan and my hip is totally fucked. The VA doesn't want to do a replacement because I'm *too young,* but my orthopedic surgeon wants to do surgery yesterday."

"You don't have to explain to me," I say, equally as short. I know I'm being bitchy, but at the same time, every time I have reached out for friendship or love, I've been smacked down. I've just never been smacked down within twenty minutes.

"Little One, look at me." He pulls me away from the entrance of the restaurant, but I don't look at him. Instead, I look out over the traffic that is starting to stack up. He gently tilts my chin until I'm looking up at him. He's stepped in close, and I can feel his body heat come off of him in waves. But I still don't look at him. I stare at the building over his shoulder.

"You can put your walls back up, and that would be fair because that was a dick move. But I'm asking for a chance. I'm going to make mistakes, and I'm going to apologize for them. And I'm going to piss you off, and I'll apologize for that too. But you are going to make mistakes, and I expect you to apologize. You're going to piss me off, and I expect you to apologize. That's how friendship works, Little One."

I take a chance at looking at him. His gaze is open and earnest. And I have to decide, right now, if I am willing to accept the chance of getting hurt. If I'm willing to open myself up to disappointment. He apologized and actually said he was sorry.

After a minute or so, I nod. "Okay."

He grins at me, puts his hand on my lower back, and leads me into the restaurant. He tells the hostess that we would like a table outside. It doesn't take long to get our beers and place our order for noodles.

Damien leans back and stretches his long legs out.

“Why won’t the VA do the surgery?” I take a sip of my beer while I wait for him to answer. To be honest, I’m fully expecting him to stop my line of questioning.

“Because according to them, I can only have so many hip replacements before there’s nothing left of the bone to replace. But my surgeon says that with *proper care* my replacement can last twenty-five years. I’m willing to do the proper care part, but the VA still won’t cover the cost.”

“What is considered proper care?” I ask. I’ve had my own run arounds with insurance, so I can definitely understand his frustration. “And twenty-five years would put you at what, fifty-five, sixty?”

“Close enough. I’m thirty-seven so it would put me about sixty-two. And I would have to stop actively logging. I could still quote jobs, haul equipment to job sites, and the like. But any overtly physical work like climbing, rigging, and that is a no-go. I’m fine with that. I would miss it, but at this point, I’m a liability, anyway. I can’t move as fast as I used to, and one slip, fall, or jar will fuck my back and hip up worse than they already are.”

“How much would the surgery cost without the VA backing?”

“About forty thousand, not including physical therapy, medications, and all that.”

I almost spit out my beer. That’s a lot of money.

“I’ve got it saved up. But I don’t want to spend it. My injuries are well documented and service related. Hell, I was medically discharged and have insurance, so the VA should be covering this and they won’t.”

"But you're in pain," I tell him. "Why wouldn't you just get your hip fixed if you have a solution to the problem?"

“Because it’s the principle. I was injured while deployed and they should pay to fix it. The reason I’m not fighting it harder is because I can work around the injury. Yes, it’s painful, but I can handle the pain. I can still work out, walk, and lift. I just have to be careful.”

“I’m sorry I suggested walking over here,” I tell him. I feel like a huge asshole.

“Why would you be sorry?” He seems genuinely confused. “You had no idea that my hip was fucked up.”

“Yeah, but still.”

“No, Little One, this isn’t on you. If my hip is bothering me, I need to say something. It’s not on you to guess.” His voice is stern and no nonsense, but also caring. He’s not reprimanding me, but he’s also not allowing me to take blame that doesn’t belong to me.

And that’s a first for me. Usually, I’m to blame when things go wrong. I’ve willingly accepted the blame in hopes that someone would stay. For the first time, someone said it’s not my fault and I’m not really sure what to do with that.

But I think I know the first step.

“Alright, Bear. What kind of scene did you have in mind?” I watch in fascination as his face morphs from concerned friend to savage Dominant.

I might have made a mistake.

Knife Chapter 4

Bear

I have to admit I am a little surprised that Jordan would even be willing to play with me. Especially after I snapped at her about my hip. But after I apologized and laid out my expectations, she seemed to relax.

The other thing that I'm concerned about is that she immediately accepted the blame for us walking. I don't like that and I shut it down quick. She's not to blame, and I will not allow her to take responsibility or blame that isn't hers to take.

I have a feeling that getting her to only take the blame that is hers to take is going to be a challenge. But first things first, I have to get her to be willing to play with me.

Over the last couple of days, I've thought about the type of scene that I want to do with Jordan. There are so many options; fire, needles, breath, and, of course, knife.

But for Jordan, it has to be something that will break down the walls that she has built around herself. Honestly, while the scene itself matters, it's actually the aftercare that she needs. She has to allow herself a chance to not be the strong one. I think that's where we will get the release she needs.

"Before I tell you what I have in mind, tell me what is the kinkiest, hardest, craziest thing you've done; in the club, out of the club, anytime, anywhere."

The waitress drops off our noodles and Jordan digs in. She thinks for a minute or two as she eats and then shocks the shit out of me.

"I let a Top take a bullwhip to me. I was in a bad place and just wanted to feel something, anything. Well, the joke was on me, because I still didn't feel anything and have the scars to prove it."

"Hold on, they whipped you till you bled and didn't stop when they saw you disappear into your head?" Confidentiality is fundamental in the club, but all I want is to figure out who did this to her and kick them out of the club. That is bullshit...and dangerous.

"I don't really know. I think I disassociated because I don't remember much. When I came back to myself, I was covered in blood and welts, but still numb."

"What did they do after? For aftercare, check-ins, anything?" It is taking everything in me not to give into the rage coursing through me.

"No. I'm not a fan of aftercare. Usually, aftercare is to make sure I'm not dead and leave me alone." She says it like an afterthought. Like it's not important, and tucks into her noodles.

"Alright, so I want to make sure I've got this right. You negotiated with a Top who took a bullwhip to your back in an effort to feel something. You disassociated, and they didn't check in with you to make sure that you were okay. Then when they were done, you came to, covered in blood, and they pretty much just left you there? Is that about right?"

I'm on the edge of exploding and she's eating her noodles like it's no big deal. But I see her eyes flick to the door and she won't look at me. She's also fidgeting in her chair. Tiny movements that I don't think she notices, but I can see through her bullshit. She's not okay. Not even a little bit.

"That's the gist, but it's not his fault, though. He did exactly what I asked for." She looks up at me. "Are you not hungry?" She gestures to my bowl of uneaten food. "You're missing out, these are some of the best noodles in the state."

I look down at my bowl. It really does look good. But I am nauseated with what I learned today. This woman is so numb, so traumatized, that she doesn't see that she was assaulted in our club. The club that has been a safehaven for so many people. That the Top that did this to her is out there treating other people like this. And she's oblivious.

This isn't consent. It's conditioning—the kind that happens when pain becomes the only way to drown out silence.

"Little One, I need to ask you something. And I need you to really think about what I'm saying and asking you—take a minute if you need to. If one of your students, a new member of the club, was to come to you and tell you what you just told me. How would you react?"

Her hand shakes just a touch as she sets down her chopsticks. She takes a sip of her beer, seemingly gathering herself. I watch with fascination as she goes from unphased about what happened to her to a mama bear ready to shred someone.

"First, I would ask them if they were alright. Then I would probably ask if they had lost their fucking mind and demand to know who did this to them."

I sit back in my seat. At least she's understanding that this is wrong.

"But again, he did exactly what I asked. He's not the bad guy here. If anyone is, it's me."

"No, Little One, you're not the bad guy. That Top should have been checking in with you regularly. Especially if you started bleeding, even if you agreed to blood play, the second he broke skin he should have been checking on you. He didn't."

She picks up her beer and starts picking at the label. I can tell she's uncomfortable with this conversation, but that's a good thing. Because I think I have an idea of how her brain works. She is so desperate for love and affection that she will let someone abuse her, just for a chance at it.

"I can go into every part and piece as to why that scene was wrong. But I'm not going to. You know that. But I can tell you now that's not how we are going to do our scene. Because, like it or not, when I do a scene and I am the one hurting, scaring, or even loving you, I am responsible for you. And if I need to be the voice of reason, that's what I'll do." I take a breath and watch her.

She stops mid-sip of her beer. Her eyes are suddenly uncertain. She thought that when she negotiated with me, she could tell me what she wanted and that's what would happen. But that's not how negotiations work. And that's damn sure not how I work.

"Little One, you won't be running the show from the bottom. We will do it my way, and when we are done, we will do aftercare. I won't just hurt you and then leave you. Are you sure you still want to play with me?"

She takes a deep breath, seeming to gather her resolve.

"Right now, yes. But I reserve the right to say no," she says and finishes off her noodles.

I chuckle and take a bite of my noodles. Fuck, these are really good.

"Good, that's smart. The scene I have in mind is going to test every limit you have. So let's start there. What are your hard limits, the things you cannot or will allow?"

"I don't really have any hard limits. At least nothing that I've gone up against yet. If I'm being honest, the only thing that makes me uncomfortable is aftercare," she jokes...at least I hope she's joking.

Knife Chapter 5

Jordan

It's been almost two weeks since I opened up to Damien about what had happened at the club two years ago. And I thought he would ghost me, but he didn't. Instead, we continued negotiations until we were both comfortable with what was going to happen.

And I am mostly comfortable, but I'm also terrified because this could really hurt. Not physically, but mentally and emotionally.

I pull my truck into the parking lot of the Wilds, my tires crunching over the gravel. I park next to Damien's truck and shut the engine off. My hands are shaking and I am starting to second guess myself.

Damien has reserved the Wilds for our scene tonight, and I am grateful to have the whole thing to ourselves. This is not something that I want anyone to witness, hell, it isn't something that I want to do in the first place. But I want the potential results. I don't want to be numb for the rest of my life.

Per our agreement, I am to follow trail four to the sacrifice space at the end of the trail. If I don't show up in the next five minutes, he will assume that I am either not interested in playing or that I'm not okay. Either way, he will come to me and make sure.

The Wilds has spent a lot of money to make the woods as safe for their primal community as possible. No one wants to ruin their feet on a chase through the woods. The trails are all moss covered instead of gravel or dirt. Fire pits are kept low and obvious, to the point where the rock has been spray painted with glow in the dark paint, so that it's obvious to see at night.

But as I make my way to trail four, I realize that I do want to do this. I want to take the chance because Damien is right, numbness is no place to live.

I take the first step onto the trail, my boots sinking into the moss that covers the hiking trail. It doesn't take long before I am coming into a clearing. I take a look around and see that it's not Damien standing there, but Bear.

He's shirtless. His burly, muscled chest and abs on full display. His entire chest is covered in tattoos, and they keep going into his jeans. His jeans ride low on his hips and showcase his powerful thighs. He's got two knives on his belt, and I'm positive one is for me.

He looks over from where he is tying rope around a tree. His eyes are dark and the fire in the pit casts shadows over his face. The tree that he is tying rope to is in the center of the clearing, the full moonlight highlighting where I'll be standing.

He turns back to the tree, showing me his back, and I can't help the gasp that leaves me. His back is completely shredded. There are puckered burn scars and what I can only assume is either shrapnel or gunshot scars. How he survived, I have no idea. But I'm really glad he did.

He glances over his shoulder at my gasp, and he gives me a feral grin. "You going to stare or come over here?"

I slowly make my way over to where he is standing. We had gone through every detail of how tonight would work, every contingency plan. But now, I'm worried that I won't be able to do it. That I won't be able to go through with this.

He must see my hesitation because he walks over to me. He runs his fingers over my face and gently cradles my jaw in his hand. He tilts my head up to look at him. "Color."

With his hand on my face, I feel grounded. Like for the first time in years, I don't feel like I am floating away. "Green," I tell him.

He smiles down at me and it's tender. "Good, Little One." He turns me to the tree where the rope has been laid out, ready for me to be his sacrifice for the night. "You can fight me, or you can go willingly, but you will be tied to that tree."

I hesitate, not because I don't want this, but because my mind is suddenly a scramble of emotions, trying to break through the numbness. He must take my hesitation as wanting to fight because before I know it, his arms are banded around me and he lifts me off the ground.

My legs swing wildly as he throws me over his shoulder and swaggers to the tree. My brain short circuits. It knows I'm safe, but my brain also knows that this is when it's supposed to shut down to protect me.

While my brain is busy trying to figure out its next move, my shirt and bra are removed. I stand with the tree to my back, the bark biting into my skin. He's got my hands tied over my head, and he's working to remove my jeans, underwear, and boots. It takes only a minute before my feet are tied to the tree and I'm completely naked and at his mercy.

He steps back and looks at me. He must like what he sees because he takes a moment to adjust himself.

"Little One, I'm going to ask again, are you ready for tonight? Knowing that I am going to break you and you are going to love it?"

I take a minute to take stock of where I am. I'm not numb, I'm excited. I'm terrified. And I'm ready to see where this will lead. "Bring it, Bear."

His laugh is savage. He stalks toward me, the firelight dancing over his bare chest. "You're going to regret that, Little One," he growls and reaches behind him.

I don't know where he was hiding that blindfold, but suddenly it's around my head and I can't see anything. Bear moves fast for such a big man.

My breathing speeds up and I feel lightheaded. I shift my weight, checking the tension in the ropes. But I freeze when I hear the snap of a twig. I sense his body close to mine, and I can't move away. The ropes are taut but not tight.

Suddenly, I feel something sharp trailing up my leg. My muscles quiver, but I can't quite tell what it is. We had discussed various tools when we negotiated, but I didn't really have a preference. My only stipulation is that he not draw blood. I've got enough scars.

He drags it further up my leg and over my hip, digging it in occasionally. I feel his breath on my cunt and I am instantly wet. I just want to grab his head and bury his face in my pussy, but I can't move.

He growls when he smells my arousal and another gush drips down my legs. "You still with me, Little One?"

"Green," I breathe out. For the first time in years, maybe ever, I am fully present in a scene. Waiting to see what happens next. My brain is engaged in what is happening, not trying to shield me.

"Good girl," he whispers. I can feel the bite of something cool and hard around my breast, trailing around my nipple. My breathing picks up and I arch against the ropes. He lands a quick swat against my nipple.

"Don't move, Little One. That's the deal." He soothes the nipple that he abused with his mouth, twirling his tongue around the stiff tip. He moves to the second nipple, his tongue circling before—what I assume is— the knife is back on me, following his tongue's path.

My fear cranks up, and I'm panting. But I hold myself perfectly still, waiting for the next place the blade of his knife will slide. I feel his hand push against my chest and I take a deep breath, letting the heat from his hand ground me.

When my breathing comes back under control, I nod once. I'm still here, still present. He removes his hand from my chest and I feel the cool air replace the warmth from his hand.

He draws the knife blade up my collarbone and I stay perfectly still. It isn't until just now that I realized how much I trust him. Because as the blade travels up my throat, I realize that he could really hurt me right now.

Suddenly, the blade leaves my throat, and I feel the rope at my wrists tug. My arms fall in front of me. Next, the rope at my ankles is cut. I'm free, but I still don't move. The knife is back at my throat. "You've done so well. We can stop now, Little One. Or we can take this further. It's up to you."

I take stock of where I am. I'm still here, I'm terrified, I'm aroused, and I want more.

"I want more, Bear. Please don't stop."

I hear the knife slide into its sheath and feel Bear step closer to me. "I'm not a gentleman, Little One."

"Please, Bear," I moan. I've never been this turned on. I've never felt like I would explode if someone didn't touch me.

He steps back from me, and I want to scream in frustration, but I hold it in. Bear isn't one to be told what to do. I feel his hands trail down my sides before resting on my hips. His finger tips dig in and he lowers to his knees in front of me and I feel his soft beard tickle my thighs.

His breath is warm across my bare pussy and I can't help the shudder that moves through me. He pulls my leg over his shoulder and I lean back against the trunk of the tree. He unleashes on me, nipping, biting, tugging on my pussy and clit until I am seconds away from exploding.

He works a thick finger into me and I can feel my pussy clench around him, dragging him deeper. "Greedy girl," he murmurs.

He shoves a second finger into my pussy and his thumb circles my clit. He moves his fingers in rhythm and before I know it, I'm coming with a scream. He continues to move his fingers and draws out my orgasm.

I'm sagging against the tree when he stands up. I hear the jungle of his belt buckle and the slide of his jeans down his thighs.

He picks me up and I wrap my legs around his hips. I brace myself against the tree and grind against him. His cock is hard and thick against me. He holds me with one hand and lines up his cock to my entrance with the other. In one smooth move, he enters me. The stretch burns, but it feels so damn good.

He starts a rhythm that has me squirming against the tree. I'm moaning and grinding against him, reaching for that second orgasm. My mind is blissfully quiet, but still fully engaged with him. I feel everything.

He continues his punishing rhythm, and it doesn't take long before I can feel my muscles clenching. "You going to come for me again, Little One?"

At my moan, he thumbs my clit again. This time giving just enough pressure to add a little pain, and my orgasm rips through me. His rhythm falters, and with a roar, he's coming with me.

He buries his face in the crook of my neck, his breath heavy against my neck.

"Bear?" I call for him. "Can you remove my blindfold?"

He chuckles and reaches up and takes it off me. The cool air hits my eyes and I blink a couple of times, clearing them.

"You did so good, Little One." He runs his hands over my hips and up my sides, up and then back down. "Let's get you off the tree."

With that, he carries me over to the fire. I let my head drop down onto his shoulder and just enjoy his arms around me and his scent enveloping me. A girl could get used to this. He moves to the other side of the fire, and I see a little nest made of mats and blankets.

"You planned for everything, didn't you?" I ask. He lowers us down with a slight grunt.

"Of course, what good is playing hard if you can't relax hard too?" He seems genuinely confused by my question. But he lays us down, me still in his arms. He snuggles me in and I rest my head on his curled bicep. He traces his hand from my ribs to hips.

"Are you okay?" he asks me, never stopping the slide of his hand.

"Yeah," I tell him. "For the first time in a really long time, I was there the whole time. I didn't disconnect. I felt safe."

"Good, I'm really glad." He places a gentle kiss on my forehead and my entire body erupts in goosebumps. "I guess you like that too?"

I just nod and try to hide my face, suddenly embarrassed.

He gently grips my chin, forcing me to look at him. "We're not doing that, Little One. You don't have to hide your body's reactions from me. I don't want you to."

Will she allow herself to be saved?

Wild Obsidian: Bruise

Vic Raven

Trigger Warnings

Bruise

Please do not try without proper education, enthusiastic consent AND mentorship!

Impact play

SVU detective

Mentions of sexual violence cases

PTSD/ Anxiety

Master/Slave relationship

Bruise Chapter 1

Jesse

As I unlock the door to my apartment, I am hit with another wave of anxiety. I barely made it out of my captain's office when I felt like the walls were closing in on me. At first, I thought it was because I've been run ragged on this case.

But it wasn't.

The captain called me into his office and told me that he was giving me two weeks. This case had been brutal for everyone, and we had done everything by the book. We caught the subject red handed and there was no way he would be able to get out of this one.

But this case hit harder than any other case I had been on in my six years in the department.

When I told the captain that I was fine, I didn't need a break, he just stared at me.

"This job takes every last shred of our humanity and leaves nothing left." He took a deep breath. "I am fifteen years sober. Before this job, I wasn't a heavy drinker. After five years in, I was drinking on the job."

I looked at him with surprise. "But I'm not drinking."

"That's not my point. You have no outlet, and it's going to be what gets you either killed or sidelined from this job."

"I'm fine," I try to defend myself. "I'm steady."

"How many panic attacks have you had in the last three days?" He raises his eyebrow at me when I don't answer. "My point has been made. You have two weeks off starting Monday. I want you to turn in your phone and radio. You are not relieved from duty and this is not discipline. This is an old man trying to keep you from going down the same path that I did."

"What am I supposed to do with myself for two weeks?"

"I can't answer that, Jesse, but maybe start with visiting your folks for a couple days. See where that lands you."

I hand over my radio and department phone, feeling like the devices on his desk are part of my very soul. Despite the fact that he said it wasn't discipline, I leave his office feeling like a failure, like I couldn't hack the job.

I walk out of his office to my rig in the parking lot, in a panicked fog, but I hold myself together through sheer force of will.

When I get into my department-issued Durango, I let my head drop against the steering wheel. I contemplate what I am going to do with myself for the next two weeks. My personal phone rings, my mom's picture lighting up the screen. I huff a laugh.

"How do you know, Mama?" I ask, leaning back against the headrest.

"Because you're my baby, I always know when you need me." My mom has always been a pain in the ass, but at the end of the day, she's probably my best friend. "What's going on?"

"I got sidelined," I murmur into the phone.

"Are you okay?" she asks. I can hear her calling out for my dad to get the car started. "I can be at your apartment in thirty minutes if your dad actually moves his ass."

I hear my dad in the background asking if I'm okay and who he has to fuck up. I can't help the smile that takes over my face. I may not agree with my parent's lifestyle, but one thing is for damn sure, they will move heaven and earth for me.

"No, I planned to come down to see you. I've got two weeks off, and my captain thinks that I need a break."

"Sit down, James, she's coming to us." I hear my dad griping in the background. "Baby, I'm so glad that you're coming down. I've missed you."

"I've missed you too, Mama," and I do. "I've got to head home and get packed, then I'll be heading down. I'll probably get there around eight-thirty or so."

"Take your time, Baby. I'll make sure I've got the stew on."

We say our goodbyes and I hang up. Feeling better already, I start my car and head towards my apartment. I don't have to do much when I get home, just grab some clothes and toiletries and clean out the fridge. I plan to spend the entire two weeks in Franklin with my parents.

I finish loading my custom sixty-six Mustang Fast Back when my phone rings again. I grimace when I see it's Daniel.

"No, I don't want to get back together. No, I don't love you. No, I don't want to have sex with you," I snarl out rapid-fire. This asshole has been relentless.

"Jesse, if you would just listen to me, you would know that it was a mistake," he whines into the phone.

"Daniel, you fucked my neighbor," I growl into the phone. "That's not a mistake."

"I was lonely, Jesse. You're always gone, leaving in the middle of the night to handle another case." He whines again. How did I ever think that this needy whining was attractive?

"You knew when we got together that I am a detective. Leave me alone, Daniel, or I'll be forced to file harassment charges." I hang up on him and start my car, the familiar rumble of the engine soothing a small portion of my soul.

I pull out of my parking spot and start towards Franklin, the only place that's ever really felt like home.

When I was eighteen and graduated high school, I ran out of there like my ass was on fire. I had gotten a full ride to UNC, and I was going to take full advantage of getting out of that tiny town. There was too much to see, too much to do to be stuck in a small town.

But it wasn't long before I realized that I missed the small town life. I liked knowing everyone and everyone knowing me. But I couldn't give up my scholarships, so I kept at it until I finally graduated.

I got a job at the department immediately after graduation and started as a beat cop. I was lucky, I got picked up by the Special Victims Unit shortly after a call where a child had been sexually assaulted. The captain, the same one that just put me on leave, saw how I handled the case and the child and pulled me off the beat. For the last five years, I have been working as an SVU detective, and I've loved every second of it.

Except the late nights, early mornings, and the completely wrecked sleep schedule. But none of that compares to the haunted eyes of children who have been brutalized. The women who will never feel safe again. The men that will forever question if they were good enough.

Give me a crackhead with a gun in a back alley any day over the silent despair of the abused.

But I will gladly be the voice of the silenced if it means that one child, woman, or man gets the justice they deserve. Even if it means I run myself into the ground.

I pull into the drive of my childhood home, right at eight-thirty.

I park next to my dad's fully restored seventy-three Porsche 911 and cut the engine. The smell of oil and gas welcome me home. I climb out of my Mustang and get my bags out of the trunk.

Duke comes trotting out of the garage, slow and steady, tail giving one lazy wag like even that takes too much effort these days.

"Hey, ole man," I murmur, bending down to scratch behind his greying ears. His fur is coarse and warm beneath my fingers, familiar in a way nothing else has been lately. "Where's Daddy?"

He huffs, turns in a stiff little circle, and starts back toward the garage with the determination of a hundred-pound senior citizen who thinks he's still in charge. I roll my eyes but follow him anyway. I would have totally missed the giant man working directly in front of me without Duke's guidance.

"You really think I'd never find him without you?" I ask the dog's swaying backside. He pauses long enough to glance over his shoulder, ears perked like *yes, actually*, then continues his slow march.

I walk into the garage and find daddy tinkering with a new project car. "Is this Mama's Bel Air?"

I set my bags down and run my hand over the raw metal of the body. Remembering the years of working with daddy in this shop. "It is. I finally got a good deal on the frame and body. The innards were trashed, but I plan on replacing everything anyway."

I watch as he continues to tear out old parts and toss them to the ground. I remember when he brought home my Mustang on the back of an old trailer. I had been fourteen and full of piss and vinegar.

Looking back now, I know I was being a shithead. But at the time, I couldn't stand what was happening inside my home. My mother and father lived a twenty-four-seven Master/Slave relationship. Growing up adjacent to that lifestyle had been incredibly difficult as a teenager.

It caused a lot of friction and was the main driving force of my leaving at eighteen. But I've been gone for almost a decade and have learned a thing or two about relationships. Specifically, the kinds I don't want.

It makes their relationship seem not so bad, though still not for me.

I'm getting ready to ask him his restoration plans when my mom slings open the door to the shop.

“Jessica Leigh, when did you get here?!” My mother is not a quiet woman, not unless my dad has told her not to speak, which is rare.

"I just got here, Mama," I say as I'm pulled into her tight embrace. Her scent of sweet vanilla comforts me.

"I'm stealing her, Hun." She picks up one of my duffle bags and turns toward the house.

"Hey," Daddy barks after her, an eyebrow raised. She stops and turns around, one hand on her hip. "Forget something?"

My mom grins and sashays—yes, sashays—back to my dad. She bends down and presses a kiss to his lips. She turns around to walk away, and he swats her ass.

This was my life growing up. I didn't think anything was weird about it. Not until I went to a friend's house and saw that her parents barely touched each other. When I asked her about it, she said that her parents just weren't very physical.

That was when I realized that there was something different about my parents. I started to pick up on other differences, and when I was fifteen, I came to my parents and asked questions.

Looking back, I realize that they were being very age-appropriate in their explanation of their Master/Slave relationship. But at the time, I couldn't understand what their relationship meant. I just knew that I didn't like what I was feeling.

"Jesse," Mama calls to me. "You ready for dinner?"

I follow her into the house, and the smell of beef stew hits me. The savory meat, spices, and fresh baked sourdough are enough to make me suddenly glad for my two week break.

I hear my dad and Duke come in behind me and head to the sink. He starts washing his hands, and my mom starts dishing out dinner. Duke curls up under the table.

"Y'all didn't have to wait for me," I say.

My parents turn and look at me like I've grown a second head.

"We eat as a family," Daddy says simply before turning around and getting the grease and oil out from under his nails.

Part of me feels like an asshole for making them wait for dinner. But the other part? The bigger part? Feels like I'm important. Like I matter. And I haven't felt like that in the years since I left home.

Dinner is chaos manifested in a small cabin in the mountains of North Carolina. The clank of spoons in bowls, Daddy's booming laugh, Mama's slow smiles. Daddy and I talk about his restoration plan for the Bel Aire, and Mama chimes in occasionally about what she wants done.

After dinner, I help Mama in the kitchen, getting dinner cleaned up. Daddy goes out and gets the animals bedded down for the night, Duke trotting after him.

Mama and I make our way out to the back porch and sit on the old porch swing. The creak of the chains and the clanging of metal in the garage are the perfect background.

"Alright, Kid. Lay it on me," Mama says as she curls up on the swing facing me.

"You couldn't give me a day before you started therapy?" I sass.

"Nope. I raised you, remember?" She looks at me with the practiced eye of a psychologist and a mother. "Kid, you haven't sat still since you learned how to move. You're about to vibrate out of your skin over there."

I take a deep breath and really look at her. Her blonde hair is turning grey. There are fine lines around her blue eyes from laughing and smiling. She's a tiny thing but would go toe to toe with a grown man twice her size.

My head falls back on the swing, and I let it out a heavy sigh.

I tell her every case, every call, every time a subject walked.

I tell her about the panic attacks and the feeling of being shredded.

The feeling that I'm failing at the one thing I've built my entire adult life around.

The best part about my mom being a psychologist is that she just listens. She doesn't judge, make pitying noises, or interrupt. She lets me get everything out.

When I'm done, I don't feel better. It's not a catharsis, just a statement of facts. Like this is happening to someone else, not me.

"Do you want the therapist or your mama right now?" she asks. Her posture is relaxed, but I can see the tension strumming under the surface.

"I don't know, Mama. I guess I didn't realize how bad it was until I came home."

"Kid, your brain is waving a white flag of surrender, but your body is still living in the trenches." She unfolds her long legs and reaches for her phone. "I want you to read an article that Cody wrote. It's about closing the parasympathetic stress loop through impact play."

My phone buzzes with her message. "Mama, I'm not interested in that kind of thing."

"Baby, it's not about kink. It's about learning to release the stress instead of letting it build inside you. It's about not white-knuckling your way through life." We watch as the shop lights start going off one by one.

"And if I don't want to read it?"

"Baby, no one is going to get you to do anything you don't want to do. We both know that." She stands to go inside. "But I think you might find some relief if you can figure out a way to close that loop."

I watch as she goes inside. I don't need to look at my watch to know what time it is. My parents had a rule: unless I was actively dying, ten pm was their time.

I pick up my phone and stare at the article like it's going to bite me. And it might.

But it could also help, and I'll take what I can get right now.

Bruise Chapter 2

Jesse

It's been a couple of days since I came home, and I already feel a lot better. Being around my parents who love me and catching up with old friends that I hadn't seen since I left Franklin has been good for me.

But that hasn't stopped the panic attacks.

I have been waking up in the middle of the night with nightmares. The haunted eyes of victims, the screams of parents, and the devil may care look of the subjects.

It's my third night at home, and I finally open the article that my mom sent me. My parents went to Obsidian for a ceremony and plan on staying the night.

I have the house to myself. Duke and I are sitting out on the back porch listening to the sounds of the mountains as I read.

I know enough about mental health and the nervous system to know that I don't know much about either. The department hosts various clinics throughout the year for their people to get help if they need it, but most of the time, we just ignore the booths.

I always figured that my mom is a therapist, that was good enough for me.

But as I read this article, I realize that maybe I need more help than I am willing to give myself.

The article talks about burnout, PTSD, dysregulation, and the stress loop. All things that I am starting to realize I have in some form. But that's not what has me sitting up straighter on the porch.

Cody talks about how BDSM in general can help regulate the nervous system, but more specifically how impact and edge play can either reset the nervous system or help close the stress loop.

Then he gets into the guts of how impact play re-regulates the nervous system. That the brain increases adrenaline and cortisol during the fight or flight response. That the system is supposed to rise, drop, and settle once the threat has passed.

But most people who are in high-stress jobs—*hello, detective*— never get the drop and actually settle. Because the threat never really passes. Most of the time, we stay stuck mid-cycle.

Stuck on the almost okay, almost steady, almost safe. The body trying to finish what the brain won't let go.

I lean forward, elbows on my knees, and breathe through my nose. Duke comes over and shoves his head between my collar and jaw. His fur is familiar and warm. I stay like that for a minute, soaking up his comfort.

I lean back on the swing, and Duke jumps up to join me, putting his giant head in my lap. And I go back to reading the article.

Cody talks about bringing in sensation, usually impact, to bring the amygdala back under control. That the brain has to have a clear signal that the danger is gone and it can rest. That signal is the steady tempo of impact—the rhythm, cadence, and breath.

He talks about how the Bottom is able to stop scanning because it found the threat and it's not as scary as the brain originally thought. That the tempo of the implement and the Top creates a safe place for the brain to actually rest.

But it's the highlighted line that gives me pause. *Pain isn't the point. Pattern is. Rhythm completes the loop.*

I stare at that line for another minute. Duke's gentle breathing brings me more comfort than I'm ready to admit that I need.

Cody goes on to explain edge play as well. That a controlled scene that suddenly activates the parasympathetic nervous system can purge a system that is overcharged. He talks about how a well-trained Top reads the body and not the words. How subspace isn't a weakness but the completion of the loop.

That it feels like the first safe, full inhale after too many months spent braced for impact.

And for the first time in years, I feel like the core of what I have been dealing with is on the big screen. Visible for everyone to see, but most importantly, I can see it.

I finish reading the article in a daze. For the first time, I have answers. I have a better idea of why my brain has decided not to work anymore. Why I was fine for years and suddenly I'm not.

I look down at the signature line of his article;

Cody Hale—Musician. Educator. Mentor. Impact Sadist.

Before I can think better of it, I click the link at the bottom and shoot off an email.

Hey, Cody,

Meredith sent me your article, and she thinks it could help me deal with some issues I've been having. I'm in town for the next week or so and would love to chat.

–Jesse

Before my phone screen goes black, there's an email notification waiting.

Jesse,

I'm glad Meredith sent you my article. I'm sorry you're going through hard shit right now. I'm available tomorrow morning if you want to meet at the coffee shop next to the winery off Johnson. Would 9am be too early?

–Cody

I wasn't expecting him to get back to me so quickly. In fact, I was hoping that he would get the email after I had gone back to Asheville. But maybe the universe has something different planned for me.

Cody,

I'll be there.

–Jesse

I arrive at eight forty-five the next morning and sit in my Mustang for a minute, trying to talk myself off the ledge. I can't believe that I'm even considering this as a viable option.

Most people go to therapy when they realize their brain is fucked up. Not me, nope. I run to the local dungeon at the behest of my Slave mother.

Fuck, I'm so stupid.

I'm getting ready to put my car in gear to go home when an old square-body Chevy pulls in next to me.

I look up at the driver and just about swallow my tongue. If this is Cody, I'm going to be royally fucked.

The man looking down at me from his truck is not what I had in mind when I pictured a music teacher at the high school. His brown hair is longer on top with a fade. He's got tattoos that just come over the collar of his t-shirt, and he's got both arms covered.

He's got just enough scruff on his face to be hot, but I can make out the cleft in his chin and if he smiles big enough, the dimples. His ears are gauged to at least an inch, and the plugs in them are the bass and treble clefs.

I can't see his eyes behind his aviator glasses, but I'm not sure I can handle seeing him look at me right now anyways.

"Jesse?" he asks, his deep voice sending a shiver down my spine.

"Hey, Cody," is all I can manage past my strained vocal cords. This would have been a hell of a lot easier if he looked like the rest of the frumpy faculty at the high school. Hell, this would be a lot better if I hadn't reached out to him last night in an obvious lapse in judgement.

"Regretting this already?" His eyebrow is arched, and it's devastating. He climbs out of his truck and opens my car door.

"Pretty much, yeah," I mumble as I climb out of my car. I thought that getting out of my car would make it better, putting us on a more even playing field.

It didn't.

I'm a tall woman standing at five foot ten, but Cody is a fucking giant. He's hovering somewhere between six five and an ice giant. I still have to crane my head back to look at his face, and I'm not a fan.

But damn if it isn't hot.

I've always gone for shorter guys, usually at or under six foot. I like to look my partner in the eye. But that's not what I'm getting with Cody.

"We're just talking, Jesse." He turns us so that we start walking to the coffee shop. "If you don't think I can help, then it's just friends catching up."

"We aren't friends, though," I tell him.

"Not yet," he says as he holds the door for me to go into the shop. He slides the aviators into his shirt collar, and I'm stunned by the deep chocolate brown of his eyes. Yup, totally fucked.

We step up to the counter, and I'm not really sure what I'm supposed to do with myself. I'm standing next to a smoking hot music teacher that is also a respected and educated Dom at my parents' sex club. And I'm asking him to help me regulate my nervous system so that I can go back to helping sexual assault victims.

We place our orders, black for me and some kind of frou-frou drink for him. I raise my eyebrow at him, and he just shrugs as he leads me over to a table further in the back. He takes the seat with his back to the wall, and I immediately start to panic.

"Your mom is Meredith." It's not a question, so I don't answer and just stare at him. He lets out a small laugh. "You can play stoic cop, or we can get to the meat of this and actually let me help you."

I peek over my shoulder when I hear the door to the shop open. When I realize it's just a customer, I turn my attention back to Cody. Those brown eyes are assessing me, like he just learned everything he needed with that one interaction.

"Let's start with this, Jesse. Why did you reach out to me at eleven thirty at night, when your parents were at the same club as me?"

"Temporary insanity?" I reply. It's good to know that my humor is still firmly in place.

"Have a good day, Jesse." He stands to leave, and as he walks past me, I grab his arm. He looks down at me, expression closed off.

"I was sidelined after a shitty case. My captain says that it's not discipline, but I can't help but feel like it is. I've spent my entire adult life working to get where I am, and I love my job. But I feel like a failure because I'm struggling with it mentally. Like I can't get my shit together."

I take a deep breath and finish it.

"I feel like I'm drowning, and I can't get my brain to stop screaming long enough to remind it that we know how to swim."

Cody sits back down. He folds his arms and leans against the table. "What part do you want help with? Remembering how to swim, or learning how to stop the screaming?"

"Aren't they the same thing?" I answer honestly.

A smile takes over his face, and for a second, I am struck dumb. Those dimples should be illegal.

"No, it's not the same. The brain and the mind are two sides of the same coin. The brain handles functions like breathing, sensing danger, reacting, and that kind of thing. The mind handles feelings like stress, happiness, and the like."

The barista calls our names, and he gets up to go get our drinks. He sits down and hands me my coffee. He takes a big sip of his drink and groans...and my body betrays me again.

"Right now, your mind is screaming that it's not okay. So your brain floods with chemicals saying, 'Swim, you idiot,' but your mind is so loud it can't hear your brain telling it to swim."

"That actually makes a lot of sense," I say as I take a sip of my coffee and try not to grimace at the bitterness. You'd think I'd be used to it after all my time drinking shitty cop coffee, but I'm not.

"Did you ever get involved in the kink community in Asheville?"

"No," I respond quickly. "Why?"

"You said that quickly. Are you ashamed of your parents' lifestyle?"

I feel like he hit my soul with that question. I want to lie and say no, that I'm not judgmental. But I really think about his question. Am I?

"I see it a lot with my students. When parents take up a lot of emotional space—even good, loving space—kids learn to shrink theirs. Not consciously. It's just a survival instinct. Your parents' love is big and obvious, so yours learned to go quiet and be contained. That's not wrong. It's just how your nervous system kept up."

"What does that have to do with being ashamed?" I ask, and yes, I am totally pouting.

"Once you realized what was behind that love, the twenty-four seven Master/Slave dynamic, you shut down your emotions. Not because you didn't love them, not because they didn't love you. But because you didn't understand, and you didn't really want to."

"...fuck," I mutter.

"Yeah, that's usually the response I get." He takes another sip of his drink. "Here's what I know and how I think I can help. Your nervous system isn't broken. In fact, I would go so far as to say that it's very active. It's just stuck. You don't allow yourself to feel things because it's dangerous. That's your mind screaming.

I want to get your mind to stop screaming long enough for your brain to get unstuck."

"What does that entail exactly?" I ask, suddenly really nervous.

"Well, that entirely depends on how quickly you want this to work. In my classroom, I have a metronome that plays in the background constantly. The tempo and volume never changes. You would be surprised how many kids come in and instantly their shoulders drop, like the weight of the world has lifted off them."

"How long does that take?"

"About three months on average." He puts his empty cup in the middle of the table.

My shoulders slump. "I don't have three months," I say quietly.

Cody studies me for a long minute—like he's trying to figure out if I'm ready to hear what he has to say next.

"The other way," he says quietly, "is you come to Obsidian and we have a scene. One where you are tied to my cross and forced to stand still and feel every bite of my flogger."

He looks me in the eye. His voice is quiet but unwavering when he drops it on me.

"And with every strike, your nervous system will finally finish the cycle it's been stuck in for years."

Bruise Chapter 3

Jesse

Tonight is the night that will either fix my brain, or break it the rest of the way. And either way, I'm ready. Because I can't keep living in this holding pattern.

I walk into Obsidian with my chin held high. I don't know what I expected, maybe to be treated like the prodigal daughter? Instead, I was treated with mild disinterest, and I was not prepared for that.

And I can't begin to explain how safe that feels.

I look around the club for Cody and find him standing next to his St. Andrew's Cross. He's wearing dark jeans, and a faded Henley shirt, the sleeves pushed up to show off those delicious tattoos.

I can't see who he's talking to. All I see is another giant tattooed man with black hair. I make my way over to him, and when he sees me, a grin stretches across his face.

That's when the second surprise of the night hits me, and I stop dead in my tracks.

Mr. Shepherd, my high school calculus teacher, turns around and laughs. I crushed so hard on him during my senior year, and now here he is, with no shirt on, covered in tattoos.

The same man who helped me through a panic attack during finals is standing next to the man that I've asked to flog me in an attempt to fix my brain.

I can feel my breathing kick up and I must have a look of pure panic on my face because Cody takes that exact second to come stand in front of me and place his hand on my chest, a firm hand moves to my jaw to tilt my head up to look at him.

He takes an exaggerated breath in. I follow his breath, letting it flow through me. We breathe for just a few moments before I see him give a small nod at someone behind me.

"Better?" he asks. His deep voice further grounds me.

I nod, and he looks at me like I'm a problem he's trying to solve. Whatever he sees on my face must be the right answer because he leads me over to the cross.

We had discussed in depth what would happen tonight, down to the aftercare. He explained that the length of the scene would be determined by my body's response to what we were trying to do.

If it took longer to get my brain unstuck, then it took longer. If we weren't getting anywhere, we would stop and find another way. He said that how I reacted to the pain would determine if he brought me to physical release as well as mental and emotional.

He said crying, screaming, cussing and arousal were all normal responses. That the entire point of this is to let all this shit out. Getting out the emotions that were stuck in my body.

Finally, he said that if anything got out of hand, I could stop it at any time with a simple *red*.

"Strip," he says gruffly as he picks up a small black box.

I reach for my t-shirt and pull it over my head. I unhook my bra and place both on the bench by the cross. I see his eyes dilate as he watches me. I've never been shy about my body. I look damn good, and I am proud of my figure. To be honest, I'm also thrilled about his reaction to it. It makes this attraction feel not so one-sided.

I shove my long blonde hair up into a messy bun and step up to the cross. He walks up behind me, his shirt brushing against my bare back, and a shiver works through me. His chuckle is low, and I feel the vibrations through my back as he secures my hands to the cuffs at the top of the cross.

"Not yet, Little One." He pulls away from me, and I feel the hard wood press against my breasts. He places a blindfold around my head, and I'm instantly plunged into darkness. My entire body tenses. "Color."

I hesitate, struggling with my need to see what's coming at me. I want to yank the blindfold off. I want to run away. "Yellow."

He places his hands on my ribs, his chest to my back, and takes another exaggerated breath in. I follow his breathing and within a few breaths, the feeling of rising panic eases a bit. "Color?" he asks again.

I take stock of where I am physically and emotionally. "Yellowish green."

He takes a step back. "I can work with that."

He places something by my head, and I hear the soft ticking.

"Your job is to breathe with that, in for two ticks, out for three. That's it."

My brain instantly starts to revolt, trying to drown out the rhythm. But I force it back and do what Cody told me. I breathe in for two and out for three. I continue on like that for a few minutes, focusing on the soft ticking.

Then the first strike comes. It's nowhere near as hard as I thought it would be. More like a gentle caress of leather against skin.

"Breathe, Little One," he says in a low voice. I let out the breath I was holding. "Good."

The strikes come with every third metronome tick. Steady. Rhythmic. Never any faster. Never any slower.

But the intensity grows. The pain of the flogger is intense, but there's an underscoring of pleasure. As the intensity continues to grow, so does the arousal and pleasure. I'm grinding against the cross trying to get just enough friction, but there's not enough to get myself off.

My brain starts screaming at me—that this is enough torture. The arousal, the pain, the blindfold, everything is too much. I am ready to call out red. But then something happens.

A switch is flipped, and I am floating.

It feels like every ounce of tension in my body has been flushed, and I am boneless. The arousal is still there, still sharp. But the tension is gone, and I feel like I'm flying.

I feel Cody come up behind me, hands on my hips and his chest to my back.

"You did so good, Little One. I'm going to help you with the rest of your tension, though. Is that okay?" Cody's breath is warm against my ear, and his deep voice drives me right up to the edge of my orgasm.

I whimper at the feel of his body against me, and I nod. I grind against him, my brain barely recognizing his hard cock pressed into my ass. My breathing picks up, and I feel his hand move from my hip to the front of my jeans. He presses against my clit, and with that one touch, I come undone with a scream.

He continues to apply gentle pressure against my clit until the rhythmic clenching subsides and I'm limp against him. The only thing holding me up are my wrists in the cuffs and him at my back.

He reaches up and unclips the cuffs from the cross and lifts me when I go boneless. He carries me to a couch and sets me on his lap. He wraps a soft blanket around me and undoes the blindfold.

I blink at the sudden burst of light to my sensitive eyes as he undoes the cuffs. He rubs my wrists, checking to make sure that blood is returning to my hands. Once he's satisfied, he positions me until I'm straddling him. My arms are tucked between us, and my head is tucked under his chin.

He pushes his hand into the hair at the back of my head and starts massaging. His other hand runs up my back gently. He holds me like that for a while, just breathing with me.

While it feels nice, it's nowhere near as amazing as the silence in my brain. There's no screaming, no haunted eyes, just blissful silence.

"Are you okay, Little One?" His deep voice is quiet.

"Shh," I tell him. "My brain is finally quiet, and you're ruining it."

I snuggle back in and grin when I hear his laugh. I think I get it now. This thing I've been rebelling against for years.

The next morning, I wake to a text message from Cody.

I'm proud of you, Little One. Take something for the pain if you need to.

I grin like a fool and send him an eyeroll emoji back. I get up and let out a groan. My back is stiff, not in a bad way, just enough to remind me about last night.

I get in the shower and let the warm water run down my back, taking my time through my routine. Suddenly, a thought hits me out of nowhere.

I didn't have a nightmare last night.

My first thought wasn't about checking my phone or my two week leave.

My brain isn't revolting, and my mind isn't screaming. The lack of anxiety is louder than the anxiety has ever been.

I finish up with my shower and get dressed at lightning speed. I grab my phone and shoot a text off to Cody.

How do you do this? I feel like a new person.

I head downstairs and find my parents cuddled up on the couch, watching one of my mom's shows.

"Hey, Kid," Daddy calls. "Want to help me work on the Bel Air today?"

"Yeah, I do." And for the first time since I was in middle school, I can't wait to get dirty in the garage with him. To do something that is enjoyable, not because of a deadline or catching a subject.

A while later, I hear the unmistakable sound of a small block 350 coming down the driveway. My dad shoots me a knowing grin before handing me a rag.

I step out of the garage, wiping my hands on an old shop towel, and see Cody pull in next to my Mustang.

"You busy?" he asks, his eyebrow raised at me. I look down at myself and see that my good jeans are covered in grease. "Never mind, that was a dumb question. I was coming to see if you wanted to get dinner."

I glance back at my dad and see him grinning like a fool.

"Let me get cleaned up." I turn back to the house and add a little extra sway to my hips.

"Take your time," he says as he walks up to my dad and shakes his hand. They start talking cars, and I know I've got plenty of time to get the grease and grit off me. My dad will have Cody talking about his truck for hours.

I walk inside and see my mom peeking over the back of the couch, looking at me with a smile on her face.

"I guess last night with Cody went well?" She's got that glint in her eye.

"Yeah, it did," I say as I start for the stairs to my room. "He's taking me to dinner."

"Good. Want some help getting ready?" The look on her face is hopeful.

"I would love some help, let me get this grease off me first."

"The body scrub you like is in the hall closet," she hollers.

It doesn't take me long to get cleaned up. And with my mom's help, my hair and makeup are soft but well done. She even managed to get my hair to actually curl. How she does it is beyond me.

I walk out of the garage in my favorite knee-high black leather boots, skin-tight jeans, and sweater that slips off one shoulder. Cody stops talking to my dad when he sees me, his breath hitching.

"Damn, Little One," he manages to get out. "You clean up nice."

"Thank you." He opens the passenger door of his truck and helps me in. "Don't wait up, Daddy."

My dad barks out a laugh and heads back into the garage, shaking his head.

The drive to town is quiet, but not in that awkward first-date way, more like the steady kind. We pull up to one of the small taverns that has a patio. The heaters are on, and there's a crowd at one of the large tables.

"Before we go in, I want to let you know, a group of us usually get together after club night to check in with each other. If you want to go somewhere else, we will. But I think it would do you some good to be around people that have zero expectations of you."

I think about what he said and how I feel right now. I've avoided socializing and people for years because everyone wanted to know what it was like to be a cop. It would dredge up work, and I would become an anxious mess.

But Cody brought me release last night, he could do it again. Plus, here in a week, I would be headed back to Asheville. Might as well figure out now if I can handle people.

"Alright, but if I need to bail, I'm out."

"Little One, if you need to bail, just tell me and we're out of here." His tone is so sincere that I can't help but believe him.

"Alright, then." He grins at me before climbing out of the truck and opening my door for me.

He helps me out of the truck and threads my arm through his. We walk through the patio entrance and his name is shouted in greeting. I freeze for just a second, but he notices.

He flexes his arm, forcing my hand against his ribs, and takes a big deep breath. I immediately follow that breath, and my heart rate lowers. He sits us next to Lock and a woman with dark auburn hair.

"Hey, Jesse." Lock grins at me. "This is Brin, my wife."

"Hey, sorry about last night. I wasn't prepared to see my math teacher at a dungeon."

Lock lets out a booming laugh. "I bet you didn't. I don't blame you, though."

Cody asks what I want to eat and orders it for me. At first, I didn't like it. But as I looked around the table, I realize that all the men ordered for their partners.

Then a couple bottles of wine start floating around the table, and I shake my head when it gets to me.

"Would you like something other than wine?" Cody asks quietly. I shake my head, but Cody isn't having any of that. "Words, Little One."

I huff a breath and look at him. "I don't like wine, it's gross."

Cody laughs. "Alright, would you like something else?"

"Do they have a local cider?"

Brin speaks up then and holds up her own bottle of hard cider. "This is what you want. It's caramel apple and absolutely divine."

I look at Cody. "I'll take that."

Brin smiles at me, and we launch into conversation about her shop and how she likes living in Franklin.

No one asks about Asheville, what it's like being a cop, nothing but acceptance.

Bruise Chapter 4

Jesse

Tomorrow, I go back to Asheville. The next day, I start back at work.

If you had asked me twelve days ago how I felt about my two week hiatus, I would have told you I was fine and I didn't need a break.

But now?

Now, I realize just how badly my brain needed the break. How much work had gotten to me. Another thing I realized is that I need someone to talk to that isn't on the job. Someone who isn't ass deep in the trenches, waving their own white flag.

I talked to Cody about it, and he had a few therapists that he suggested. All of them are trauma informed and ready to help with the heaviness of public safety.

But that wasn't the best part of the last two weeks.

The best part was finding ways to relieve the pressure valve in my brain before I went numb or burned out. Things that didn't include heading to a dungeon.

Cody had taken me hiking a few times in the last week, usually after he got off of work. We talked, and he taught me various grounding techniques that worked for him.

I had forgotten how much I enjoyed hiking, being around people, and generally being a functioning human being.

Cody even offered to sponsor my membership at Obsidian since it's only a little less than an hour drive from Asheville to Franklin. I didn't really know what to say to that, but I told him I would think about it. Baby steps are key for me right now.

I don't know what to call the relationship between Cody and me. It's grown while I've been in Franklin. And there is definitely something there. The way he watches me, the heat and desire in his eyes, isn't something that my mind made up.

Tonight, though, is my second scene with Cody. When we first talked about the first scene, he had warned that a second scene would be necessary to make sure that any residual tension was gone and that my brain could figure out how to unstick itself after a shitty case.

But I don't think the scene is only to do with my mental health. Especially not after the hot and heavy makeout session in the bed of his truck as we watched the sunset. I felt like a teenager again, and I want more of that.

As I approach the doors to Obsidian, I think back on the difference a week can make. When I first came here, I was expecting shame, judgement, and to be the prodigal daughter when I walked through the door.

And I knew better. The kink community is the least judgmental community. No one cares that I am Meredith and James' daughter, returning from Asheville. They care if I am safe, non-judgmental, and consensual.

And that's something I never thought I would be proud of.

I hand security the card that Cody had given me, and I am excited for the drop that is waiting for me. Security gestures for me to go inside, and I am immediately swallowed by the dim lights, heavy bass, and sounds of the dungeon.

Cody said to meet him at the same station as last time and I start making my way back there. I see my parents out of the corner of my eye. My mom is kneeling at my dad's feet on a pillow with her head bowed.

She doesn't see me, but my dad catches sight of me and gives the barest hint of a smile. He touches the back of my mom's neck in the same quiet cue I've seen a thousand times growing up, the signal for her to lift her head.

She turns just enough to see me, and her smile is warm and genuine before she lowers her gaze again and rests her cheek lightly against his thigh. The devotion there is unmistakable, and, for the first time in my life, not something that confuses me.

And that's something else I've realized in my two weeks at home. I don't have to understand it to support it. I finally understand what my parents had been trying to tell me all those years ago when I came to them with questions but not willing to hear the answers.

I walk to where Cody is waiting for me, the metronome already ticking time. He's dressed in leathers this time. Leather pants encasing his thick thighs, leather harness crossing his chest.

His tattoos are on full display, and I finally get to see him cleanly shaven. Those dimples when he smiles are big enough for me to curl up in.

Tonight, though, his cross is against the wall. It's to give me privacy as much as it is to provide me the ability to drop. He said he wants to give me the chance to learn how to ground and drop even with distraction.

I walk up to Cody and wait for him to give me my next instructions. He places a hot kiss to my mouth before ordering me to strip. I won't get fully nude, not while my parents are here. Granted, they are on the other side of the club, but it's still too close for any of our comfort.

I face the wall when I take off my shirt and bra. I place them on the bench next to the cross before pressing my chest against it. I lift my arms to the top of the cross and wait for Cody to secure my wrists in the cuffs.

He doesn't blindfold me this time, and I see the club moving in my periphery. I hear the soft ticking of the metronome by my head. Within seconds I'm already sliding into that fuzzy space that I'm learning to live for.

He presses his chest against my back. "Are you ready, Little One?"

I nod, already feeling my joints loosen.

The first strike is soft, barely a whisper of leather against flesh. I breathe in for two and out for three, letting the metronome take me away as he gathers intensity.

Now that I know what it feels like, the drop is damn near instant. I don't think he has gotten a full dozen lashes in before I am boneless against his cross.

He stops and comes up behind me. "Can you make it until I can get you to my apartment, or do I need to get the rest of this tension out?"

"Now, Sir," I beg. "I can't wait."

"Little One, you are on the verge of something I don't think either of us can stop. You better be sure." He caresses my arms before reaching up to unhook the cuffs from the cross.

I push my ass back against him. "Please," I moan.

He reaches to the front of my jeans and presses just hard enough to give me a taste of what's to come. But I'm already wound so tight, I come with a scream. Lights flash behind my eyes, and I can't stop grinding into his hand.

It's the most powerful orgasm I've had in my life.

"Please, Sir," I beg. "I need more."

He pulls me away from the cross and before I fully realize the change in position, he's got me over his shoulder and headed to the suites on the upper level of Obsidian. He's taking the stairs a sprint.

He uses his keys and opens the door. Then I'm on the bed, and he's ripping my jeans down my legs. I reach for the laces on his leather pants, but he pushes my hands away.

"Oh no, Little One. You've teased me enough over the last week. It's my turn now."

He undoes the buttons and zipper of my jeans and yanks them off before I can even move to help. He makes quick work of his leathers and has them off and across the room before I know what's happening.

He shoulders my thighs open and stares down at my bare pussy. He licks his lips and then dives in like he's been starving for years. He devours me—that's the only way I can describe how he falls on me.

He licks and bites my lips. He sucks on my clit, and within minutes I am right at the edge of another orgasm. He shoves two fingers into my cunt, and I feel like I'm about to come undone. "More," I beg again. I need more.

"So greedy," he murmurs against my cunt as he shoves his fingers into me and curls them towards my front wall and hitting that sweet spot inside me. A silent scream leaves me, my brain short circuits, and I'm floating again.

"Oh, my naughty Little One, squirting all over the bed," he praises. But my brain isn't working, it can't be if I squirted. I've never been able to do that.

He moves out from between my legs, wiping his mouth with his hand. But his chest is damp, and it's not from sweat. He opens the drawer of his nightstand and pulls out a condom.

He rolls it on and climbs up onto the bed. He leans down and presses a kiss to my mouth, his tongue forcing my lips to open. Like everything else tonight, he is savage. Pulling moans from me like it's the easiest thing in the world.

I wrap my legs around him trying to get him to fill me, but he won't. He just continues to kiss me until I've had enough teasing.

I roll him to his back and straddle him. I hold his thick cock up and slowly lower myself onto him. His thick, long cock nearly splits me open.

"You gonna ride me, Little One?" He lands a firm swat to my ass. "Then fucking ride me."

He grabs my hips in a punishing grip and sets a rhythm that is pure torture. My eyes roll into the back of my head, and I am one big ball of feeling and need. I feel every-fucking-thing and I can't imagine sex any other way ever again.

"What have you done to me?" I ask in a gasping voice, riding him hard and fast.

"Set you free, Little One," he grunts. "Now fucking come or you will be left waiting until next time."

He lands a few rapid-fire slaps to my clit, and I'm screaming like my soul is being purged from my body. My cunt clenches around him, trying to strangle his cock. He's right behind me, holding me still as he pumps jet after jet of cum into the condom.

I collapse onto his chest, tucking my face between his collar and jaw. I breathe him in, sweat and leather, the scent of us mixed in. A feeling of peace washes over me.

"You okay, Little One?" he asks, running his hand up and down my back before burying it in my hair.

"Why do you always have to talk after you scramble my brain?" I mumble against his throat.

He laughs into my hair, still massaging the back of my neck. "Because I want to make sure you are good."

"I'm fantastic, until you start talking. Then I want to stab you," I grumble.

"Noted," he says with a laugh. He wraps his arms around me, and we stay like that for a while.

I must have dozed off at some point because I jerk awake. I'm still snuggled into his chest, his breathing deep and even.

I look up at him, and he's still asleep, his lips barely parted.

"You could take a picture," he grumbles.

"I could, but I don't think it would do you justice," I sass back.

His arms squeeze around me, and I place my head back on his shoulder. I don't want to go back to Asheville. I want to stay right here.

"I'm scared to go back to work," I mumble into his chest.

"I'd be worried if you weren't scared. But you've got this, Little One. You know how to get unstuck," he says, his voice still gravelly from sleep.

"I know, but what if I can't get unstuck? What if my mind starts screaming again?"

"Then you use the metronome app you downloaded and call me. I'll talk you down every time."

"But—"

"But nothing." He uses his finger on my jaw to bring my face up. "You are borrowing tomorrow's troubles. We will face tomorrow, tomorrow."

"You make it sound so simple," I grumble. I wish I could achieve that level of Zen, but I am a chronic worrier.

"It is that simple, just not right now for you. And that's okay. We'll get you there," he says simply. "Now, let's get you home. You've got a big day tomorrow."

I didn't know it then, but that morning would become the first of several turning points for me. Not once had my heart rate spiked. There was no panic, no tension, no anxiety. Just a quiet confidence. Peace. Safety.

When I came back from my break, my captain had given me good news. We were all going on rotation for on-call status. No more random calls in the middle of the week. If we were on call, we would get dispatched. If we weren't, we wouldn't be bothered.

That helped spread the workload across all the detectives.

I've been at work for a week now, and I was sent to the hospital last night around three am. A woman had been assaulted, and I was not only helping her through it, but also gathering evidence to put the subject behind bars.

Last month, it would have caused a total systemic meltdown that I would have to white knuckle my way through. Now, I am able to honor my own boundaries and not bleed myself dry on every case.

Cody is coming up this weekend. He texted me a map of all the breweries and tap houses he wants us to hit. Since my apartment is so close to downtown, we can walk to all of them.

I get to see my parents more, and I am settling into my new routine.

I've got a ton of work left to do, but now it feels more manageable.

He takes her, but gives everything back.

Wild Obsidian: Taken

Vic Raven

Trigger Warnings

TAKEN

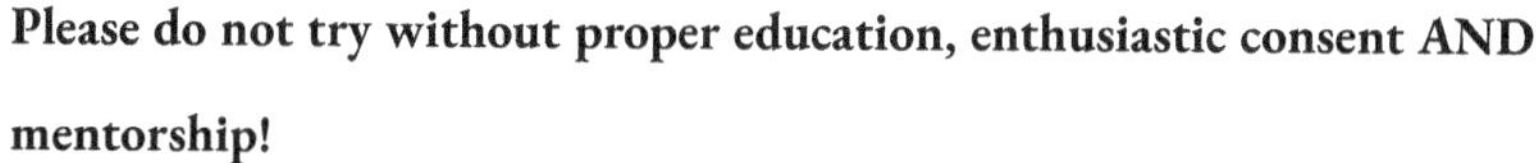

Please do not try without proper education, enthusiastic consent AND mentorship!

Please do not read if until you have read the trigger warnings!

ON PAGE Consent non consent (CNC)

Off page mention of rape; marital and roofie'd

Chase/ Primal

Talk of religious trauma

Anal penetration

Taken Chapter 1

Becca

Today, I will either be committed to a psychiatric hospital or finally move past the trauma that has shaped my life for the last ten years. It's really a toss-up at this point.

Last week, I talked about using consent-non-consent with my therapist. While I had done a fair amount of research into it, I wasn't totally sold on the idea that this was a viable option for a rape survivor.

CNC didn't make a lot of sense to me, but other rape survivors said that it helped them overcome the trauma and allowed sex to be okay again. And I desperately want to be normal...whatever that is.

My therapist looked at me like I had grown another head, but after taking a second to gather her thoughts, she asked what I knew about CNC. I told her that basically I was consenting to being raped.

She just shook her head and said that is why I didn't understand how it was a viable tool for survivors. CNC is much more than that. In fact, she said that if I were to talk to someone about CNC and said that, a good practitioner would run away screaming. She also said that if I said it like that to someone and they didn't run away, I should be really worried.

When I asked her about the research done about CNC, she told me that not only can CNC extremely therapeutic for rape survivors but just about all of BDSM can be therapeutic to all traumatized and neurodivergent people.

We continued to talk about it for the rest of the session, and I walked out with more questions than answers. But she suggested going to an Obsidian munch or class and just talk to the people there.

I was shocked that she would suggest that I go to a sex club. But I figure after seeing her for the last seven years and seeing the progress that I've made in that time, I can trust her. She told me to tell them that Beth sent me, whatever that means.

I get out of my car in the club parking lot. I'm nervous, but after everything I've been through, this is nothing. I walk towards the doors with my head high, my heels clicking on the ground, and the summer breeze pulling at my sundress. I left my long, brown hair down today, and now I am regretting not having it pulled back in my signature messy bun.

I'm not sure what I expect when I walk in, but seeing normal people in normal clothes isn't it. No leather, no masks, no whips or chains swinging from the ceiling—just a handful of people talking like old friends and a folding table at the entryway. The sign says to "sign in," and I freeze. Do I really want my name on record at a sex club?

One of the women behind the table must see my hesitation. "You don't have to use your real name," she says kindly. "Just whatever you're comfortable with—and your pronouns, so people know how to address you."

I let out a breath I didn't realize I was holding. Okay. Still strange, but slightly less terrifying. I scrawl "Becca" on the tag, stick it on my dress, and try to pretend this is just another conference check-in. This is beyond odd—but maybe odd is exactly what I need.

They point me in the direction of the tables, explaining that lunch is buffet style and to help myself.

I nod and walk towards the tables that have been set up classroom style. I notice a woman flanked by two men chatting with another woman with her back to me. I also see a line of people along the back wall filling their plates. This is shaping up to be the weirdest thing I've done in a hot minute.

One of the women at the front notices me and waves me over. As I walk over, I see that Beth is the other woman that I couldn't see.

"Hey, Becca, I'm glad you made it." Beth gives me a quick hug and turns us back to the group. "This is Maris, Rhett, and Cam. Maris is our educator here at the club and is putting on the class today."

"Oh," is all I can say. I'm shocked. Not because of Maris, but because my therapist is at a sex club munch.

She takes my arm and pulls me off to the side.

"I have to be very careful in my line of work. If the boards in this state think that I am sending people to a BDSM club, my license will be pulled. However, if you just so happen to walk into a munch, then that is circumstantial...does that make sense?"

"I understand, I'm just a little shocked is all. I am trying to process what I'm seeing," I say, gesturing to the space.

"Did you think there would be leather, whips, and chains?" She chuckles. "We save those for demo or club night."

My eyes must bug out of my head because she laughs harder.

"Becca, it's okay. I know that you had a sheltered upbringing, and I know that this must be really weird for you. But I promise, this is the best place for you to get the information for what you want. I am absolutely terrified that if left to your own devices, you will end up hurt again. Coming here, to Obsidian, means that the danger to you is minimal."

"I'm okay. I just don't know that I was expecting *this*."

"It's okay to be overwhelmed. I would be concerned if you weren't. I'm sitting on the edge of the second row, if you want, you can sit with me. If not, no pressure. But today's class is the reason I suggested this munch."

With that, she walks back over to Maris and starts chatting. I put my purse down by hers and go to the buffet line. It's a good spread and I load up my plate. As I reach for the salad dressing, a hand grabs it before I do.

I look up and see a tall man with black hair and green eyes talking to another man in line. He's wearing a button down black shirt with the sleeves rolled up his forearms and tucked into his jeans. He's tall, over six foot, with an athletic build. I'm getting ready to say something when he turns his head and sees me. He freezes, just for a second.

"I'm sorry, I wasn't paying attention when I grabbed it. Here," he says and hands me back the bottle.

"Thank you," I say, and when I'm done, I hand it back to him.

He continues to stare at me, and I wiggle the bottle in an effort to get him to take it. He takes it from me slowly. "Where are you sitting?"

"I'm in the second row, on the edge," I tell him. One of the things that I'm really good at is wearing a mask of complete confidence when I'm in new situations. It is a skill that has come in very handy over the years. Because outside I am a calm, confident woman. Inside, I am a nervous wreck.

I take my plate to the table and sit down. It's not long before Beth comes and sits next to me. We chat as we eat and wait for the class to start. As we are talking, Beth looks over my shoulder, and a smile takes over her face.

She gets up and rushes around me, giving the man from the buffet line a hug. He lifts her up with arm, balancing his food with the other. Beth hangs there for a second before he puts her down.

"Becca, this is Derrick. Derrick, Becca," she gushes. "I'm so glad that you're teaching this class with Maris, Derrick."

"I wouldn't miss it for the world." He looks over at me. "Mind if I sit down and eat before we get started?"

I nod and scoot my chair over a touch. I look back at Beth and she looks giddy.

We continue talking as Maris walks up to the front of the room.

"Good afternoon, everyone." She raises her voice to be heard over everyone and almost immediately everyone stops talking. "Today is a special treat. Derrick is here to talk to you guys about one of my favorite topics, consent-non-consent."

The whole room erupts in applause, and my heart stops. I turn and look at Beth, and she gives me a guilty smile.

Derrick gets up and walks to the front of the room. "Good afternoon, y'all. For those that don't know me, my name is Derrick and I am an attacker."

He pauses and looks right at me. I turn to Beth and whisper, "Did you tell him?"

"No, Becca. I would never do that. But he has a sixth sense about these things and he's taken a liking to you," she whispers back.

Derrick launches into his talk about consent-non-consent, and the different variations of it. He talks about what it means to be hunter/prey and captor/captive. He talks about the art of negotiations, and how important they are for both the Top and Bottom.

Finally, as the discussion starts winding down, he talks about what both the Top and Bottom get out of the scene. He looks directly at me as he goes into the gritty details of power exchange, the difference between non-con, CNC, and actual rape.

I feel myself becoming aroused under his direct stare, hearing him talk about the hunt and chase. The way he talks about breaking into a home or chasing someone through the woods. Pinning them down and taking their choice away.

But he isn't really taking their choice away. The scene is negotiated down to the most minute of details. The control rests completely and solely with the Bottom. They carry the most mental and physical risk.

The Top is the facilitator of the scene, but carries the most legal risk.

And that is the consent. That is the P.R.I.C.K.

Derrick opens the floor for questions, and my mind blanks. I'm not as confused as I was before. I can see how negotiating even the smallest of details and both parties agreeing to them takes the victim narrative away. It gives power back to the victim—or survivor.

Beth looks at me and tilts her head, asking silently if I have anything to add. I shake my head. I need a minute, or year, to process what I have learned today. My mind has been cracked open and everything I thought I knew about sexuality, trauma, and healing has been scrambled.

Derrick finishes questions, and Maris takes over, offering the prey or captive viewpoint. He comes back over to his seat. "Was that educational enough?" he whispers in my ear.

"Very," I respond. I can smell his cologne: citrus with sage and a hint of lavender. "I still have a ton of questions, though."

He nods but turns back to Maris and listens to her portion of the talk. It's not long before she wraps up and everyone breaks into groups to chat and relax.

"I would love to talk with you more about CNC and non-con, but I have a meeting to get to. Beth has my number, and I'd like for you to call me when, or if, you are ready."

With that, he gets up and heads out of the building. I watch him go, my panties uncomfortably damp and my mind spinning.

Beth taps me on the shoulder and gestures for me to follow her. She gets Maris' attention and gestures to one of the tables in the back. Maris nods and untangles herself from Rhett and Cam.

We all reach the table in the back and sit down. But Maris doesn't talk and instead settles on the chair. She seems really uncomfortable, and Beth starts talking first.

"Maris, I want to talk to you about being prey. It's something that I've been thinking about for the last couple of months, but I'm not really sure where to start," Beth lies through her teeth. I'm grateful, though. I don't think I would have had the lady balls to bring this up on my own.

Maris looks at me and then Beth. She nods and starts talking. Slow at first and then with more and more excitement. She talks about the first time she talked to her husband, Rhett, about it.

How he voiced his concerns about her past sexual trauma from her family. How they negotiated and talked until they had every single detail planned out. She said that it was the most cathartic scene she had ever had because it was hers to control. She knew that she could stop it at any time.

She said the aftercare afterwards was the best because the man that she felt safest with was there to bring her back.

She continues to talk about how now she loves being chased through the woods and captured by her men. That sometimes she does the chasing. That being prey doesn't mean that you're weak, just that you got caught.

And being caught isn't a bad thing.

"Does that answer your question?" She looks right at me as she asks Beth.

"I think so. If I have more questions, I'll reach out."

With that, we leave the table, and watch as Maris walks back to her men. They wrap her up in a hug, sandwiching her between them. The love they share is obvious and heart-melting to witness.

"I want you to really think about what you've seen and heard today. I'll text you Derrick's number, and I want you to talk to him. You don't have to agree to anything, just talk."

"Okay." We walk over to the table and grab our purses. I dig out my car keys. "Same time next week?"

She laughs. "No, our normal time at my office on Monday."

"Sorry, it's a habit." I laugh.

Taken Chapter 2

Becca

It's been a few days since the munch, and my brain has processed a lot of the information since then. I texted Derrick when I got home after the munch and we chatted long into the night multiple times. Thankfully, I work as a freelance editor from home, so the lack of sleep isn't a big deal.

Today is the first day of our negotiations, and I am nervous. I want to do this. I *need* to do this. But I am terrified that I will end up in a worse position than where I started. But I feel stagnant, like I can't move on, and I desperately want to move on. I want to date, I want to have sex, I want to not be terrified of men.

I drive up to the restaurant where I am meeting Derrick, and I see him waiting outside for me. He's in dark-wash jeans and another button down shirt. The sleeves are rolled up again, showing his muscled forearms, but this time, it's a dark green shirt and he's wearing a black leather vest.

His black hair is slicked back, and the sides are skin short. His beard is trimmed to stubble on his face, and he looks delectable. I park my car and he starts walking toward me. Derrick opens the door and helps me out of the low-slung car.

"I didn't peg you for a muscle car kind of girl," he says, taking stock of my blacked-out Challenger.

"Would it surprise you more that Hecate is a manual or that I actually know what's under the hood?" I ask. I'm not offended. Most women don't really know their cars. But I'm not most women.

"Hecate, huh. That is the perfect name for her." He looks impressed and closes the car door. "Lock it," he says gruffly.

I raise my eyebrow at him but hit the clicker, a chirp answers us.

He places his hand on my lower back and leads me to the restaurant. I'm not really sure how I feel about a man touching me. But if I'm going to ask this man to break into my home and fuck me, I should probably get used to it.

He opens the door for me and tells the hostess that we have a reservation. I watch as the hostess eye-fucks him and ignores me. She continues to flirt with him, and I'm getting ready to say something when he shuts her down. Hard.

"Ma'am, I'm here with her. Please just seat us." His shut-down is polite but direct, and I am secretly thrilled that he didn't play into her flirting. It makes me feel special that he handled it so I don't have to.

The hostess scoffs at me but grabs our menus and leads us to our table. It's in the back corner of the restaurant, away from other people. He helps me into my seat before placing his bag next to my purse on the chair beside us.

The waiter comes by and drops off our waters before taking our drink order: a beer for Derrick and a glass of wine for me.

"What do you do for work?" he asks while looking over the menu.

It's an innocent question, but it's suddenly hard to answer. "I'm a freelance editor."

"Really? For what genre?" I have his total attention now, those dark green eyes match his shirt, sharpen on me. That inky black hair is starting to fall in front of his face.

"This and that. Really whatever pays the bills," I tell him. I'm not sure how I explain that I edit romance. Sure, I do the occasional non-fiction or young adult, but for the most part romance is my bread and butter. Most men think that romance is written porn, and I don't know him well enough to know how he will react.

The waiter takes that time to come up with our drinks and ask if we've decided what to eat. Derrick places an order for appetizers. I'm ready to order, but he seems to want to take his time.

"Okay, so you're an editor. What else do you enjoy?" He takes a quick sip of his beer.

"Uh, I don't really do anything else. I enjoy editing and I dabble in writing, but that's really it. What do you do?" I ask, trying to get the spotlight off me.

"The short answer is that I'm a psychologist by trade and have a couple of journals and papers published. The long answer is that I was sexually assaulted when I was in college. A girl roofied me at a party after I told her no repeatedly. When I woke up the next morning, I was sick, dizzy, and couldn't remember anything from the night before."

He looks at me like he's trying to get a read on me. Like he has told this story before, and no one believes him. But I do. I know what it's like to not have people believe you.

"What did you do?" I ask with a calmness I don't feel. Instead, all I feel is rage that his choice was taken from him. Just like mine was.

"I went to the emergency room and told them what happened. No one really believed me, *because men can't be raped*. But one nurse did. She stuck with me the whole time."

He takes a deep breath and continues, "I don't drink heavily. I am a two beer max kind of guy and always have been, even in college. The doctors did a toxicology report, and it came back that I had been drugged with Rohypnol. Unfortunately, there was no way to prove who did it because there wasn't any evidence."

"I'm so sorry, Derrick." I reach across the table and put my hand on his. I understand his pain, not as a man, but as someone who has survived too.

"So I went to therapy. I stopped hanging out at parties and I changed my major. I was going to be an investigative journalist. But after what happened, I knew I wanted to help others who had been hurt too."

"So you're a trauma therapist?"

"Again, the short answer is yes. But the long answer is that I pretty much help anyone dealing with sexual issues. I have clients that are rape or assault survivors. I have clients that struggle with repression from culture, religion, or childhood traumas. If it deals with sexuality, I have a hand in it."

"Is that how you know Beth? Was she a patient or your therapist?" I know I'm digging for information, but I don't know if I can have sex with a man that my therapist had sex with.

Derrick laughs. "No. I know Beth from college. She was friends with a lot of my classmates, and we did a couple of projects together. We became friends and have stayed in touch over the years. When I moved back to Franklin from Ashville, we caught up. Plus, she is madly in love with her girlfriend."

I sat back, stunned. I had no idea that Beth is lesbian. Not that it matters to me, but I had no idea. Which I guess is the point. Therapists have to remain closed off and professional. Otherwise, they can't be effective in helping their clients.

"Now that I've given you my down and dirty, what makes you want to try CNC?" He asks it like he's asking about the weather. Like it's no big deal.

"Uh, well..." I swallow hard. This isn't something I usually share with someone I don't really know. But if I want to do this, if I want to try to take my life back,

I need to speak up. I need to tell him what I want. “Short story is that seven years ago, my ex-husband broke into my house, beat the shit out of me, and then raped me after I had sex with another man.”

Derrick’s face morphs from interest to fury. His jaw tightens and his eyes darken.

“And the long answer?” he asks gently.

“The long answer is that I was raised in a controlling home that was deeply rooted in religion. I was raised to marry the pastor’s son when he came back from college. The day I graduated high school, I was married to him. The abuse started immediately, but since I grew up with it, it didn't seem weird to me."

I take a minute to collect myself. I am trying to keep this short and concise, but it's hard to condense years of trauma and abuse into a few sentences.

"But one night, I was late with dinner. I had been dealing with hellacious nausea from the minute I got pregnant and was running behind. He grabbed me by the hair and beat me until I lost consciousness. I woke up in a pool of my own blood. I called 911 and they took me to the hospital. I gave birth to my nineteen week old baby girl alone."

I look up at him, waiting for him to tell me to stop. But the look on his face is a mix of fury and compassion. Derrick takes my hand in his and rubs his thumb across my knuckles. It gives me the strength to continue.

"I left him and pressed charges. The state wouldn't charge him though. He was a pastor and I am just a woman. So I moved out of state. I started seeing a therapist and was getting better. I started dating after a couple of years, and when I finally found someone I felt safe enough to have sex with, my ex-husband broke into my house, beat me, and raped me. This time though, I wasn't in a state that took the man's side. The state charged him and with my testimony, his record, and the evidence, he was sentenced to fifteen years."

"And now?" he asks gently. His hand never removes from mine.

"Now, I am ready to get the rest of my life back. I want a husband and family, but I can't stand the touch of most men. I don't trust that when he gets out, he won't come looking for me. I read a couple of articles about CNC and did some research. I've been doing a ton of research and a lot of introspection over the last year, and I'm ready."

With that, he nods. Our waiter takes that time to come up and take our order. He says the appetizers will be out in a few minutes. When he leaves, Derrick looks at me. I'm not sure what I see in his eyes. There's compassion and understanding, but also fury and maybe a little bit haunted too.

"I want to help you, and I think I can. But first, I have to talk about some of the things that I do and how I do a scene before we go any further. This isn't something that I play with because my freedom is extremely important to me."

The waiter drops off the appetizer and plates and leaves again.

"I am an *attacker*. Basically, that means after we negotiate the scene, I will break into your house when you give me the signal. I will be rough with you. I will do to you the things that you need and want. Nothing that you don't consent to will be done. If you don't want my hand around your throat, it won't be. If you don't want me to pin you down on your stomach, that won't happen. But

I will be rough, I will hurt you, and I will fuck you. If you safe-word, we will stop. Period. When we are done, I will take care of you in the way that you have indicated you want."

I realize that I have started panting and my panties are soaked. But I manage to nod, and he continues.

"However, in order for your experience, and by extension mine, to be pleasurable, healing, and ultimately positive, you will have to be willing to push your boundaries. If you struggle with touch, you have to realize that I will be touching you. If you have a problem with choking, you are tying my hands and not allowing me to offer you everything that you want and need. Tonight is not about negotiations, that's another night. Tonight is about setting expectations for both of us."

"Okay." I pause as the waiter sets down our dinner and clears away the appetizer. I didn't realize that we had both eaten everything while we were talking. "What if there's something that I just can't do?"

"Then we don't do it. Are you familiar with RACK or PRICK?" he asks as he cuts into his grilled chicken.

"Risk Aware Consensual Kink and Personal Responsibility Informed Consensual Kink?" I tell him. I bite into my cheesesteak and moan.

He laughs at my antics but nods. "Yes. Do you understand what it means?"

"I think so. Basically, that both of us walk into a scene or situation where we understand the risks associated with what we are doing. If someone was to sign up for an impact scene, they know, understand, and consent to being hit or doing the hitting. For us, I have to understand and consent to you forcing the scene that we agreed upon, trusting that you will stop when I say stop."

"More or less. My expectation of you at this point is to make sure that you are clear on what you are getting into and what I am getting into. I also need you to understand that this isn't going to happen anytime soon. There is a lot of negotiation that goes into this, and I'm not willing to rush this and hurt you."

I let out a relieved breath. I didn't realize that I had been expecting this to happen quickly. That we would have negotiations tonight and then tomorrow night he would be breaking into my house.

"I'm really glad to hear that," I tell him. With that, I work on finishing my meal. The cheesesteak really is divine.

He finishes his meal and his beer and leans back in his chair. "Are you open to homework?"

I nod because my mouth is full. I've always been an enthusiastic eater. It was something that I had rediscovered through therapy. I love food, but when I was growing up and then married, food was fuel for our bodies and nothing more.

My weight was constantly managed, first by my father and then my ex-husband. The first thing I did after getting divorced was gorge myself on all the food I had been missing out on.

"This week, I want you to revisit that night with your ex. I want you to really think about the things that he did to you. I want you to think back on the perceived shame of finding that you were aroused by something. Maybe his hand around your throat or him pulling your hair. I want you to think about things that trigger you, really trigger you. Like a smell, the sound of glass breaking, anything. If you see Beth, talk to her about this. She is well-versed in CNC and can help you navigate a lot of this."

I wipe my mouth with my napkin and finish my glass of wine. "I don't like this homework."

He laughs. "I know, but when we talk again next week, I need to know the answers to these questions. Plus, this will let me know that you are taking this seriously and that I can trust you."

With that, Derrick pays the check, and we head to the front of the restaurant. He keeps his hand on my lower back as we leave the restaurant. When we make it to my car, he opens the door and helps me inside. I start the car and roll down the window.

"Same time next week?" I ask with a laugh.

"Same time next week," he returns with a smile.

Taken Chapter 3

Becca

THE LAST SEVERAL WEEKS have been really bizarre, but in a good way. Before my divorce, my ex hadn't given a single fuck about what I wanted sexually. The church believed that a woman wasn't supposed to enjoy sex, and if she orgasmed, it was a mark of evil.

I have never in my life put so much thought into sex. Did I even like sex, what made me feel good, did I know my sexual orientation, had I ever had an orgasm... These thoughts and questions and more had been brought to the table over the last several weeks since Derrick and I started negotiating the CNC scene.

And even after all the research I have done on BDSM, CNC, and kink in general, I don't really have answers to these questions. I have been leaning heavily on Beth to help me find answers, and it is maddening. I just want someone to tell me what to do, what to feel.

Unfortunately, that's not how any of this works.

But I did learn a lot about myself over these last couple weeks, and I have a feeling I am going to keep learning. But instead of feeling like a failure because most women my age have figured out what they wanted sexually, I feel liberated.

Like the weight of all the childhood, religious, and marital trauma I have been through is lifting.

Tonight is the final negotiations with Derrick. Though he did say that it would depend on how tonight goes. He has been very thorough, asking if I have ever had anal sex, had an orgasm, or even masturbated. He even asked if I had a recent STI/STD checkup.

Since I haven't had sex in over seven years, the answer was a resounding no. But he insisted that I get one done. I had never felt so anxious as I did waiting for those results. But when they came in, I breathed a sigh of relief and then emailed them to him. He sent me his, dated the week prior.

It got me thinking about whether he would be using a condom and he said yes, but a condom doesn't protect against all STIs.

We talked about birth control and the morning after pill, whether or not I have been using penetrating toys to masturbate, and more. I told him that I'm not on birth control since I'm not sexually active, and he requested that I start. It isn't a hard limit for him, but it is an extra layer of protection.

When he mentioned getting the morning after pill, I had to really think about if that is something I am comfortable with. I decided that I am more uncomfortable getting pregnant, and got the pill.

I didn't really understand a lot of his questions and I ran them by Beth during our sessions. While Beth is a sexual trauma therapist, I don't think she was expecting to have give a sex ed class to a twenty-nine-year-old woman. To be honest, I didn't realize how deficient my education was.

I went to a private Christian school in Utah and married a pastor right out of high school. My sexual education was severely lacking. But I am catching up now.

I mentioned a safe-word to Derrick, and he said that he wasn't a fan of a word. He preferred to use the stoplight method. He said that if I wanted to use a safe-word, then we could use one, but sometimes, especially in CNC, it was hard to remember safe-words. But everyone remembers a traffic light.

He also told me to use hand signals or tapping. One was the same as green. Two was the same as yellow, and so on. I actually think that is really smart. I'm probably never going to remember to yell out *pineapple*.

When I brought that little tidbit to Beth, she agreed, but said that it was up to me. She also brought up that if I started shouting random words, Derrick would stop because obviously I wasn't okay. That made me feel a lot better, too.

I am just finishing up getting ready when there is a knock on the door. Derrick offered for me to come to his place or for us to meet in public, but I wanted to be in my own space tonight.

I look through the window and see his Harley sitting at the curb. I didn't know he rode, and now I like him even more. I wonder how shocked he'll be when he sees my Scout sitting in the garage next to the Hecate.

I open the door and he's holding his helmet in one hand and a bag of takeout in the other. His black hair is a mess and flops into his face. He shaved his face clean, and I feel my pussy spasm.

"Hey, Pretty Girl." He holds up the back of takeout. "It's splurge night, and I got all the goodies."

I step back to let him inside, and I melt a little. He started calling me *Pretty Girl* after our second meeting, and I decided then and there that I was a nickname girl.

"What kind of goodies? Are they my kind of goodies or yours?" Derrick is extremely health-conscious. Every time we have dinner, it's been lean proteins like chicken or steak and vegetables. Minimal carbs, never dessert, and only one beer.

"How do you know that my goodies aren't your goodies?"

"Please, I've seen how you eat. I highly doubt that you are going to be wolfing down a burger and fries."

He laughs and holds up the bag. "Not a burger and fries, but they opened up a new Thai place by my house and I wanted to try it. You said you loved Pad Thai, so I got the house Pad Thai for you. Beef Pad See Ew for me."

My mouth waters. I show him where he can put his helmet and motorcycle jacket, which is right next to mine.

"You ride?" he asks, clearly shocked.

"Since I moved to North Carolina. Duchess is in the garage."

"Can I see it?" He looks like a kid in a candy store. His excitement amps up mine, and I grin.

"Follow me." I lead him to the back of the house, to the garage door, and open it up. Next to my Challenger is my Indian Scout, blacked out just like the car. He walks over to her and takes her in.

"You are full of surprises, aren't you?" He grins at me. "If I had known you rode, I would have taken you to my favorite spots."

He continues to walk around the bike, taking in all the accessories I've added over the years. I'm about to give him the rundown on her when my stomach lets out a howl.

"Let's get you fed, Pretty Girl," he says with a laugh. He places his hand on my lower back, and we head back to the living room. He opens up the bag and starts taking out containers. I smell the spice, lime, and peanuts.

I head into the kitchen for a beer for him and a cider for me. When I get back to the living room, he has removed his boots and placed them by the front door.

He hands me my Pad Thai and a pair of chopsticks, and I hand him his beer. Derrick sits next to me on the couch with his own container, and we tuck in. We trade bites of our meals, and I realize that his spice level is significantly lower than mine, if his coughing is anything to go by.

Once we are finished eating, he cleans up and takes everything to the trash. When he gets back, he stops at his book bag to grab a notebook. I tilt my head in question.

"Every time you and I talk about what you want, what I want, your boundaries, etc., I write it all down. I don't want to miss anything and I don't want to accidentally trigger you during a scene."

"Well, I'm glad that someone is tracking this," I joke.

"This is really important to me. I don't take this lightly. Not only is your mental health on the line, but so is my freedom. I don't want to fuck that up."

He sits back down next to me and turns so that he's facing me. He opens the notebook to the first page, and we start going over everything that we have talked about over the last six weeks.

At this point, I'm not as surprised that he is so thorough. Since we started these negotiations, he has brought up things that I had totally forgotten we've talked about.

When he gets to my hard limits, he stops. "Has anything changed with this? Do you want to add to this or change anything?"

"The hair pulling is still a hard limit. It's just not something that I can handle. That's how my ex would grab me before he beat me. Anal is a softer limit now though. My concern with that is I don't have any experience with it. I'm on the fence about breaking glass. We talked about how my ex broke into the house when he raped me. But if I am doing this for healing, I wonder if it would be a good idea to do it so that I can take that noise back. So it doesn't scare me anymore."

Derrick is making notes in his notebook but stops on that last part. "I don't think this will be the time to work through taking that noise back. You are already going to be stretching your limits by doing the scene."

I nod, and we continue working through his notebook. As he reaches the end of his notes, my panties are drenched and I am panting. Derrick has shifted a few times. This happens to me every time we have negotiations. When I get home afterwards, I have to pull out one of my toys to take the edge off.

Derrick closes the notebook and puts it on the coffee table. He leans back into the couch and runs his hands through his hair. "Come here," he growls.

My heart stops for a split second and then starts galloping. I take stock of where I am mentally and emotionally: aroused, safe, trusting. I take stock of my body: nipples hard, shallow breathing, panties soaked. I ask myself, *Do I want this?*

I decide that I do, and I get up and move to stand between his legs. He leans forward and runs his hands up my thighs. He nuzzles his face against my cunt. He inhales deeply. "I have been smelling your arousal for the last two hours and it's been driving me insane."

His grip is firm on my thighs but not bruising. "If you don't want this, tell me to stop."

When I nod, he jerks me down and I straddle him. He moves his hands to my hips and up my sides. He continues until he has my breasts palmed in his hands, his thumbs feathering across my nipples.

I moan and arch my back to push my breasts further into his hands. "Harder," I groan. He starts pinching my nipples and I moan louder.

I place my hands on either side of his face and drag his face up so I can kiss him. His lips are soft but firm. I run my tongue over the seam of his lips and he opens. When his tongue brushes mine, he turns savage. He flips us so that I am lying on the couch and he is over me.

He grinds against me, and I raise my hips to meet him. It feels delicious and I am close to coming. His mouth is back on mine, and I need just a touch more friction and I will be coming.

"No, Pretty Girl. You aren't allowed to come until I say so," he growls in my ear and pulls away from me.

I want to scream in frustration. I am so close.

But then he shocks me. His hands move to the waistband of my leggings and start to tug them off. I stiffen.

"Give me a color, Pretty Girl."

I take stock of where I am. Did I stiffen because I don't want this or because I haven't done this in a long time?

After a minute, I tell him, "Green."

His eyes shine with pride, and he nods. He continues to work my leggings off, taking my underwear with them. "Good girl."

My heart melts, and my skin prickles as his hands trace my mound. He lowers his face to my cunt. He inhales again, breathing in my arousal. Derrick lets out a guttural growl when his fingers slip through my folds and finding me soaking wet.

I buck my hips into his face and without warning he lands a light swat to my clit. My pussy clenches around his fingers and again I am seconds away from coming. But he pulls his fingers out of me, again keeping me from coming.

"I told you, you will come when I tell you to, not a second before." His voice is deep and silky.

"Didn't I say edging was a hard limit?" I ask sarcastically as I roll my hips into his face again.

"Nope. Nice try, though." He chuckles against me. He puts his mouth back on me, licking my outer lips before moving to suck on my clit. His fingers are back inside me as well. Within minutes, I'm back at the edge, ready to come and praying that he'll let me.

But he doesn't. He backs off again.

He continues to edge me, teasing me, and just when I'm ready to kill him, he takes me back up to the edge and holds me there. I've never felt this kind of pleasure and pain before.

Right as I'm expecting him to back off the edge again, he lands three rapid-fire swats to my clit. The stinging suspends me right at the very edge of the cliff that he's been holding me at. But I don't come immediately. I hover right on that very edge of pleasure and pain, suspended in my orgasm.

Finally, he brings his mouth to my ear and growls, "Come for me, Pretty Girl."

My orgasm rockets through me, and I am suddenly in a free fall. Lights are flashing behind my eyelids, and I'm pretty sure I sound like a demon as I am coming.

I feel like my orgasm won't stop and I'm a sobbing mess. Derrick wraps me in his arms and I am against his hard chest, his leg between mine. I am still grinding against him, still orgasming. One orgasm rolls into two, and then three. It's not stopping.

Derrick pushes the hair out of my face and kisses the tears off my cheeks. He is murmuring in my ear, but I can't make out what he's saying. My brain is too busy short-circuiting.

After what seems like a lifetime and a million orgasms later, I finally come back to my body. My body is light and heavy at the same time. Derrick is still petting me and I have snuggled into him.

"You did so good for me, Pretty Girl," he murmurs. "You're safe. Do you want some water?"

At my nod, he disentangles himself from me and heads to the kitchen. I hear him moving around the kitchen, and when he comes out, he is carrying the water along with the chocolate bar that I keep in the fridge.

"Starting your stalking early?" I ask.

"Pretty Girl, I have been cataloging your house since I pulled up tonight." He chuckles.

"Oh...that's slightly terrifying." I sit up and wrap the fuzzy blanket around myself. I motion for the water and candy bar. "Gimme."

"This is what we both signed up for, Pretty Girl." He hands me the water and candy bar and I dive into both. "Are you okay?"

"I'm fucking fantastic," I mumble with my mouth full. "But I swear I will kill you if you do that to me again."

He laughs. "Noted."

Taken Chapter 4

Becca

It's time. I finally feel like I am ready for Derrick to take me. Part of our agreement was that when I was ready, I would put a green light in my front window. It had taken a couple of days and an emergency session with Beth to get me ready to turn the light on.

I had been a wreck the whole day, thinking that he could show up any minute. But he didn't.

He didn't come the next night either. But I've kept that light on twenty-four hours a day, and he still hadn't shown up. He wasn't responding to my text messages or phone calls either. My next session with Beth, I complained about the whole thing.

She told me that's not how CNC works. Sometimes, sure, there was an agreed upon day and time. But for the scene to feel real and authentic, it had to come as a surprise. She told me that I had no idea when someone was going to break into my house, and this is no different.

We are entering week three of no contact from Derrick, and I'm tempted to turn the light off and tell him to fuck off for ghosting me. But I don't. I want this too badly.

Tonight, I am up late editing a dark romance novel. I'm almost finished with it, but my brain is turning to mush. Thankfully, my deadline isn't for another week, and I decide to go to bed.

I go through my nightly routine: a quick shower, night cream on my face and hands, and checking the locks on the doors and windows. I crawl under the covers and I'm asleep before my head hits the pillow.

I couldn't have been asleep for more than a few hours at most when I hear the front door open.

At first, fear pours through me, taking me back to that night seven years ago. I'm a twenty-two-year-old woman who is about to be brutally raped and beaten.

But then a shot of rage shoots through me and I'm out of bed before I can think to grab the pistol in my nightstand. I will not be a victim, not again.

I creep down the hall that leads to the living room and wait at the doorway. I don't hear any movement and I can't see anything. I should have gotten a fucking dog.

I move away from the wall and step into the living room; the front door is shut and locked, the windows are still shut, and the green light is still on.

Just then, I'm shoved face first against the wall, hard enough to rattle the knick-knacks on the bookshelf next to me. I let out a shriek and start fighting back. This can't be happening. Not again.

My hands are wrenched over my head and held there. My hips are pinned against the wall. I can't move. I try to sling my head back to headbutt my attacker. He must be really tall because I only hit his chest, maybe shoulder. But my head hits something hard.

"My Pretty Girl has some fight in her," a muffled voice growls in my ear. "Good, I like it when they fight."

My heart stalls out. Derrick. I forgot about the green light.

But now I'm pissed. I manage to get my leg free from his and I stomp on his foot. Unfortunately, he's wearing boots and just laughs in my ear. He spins me so my back is against the wall and pins his hips against me.

I take him in.

He's wearing a military vest with tools and other odds and ends attached to it. The flashlight clipped to his shoulder must have been what I smacked my head on when I was trying to get away. He's got a name tape on the front of his vest that reads *Punisher*.

He leans down into me, his hands still holding mine over my head, and I can feel his breath against my face. He's got on a balaclava and all I can make out is his dark green eyes and the bridge of his nose.

"Are you going to run for me, Pretty Girl, hmm? What about scream for me? Or you going to drop to your knees and beg?"

My legs are shaking and my pussy clenches at his harsh words. This is not the Derrick that has been talking to me for the last couple of months. This is Punisher, the persona that I have agreed to play with.

I go limp.

"Begging is always a good choice," he says. He loosens his grip so that I can slide down to my knees, but that's not what I do.

I push him, and he releases me. I take off down the hall and before I can get more than a few steps, I feel him push me back into the wall. My hair gets caught between his hand and my shoulder, and my head gets wrenched at an angle.

He immediately freezes.

I'm breathing hard, memories bombarding me all in a split second. He gently spins me around until I am facing him. He pins me against the wall, but this time leaves my hands free.

"Color," he says gruffly.

It takes me a second, and I realize that I am okay. I know exactly where I am and who I'm with.

"Green," I tell him.

He takes a second to look at me. Whatever he sees must convince him that I really am okay because he growls *good girl* into my ear.

With that, he leans down and throws me over his shoulder. I squeal and start beating his back with my fists. But all I do is hurt myself because his vest is thick.

He lands one solid smack to my ass, the crack echoing down the hallway. It burns, but my pussy clenches. He puts his hand over my butt as he continues down the hall and the other holds my legs tight so I can't kick him.

When he gets to my bedroom, he throws me on the bed. I push my hair out of my face and scramble off the bed. I'm going to make him earn this.

I rush for the door and he grabs me again, this time bringing my back against his chest. His hands hold my arms in front of me and he shoves me back onto the bed, this time trapping my arms in front of me. I try to kick out but I can't get enough leverage.

He wrenches my sleep shorts down and growls when he sees I'm not wearing underwear. "Were you waiting for me, Pretty Girl?"

He drags his fingers through my folds, gathering my wetness on his fingers before tracing my asshole. He forces a finger inside me and the invasion burns. I let out a scream. He continues to fuck my ass with his finger.

"Such a dirty girl," he says softly in my ear. "But you like it, don't you?"

My heart feels like it's going to explode. My adrenaline is pumping, and I am simultaneously aroused and terrified. My hair is sticking to the sweat on my face.

I hear the jangle of his belt and take the opportunity to try to get out from under him, but his finger in my ass curls down and I am coming with a scream.

"Nice try," he growls in my ear. He keeps his finger in my ass, though he's not moving it much now. I'm trembling all over from my orgasm and my brain is working double time to figure out what the hell is going on.

I feel him notch his cock at my pussy, and it's the only warning I have before he slams into me. I let out a scream, and he bucks into me hard and fast. I can't brace myself because my arms are still pinned in front of me. He forces my face into the blankets, and it does nothing to muffle my screams.

The friction and pressure is just right, and within moments I'm coming again. My entire body goes lax and I feel like I'm floating.

I feel him slide out of me and flip me over. He takes my arms over my head again and he slams inside of me again. This time, my scream is silent, and I see stars. He continues to fuck me hard, one hand securing my hands over my head and one grabbing my throat.

He applies a little pressure, never breaking his rhythm and never taking his eyes from mine. He applies more pressure until I can't breathe and my vision starts to darken. My pussy tightens and I can feel another orgasm building.

He releases my hands and delivers three sharp slaps to my clit. My orgasm rips through me and he releases my throat. Oxygen burns down my throat and into my starving lungs. It amplifies my orgasm and I am orbiting Saturn.

I feel him slam into me one more time and let out a roar.

He collapses on top of me, and I gladly take his weight. It's heavy and grounding. He rolls to his side and brings me with him. I'm wrapped in his arms, and I snuggle into his warmth.

"You did so good, Pretty Girl. You're safe," he murmurs in my ear.

"Can you take off the vest?" I whisper. "It's very uncomfortable."

"Sure." He rolls out of bed and takes off the vest and his shirt. I'm met with a wall of muscle and tattoos.

"I'll stop making fun of your eating choices," I murmur in awe. There isn't an ounce of fat on him.

"I'm glad you approve. Give me one second, I'll be right back." He leaves the room and I hear him moving around in the living room.

He's back a few seconds later with my favorite fuzzy blanket, a bottle of water, and my favorite candy bar.

He kicks off his boots and places the water and candy bar on the nightstand before he climbs into bed with me again. He wraps me up in the blanket and then pulls me into his arms. We lay down like that for a while, me quiet and him murmuring sweet nothings into my ear.

For the first time, I feel safe. I feel like I have been given my life back. Oh, I know there's still work to do. But the work doesn't feel so endless anymore.

"What are you thinking about so hard over there?" Derrick asks. I pull back just enough to be able to look at him.

"Just that I finally feel free. Like the weight of my trauma is lifting. It's not gone, but I feel like I can actually get free of it."

"You are free, Pretty Girl, you just had to get out of your head enough to see it."

Taken Bonus Chapter

Derrick

The first night I saw the green light on in Becca's window, it took everything I had not to break into her house. I had to remind myself that's not how this works. There has to be distance. No texts, no phone calls, radio silence.

For the last three weeks, I had to use every ounce of self-control that I possessed to not go to her.

Because unlike other prey that I have played with over the years, Becca hits different. I don't know if it's her trauma, her desire to overcome it, or if it's just *her*.

She's stunning. Beautiful, long brown hair with deep red highlights. Bright green eyes that show every expression she feels. She's probably five-six, but she barely reaches my shoulder. Her curves are thick and perfect.

But it's her kindness despite everything she's been through. It's her attitude and the fact that she has a Challenger and a motorcycle. She is the complete package, and I want to hunt her every day for the rest of my life.

But first, we have to get her through her trauma without triggering regression.

Tonight is the night that we are going to really work on that, though. I am equal parts aroused, excited, and terrified.

I've been an attacker for years, and I've gotten good at it. While I take every encounter with prey seriously, I don't want to fuck this up.

I drive past Becca's house and park on the street. This is the most dangerous part of any CNC scene—the break in. If I'm caught, it will be hell to explain to the police. But that's part of what's so arousing about this. The potential of getting caught.

I watch as her lights turn off one by one. I set the alarm on my phone for an hour. When we were talking about how she learned to feel safe again, she said that since moving to Franklin she has been able to fall asleep quickly and sleep like a rock.

So I wait, breathing slowly and getting my mind right before I do what I crave, and what she asked for. I go through every list of triggers, wants, and soft limits. I go through my game plan and contingency plans.

It doesn't take long for the alarm to bring me out of my meditative state. My eyes snap open, and I am no longer Derrick, the trauma-informed therapist that helps survivors thrive.

I am Punisher, the persona that loves to hunt and track his prey. That wants fast, hard, rough sex where my prey fights back.

I adjust my vest as I get out of my truck, making sure that everything is where I want it, and grab my bag out of the back seat. I pull the balaclava out of my pocket and push my hair out of my face before sliding it on as I walk up to her front door.

I pull the lock pick set out of the pouch on my vest and start working the lock. I hear the lock snick, and open the door. I shut the door quietly behind me and lock it again. The green light glows in her living room window like a beacon

My eyes scan her living area, and I track the shadows and places to hide. I hear a creak of a floorboard and grin under my balaclava. She's going to fight me. I stand next to the hall entry, my back against the wall. When she comes out of the hall, she looks to the front door, and it gives me an opening.

I grab her and push her against the wall. I snatch her hands over her head and pin her against the wall with my hips. She goes wild, but she can't move. She tries to slam her head back, but her head slams into the flashlight strapped to my shoulder.

"My Pretty Girl has some fight in her," I growl in her ear. "Good, I like it when they fight."

She stops moving for a split second as her brain registers who I am. But it only lasts for a second before she starts fighting me again. She manages to get her leg free and stomps on my foot, but I'm wearing boots and barely feel it.

I chuckle at her attempts and spin her around so she can see me. Her eyes run over me, and I watch as her pupils dilate and a small shudder runs through her.

"Are you going to run for me, Pretty Girl, hmm? What about scream for me? Or are you going to drop to your knees and beg?" I ask her as she squirms in my arms.

But she goes limp instead, and I'm a little let down that she's not going to fight me.

"Begging is always a good choice," I say as I loosen my grip for her to slide onto her knees.

But she doesn't slide to her knees. Instead, she shoves me and takes off down the hall. There's the fight I was after. I grab her by the shoulder and shove her into the wall. Some of her hair gets caught, and I watch as her neck is wrenched to the side.

I freeze. Silently praying that this doesn't trigger her. I spin her around gently, pressing her back against the wall. "Color," I ask.

I watch with awe as she checks in with herself. She knows she's safe because she tells me, *green*.

I check her anyways. Her breathing is fast but not terrified. Her posture is ready for a fight, not fear.

"Good girl," I growl into her ear.

Author's Note

YOU AREN'T WEIRD, YOU'RE curious

Let's say that again for those that didn't really feel it. *You aren't weird, you're curious.*

I can't tell you how many times I heard some version of "you can't" or "you have to" while growing up and even into adulthood.

You can't have weird hair.

You can't have that piercing.

You can't have that tattoo.

You can't say no to a hug.

You can't act like that.

You have to work a 9-5 job.

You have to have kids.

You have to fuck your husband like a porn star, but not act like one.

And you know what happened when I listened to the people that told me I have to or I can't? I turned into a nervous wreck, a people pleaser, emotionally stunted, repressed and someone who had come to resent *some* of my life choices.

Don't get me wrong, I LOVE my life and I wouldn't change it for the world. But sometimes, I look back and think, what would have happened if someone, ANYONE, had listened to me? If I had been strong enough to say NO.

What if someone had actually paid attention to me?

What if the people who were supposed to protect me, actually did?

What if my voice had mattered?

What would have happened if I was allowed to dye my hair as a teenager?

What would have happened if I was allowed to get that piercing or tattoo?

What would have happened if I was heard and action was taken when I told someone that I was touched inappropriately as a seven year old?

And I realized, through therapy, that I don't have to live my life by the expectations of others. After working to heal the inner child, I moved into the pissed off teenager phase and I was ready to go to war against those that hurt me in my past and continued to do so in my present.

I worked with my therapist and wrote letters, though never sent them. I dug deep to find the courage to use my voice, because my voice does matter.

I talked with my husband of twenty plus years and our relationship got stronger. I explained that sometimes physical touch fucking HURTS. That my brain naturally goes in a million different directions and sometimes, he needs to be the *Vic Wrangler* instead of the *Vic Supporter*. That I can't handle 100% of the finances alone, that I need help.

And you know what happened?

I went from being a resentful wife that carried nearly the entire load on her own, to an actual partner. I went from constantly failing at things I wasn't good at, to having a partner who handled those things because he is good at them. I fell in love with my husband all over again.

But in that process, I isolated from people that had hurt me while growing up and continued to hurt me as an adult. I pulled away from people that did not support me, protect me, and enjoy me.

I learned to protect my peace and set boundaries.

And you know what happened?

Nothing... and everything.

The people who were supposed to support me, didn't. The people that I wanted to have relationships with, walked away when I learned to stand up for myself. And that's okay.

And the people that loved and supported me, they continued to do so.

And while I am all about demanding respect and not accepting blame that isn't yours to take, there is something within the kink community that needs to be spread throughout the world and that is **personal responsibility**.

We should not bleed on those that did not cut us.

We should not force others to endure the pain that we have endured.

We should not reject ideas simply because we do not agree with them.

And most importantly, we should ALWAYS be kind to others.

However, there is a phrase in EMS that should be everyone's mantra: Do no harm, but take no shit.

Stay Kinky, Friends

Vic Raven

www.ingramcontent.com/pod-product-compliance
Lightning Source LLC
LaVergne TN
LVHW010627110826
845149LV00014B/2792